Luke

Jenny returned his stare — and his smile. Her heart seemed to beat stronger, her cheeks flushed, her breath lodged in her throat, and a sudden aching warmth spread down from her breasts to her hips.

The very first time Luke Benning had gazed into her eyes, she'd experienced the same symptoms — the blushing, the breathlessness, the vibrant desire humming through her nervous system. But now, after so many years, so many changes . . . She wasn't supposed to feel this way. Not anymore.

She wasn't *really* feeling it, she convinced herself. What she felt was merely a memory. She was no longer the Jenny Perrin who had fallen in love with Luke one idyllic summer. She no longer believed what that innocent child had believed. She no longer wanted what she'd wanted then. Everything was different, including Jenny. Especially Jenny.

I wish to thank Nancy Richards-Akers for telling me all about the City Tavern in Georgetown, and Kathleen Gilles Seidel for putting me in touch with Nancy.

Also, my gratitude to Tania Gray for answering my many questions about the Middlesex County District Attorney's Office.

Finally, a special thank-you to Anne Stuart Ohlrogge for supplying me with three perfect words.

Other novels by Judith Arnold

Silhouette Sensation

Twilight
Comfort and Joy
Going Back
One Whiff of Scandal
Change of Life

JUDITH ARNOLD
One Good Turn

Silhouette Sensation

First published in Great Britain in 1991 by Silhouette Books, Eton House, 18-24 Paradise Road, Richmond, Surrey TW9 1SR

© Barbara Keiler 1991

Silhouette, Silhouette Sensation and Colophon are Trade Marks of Harlequin Enterprises B.V.

ISBN 0 373 58274 9

18 – 9110

Made and printed in Great Britain

Prologue

"Hey, somebody turn on the tube and catch a weather report," Taylor hollered as he carried the platter with the steaks outside to the deck, where the gas grill was heating up. "Find out whether or not we're going sailing tomorrow."

The blond woman filled two stemware glasses with Chablis and beckoned Luke to follow her out of the kitchen. He couldn't remember her name—Allie or Ellie—but he understood that he was supposed to entertain her. Taylor was obviously in hot pursuit of her dark-haired cousin, whom he'd ushered out onto the deck to keep him company while he barbecued the steaks. Both cousins were pretty, both slim and smart and stylish in their white slacks and brightly colored T-shirts. It amazed Luke to think that Taylor actually knew women like this. Most of the women Luke knew back home on Long Island were either too young, too old, neurotic or married.

These two—Suzanne and Ellie or whatever—couldn't be so easily categorized. If they were older than Luke and Taylor it wasn't by more than a year or so, and in the half hour since they'd arrived at Taylor's house in Harwich Port they hadn't exhibited any obvious neuroses. Taylor had promised Luke, when he'd invited him to spend the summer at his beachfront house on the Cape, that he would meet plenty of women in the Bay State's vacationland. It was an offer Luke couldn't refuse.

"There's the TV," said Ellie, gliding across the living room to turn the television set on to the six o'clock news broadcast out of Boston. "Pray for sun, Luke. I love sailing, don't you?"

"Oh, are you going to be coming on the boat with us?" Luke asked, then gave himself a mental kick. He should have said, "Would you like to come on the boat with us?" and then she would have said, "Sure," and he'd have gotten to spend the following day watching her fine blond hair blow in the breeze as Taylor navigated his twenty-eight-footer through the tranquil waters of Nantucket Sound. That was the way these things were done: the woman hinted and the man picked up on the hint.

Luke wasn't used to this. Four years as a public school teacher in a family-oriented community, two of those years as one-half of a steady relationship, and he'd forgotten the way the game was played. Taylor had insisted that before long Luke would remember all the rules and the moves, but at the moment he was feeling kind of rusty.

Ellie stepped over the glass-topped coffee table, scooping up the remote control on her way, and dropped onto the leather couch. She nestled into the cushions and took a sip of wine. "Have you got a preference?" she asked.

"I beg your pardon?"

"Which news show do you prefer?"

"Oh, I don't care," he said, sitting next to her. Her subtle smile informed him she was glad to have him there, and he leaned back and extended his legs under the table. "I've only been here a couple of days—not long enough to develop any viewer loyalty."

Ellie chose a channel and tossed the remote control back onto the coffee table. Then she curled her legs up under her and turned to Luke. "Taylor said you live on Long Island."

Luke nodded. She had pretty eyes, he noticed, an unreal turquoise color. One of his students had arrived in class one day with her previously pale blue eyes transformed into that odd turquoise shade, and when he'd questioned her about the change, she'd explained that the contact lenses currently being manufactured had really bodacious tints.

He wondered whether Ellie was wearing contacts. He couldn't believe her eyes were that color naturally.

"I live in Bethpage," he said.

"Bethpage?" Ellie trilled a laugh. "It sounds like a girl's name."

"It does," Luke concurred.

"Is it nice there?"

Small talk. He'd forgotten how tedious it could be. "It's a typical New York middle-class suburb," he answered politely. "I like it all right. I wish the school system was a little more progressive, but it's not a bad place to work."

"That's right—Taylor told me you're a teacher."

"High school social studies."

She contemplated him, curiosity sparkling in her blue-green eyes. Luke presumed that she didn't make a habit of socializing with schoolteachers. According to Taylor, Ellie was a consultant who specialized in putting together financial packages for the construction of mini-malls. Her cousin Suzanne, Taylor had informed Luke, managed a mutual fund for one of Boston's major investment firms. They were going to be staying at the Wychmere Harbor Club for only a week, but Boston wasn't so far away if Luke took a fancy to Ellie.

He ought to take a fancy to her. His first impression of her was positive. She had plenty going for her.

"Taylor's so lucky, being in the restaurant business," Ellie remarked. "He can go sailing in the morning, host the occasional barbecue and still take care of his professional obligations. He has such flexible hours. Then again, teaching has great hours, too, doesn't it?"

Luke shook his head. "People assume it does," he said, "but just because the kids leave at three-thirty doesn't mean the teachers do. I coach the soccer team, and then there are meetings, prep work and all—and invariably I bring work home to do in the evenings."

"Yes, but you've got the whole summer off," Ellie pointed out.

"This is the first summer I've taken off since I started teaching. I usually teach summer classes and help run a neighborhood soccer program. This summer, though..." He shrugged. "I decided to give myself a break."

There was more to it than that, of course. There was the inheritance he'd received after his grandfather's death last January, a sum of money the likes of which Luke hadn't contended with since he'd turned his back on his father and law school seven years ago. There was the fact that Taylor was considering the purchase of a second restaurant and was looking for a silent partner just when Luke was hoping to invest part of his windfall.

And then there was the breakup. There was the gradual, irrefutable realization that he didn't love Linda as much as he wanted to, that after two years he hadn't been able to convince himself that she was the woman with whom he wanted to spend the rest of his life. There was the pain of facing that unpleasant truth with her, the harrowing fear that no woman would ever measure up, the bewilderment over why, when he was a tolerant, easygoing man in every other aspect of his life, he continued to demand perfection in a woman—especially given that he wasn't sure what such perfection entailed. All he knew was that Linda fell short, and that Ellie—bright, ambitious, attractive Ellie—would probably fall short as well.

On the television, the male half of the anchor team was reporting on a community march against drugs in Dorchester. Luke asked Ellie to tell him about her work.

She launched into a monologue about her strategies for financing commercial construction. He should have found the subject fascinating. Even during the lean years, when his modest salary barely spread thin enough to cover the rent on his house and the grad-school loans he'd had to take when his father had cut him off, Luke had enjoyed reading the business pages, following the markets, theorizing about investments. He'd never had anything against wealth.

Now the lean years were over. He had a lot of money, and he was looking for something to do with it. He would be wise to pay attention to the opinions of a woman with a Harvard M.B.A.

Yet he had to exert himself to listen to Ellie. He struggled against the temptation to gaze out the picture windows at the expanse of dune grass leading down a steep slope to the beach, or to watch the television report on the indignant law-abiding citizens of Dorchester. He had to force himself to nod and look intrigued and say, "Oh?" at the right junctures.

This should be easy. Ellie was fantastic. Why did he have to work so hard at it?

"Can I get you some more wine?" she asked after draining her own goblet.

He looked at his scarcely touched wine. "No, thanks," he said, exercising etiquette by rising to his feet. "I'll get you some more, though."

Grinning, she stood and pushed him back onto the sofa. "No, I'll get it. I've got to powder my nose, anyway."

Returning her grin, he watched her saunter confidently out of the living room. Then he slumped against the cushions and groaned. He wished there was some discreet way of assuring her that if this dinner party turned out to be a bust the fault lay solely with him. He took a sip of his wine and grimaced at its watery flavor. What he needed was a beer. And maybe a new personality.

On the television, the story about the drug protestors ended, and the male anchor said, "Could there be some rain on the way? We'll have a complete forecast coming up."

"Also," the female anchor said with a somber expression, "date rape on the increase. We'll have a special report from Mary Ann Gavin when we get back."

Theme music, fade out, and then a commercial for a brand of motor oil. Luke contemplated his wineglass for a minute, then stood and crossed to the window. Straight ahead he viewed the grassy slope, the weathered wood steps leading down to a narrow strip of white sand, the gray water stretching out to the horizon and a few innocuous clouds scattered across the evening sky. If he angled his head, he could see part of the deck that extended out from the kitchen and dining room. He glimpsed the jaunty umbrella shading the circular table, which was set with four matching place mats, silverware and napkins. Suzanne lounged in a chair, sipping a tall drink. Taylor was arranging the steaks on the grill and telling her something, apparently a joke. She threw back her head and laughed.

"Date rape," the anchor woman's voice intoned through the television's stereo speakers. "It's also called acquaintance rape, and it's on the rise in the Bay State and elsewhere. Here with a special report . . ."

Luke watched through the window as Taylor leaned over Suzanne, whispered something in her ear and ignited a fresh gale of laughter. Taylor was as good at the game as ever.

When they'd roomed together at Princeton, Luke had managed to hold his own with women, but Taylor had always been a pro.

"...And closer to home," came the reporter's voice, "jury selection began today in the case of a man charged with the rape of a Tufts University student he'd been dating for several months. Some observers claim that the length of the couple's relationship will make it impossible to prosecute this case. Not so, says attorney Jennifer Perrin from the Middlesex County D.A.'s office."

Jennifer Perrin? Jenny? Luke spun away from the window and sprinted across the room, halting just inches from the TV set and dropping to his knees. He stared at the woman shown sitting at a broad desk in front of a wall lined with shelves of leather-bound legal volumes. The woman had a delicate face, a pointy little chin and vivid red hair cut in a sleek chin-length style. She was wearing the sort of gold button earrings Luke tended to associate with his mother, and a severely tailored blazer and high-necked blouse that seemed inappropriate to the late June weather. She clasped her hands primly on her blotter.

Jenny Perrin. Not the most common name in the world, nor the most unusual. That fiery red hair, though—the red hair and the hazel eyes and that wonderful stubborn chin of hers... It was Jenny, all right.

He struggled to overcome his shock in time to absorb her words. "The issue in this case isn't whether the victim knew him, whether she dated him, whether she believed herself in love with him." Much about this Jennifer Perrin on TV was nothing like the Jenny he remembered, but her voice was exactly the same. It still had that slightly husky edge to it, a quality reminiscent of someone just coming off a mild case of laryngitis. "What this case—like any other rape case—is about," she asserted, "is that the victim said no. Unfortunately a lot of men still refuse to accept that when a woman says no she means it. That's why we have laws, and that's why we're prosecuting Matthew Sullivan. His girlfriend said no and he forced himself on her. It's rape, pure and simple.''

The camera cut away but Luke remained where he was, transfixed. Jenny Perrin an *attorney*? He laughed in disbelief.

''What's so funny?'' Ellie asked as she glided across the room to join him on the rug in front of the television, her glass refilled.

''Nothing,'' he said, shaking his head to clear it.

''That was about rape.''

''I know.'' He suppressed the impulse to continue laughing, although every time he thought of Jenny seated in that stern blazer in front of all those law books he felt a strange tickle in his chest. Jenny a lawyer. Jenny a *prosecutor*. Incredible.

Ellie was giving him a peculiar look, and he hastened to justify his reaction to the news report. ''It was the attorney they just interviewed,'' he told her. ''She was a friend of mine years ago. I never imagined she'd wind up being a lawyer.''

Ellie continued to study him, a knowing smile teasing her lips. ''An old girlfriend, hmm?''

''Well... I guess you could say that.'' No point trying to explain the mystifying complexities of the summer he'd spent with Jenny Perrin, the intensity of their bond, the need that had evolved into profound love. ''Girlfriend'' didn't begin to describe what Jenny had been to him.

But it had all been so long ago. Why strive for precise definitions at this point?

A meteorologist appeared on the screen, backed by a map outlining the six New England states. He gesticulated toward various isobars, singled out various highs and lows, discussed a weather system moving south out of Canada. None of it registered on Luke. All he could think of was that Jenny Perrin was a lawyer—somewhere in the Boston area. Jenny Perrin. Jenny.

The woman who'd saved his life.

"The steak is done," Taylor announced from the living room doorway. "Pink in the center, dripping with juices. Grab it now or forever hold your peace."

"Fifty percent chance of rain for tomorrow," Ellie informed him as she turned off the television. She lifted her glass and stood. "Come on, Luke," she said, extending a hand to him.

He was supposed to help her to her feet, wasn't he? Well, Ellie was apparently a liberated woman, as willing to initiate chivalrous measures as to be the object of them. Attempting a weak smile, Luke took her hand and let her hoist him off the rug.

"What's with you?" Taylor asked, eyeing his friend. "You look like you got bitten by something."

"An old girlfriend of his was just interviewed on the news," Ellie explained.

"Linda?" he guessed, surprised.

Luke shook his head. "Jenny Perrin."

"Jenny?" Taylor grimaced and made a gagging noise at the back of his throat. He knew better than anyone else how Jenny had demolished Luke. He'd been the one to pick up the pieces and glue Luke back together again. Despite the passage of seven years, Taylor obviously hadn't forgiven Jenny for breaking his best friend's heart.

Luke had forgiven her—more or less. Truth was, he had simply forced himself to stop thinking about her. He had embraced the good things she'd taught him, the values she'd imparted to him, but he'd deliberately put thoughts of the woman herself out of his mind.

"She's a lawyer in the Middlesex County D.A.'s office," he told Taylor, stepping aside so that Ellie could precede him out onto the deck.

"Jenny Perrin? An assistant D.A.?" Taylor's snort implied that he found the idea as preposterous as Luke did.

Suzanne was already seated at the table when they reached it. Ellie sat across from her, Luke between them with his back to the house. Taylor tossed the salad with a flourish, ground a liberal amount of fresh pepper onto the greens and then sliced the warm loaf of sourdough bread.

"Who was this woman?" Ellie asked Taylor.

"Luke's first love."

"Ahh."

"Eons ago," Taylor added, smiling at Suzanne. "A summer romance. You know how these torrid summer romances can be."

Suzanne returned his cryptic smile. "No, but maybe I'll find out soon."

"Maybe you will," Taylor agreed with a wink.

Luke followed the conversation superficially. He laughed with the others, made a few jokes, passed the butter and the salt. But his gaze kept straying to the beach beyond the deck, the rhythmic roll of the waves breaking on the sand, the pale clouds hovering above the horizon. A breeze danced through the tall dune grass and ruffled the untrimmed locks of his tawny brown hair. To his right the sun was setting.

He recalled a sunset he and Jenny had watched from the Mall. The sky behind the Washington Monument had turned the color of burnished gold, with streaks of coral and sapphire and amethyst, like some jeweler's stunning confection. He'd been holding Jenny's hand, her slender fingers woven through his, the hot, humid air fluttering along the hemline of her loose-fitting cotton dress, her long hair pulled up off her neck in a slowly unraveling braid.

"It's so beautiful," she'd whispered, watching as the monument darkened into an imposing silhouette in the waning light. "There's so much beauty in this world, Luke. Don't ever let it get away from you."

He remembered thinking that the most beautiful thing in the world was Jenny.

And she'd gotten away.

PART ONE
July, 1984

Chapter One

"Rich and blitzed," Sybil drawled.

Jenny turned and acknowledged her roommate with a fleeting smile. She had known Sybil only two weeks; they'd met the day they had moved into their summer sublet, a two-bedroom flat on 36th Street NW that housed a quartet of Georgetown students during the school year. Like Sybil and her other two apartment mates, Jenny had learned about the sublet from an ad in her college newspaper. The luck of the draw had placed her in the same bedroom as Sybil, a theater-arts major from Emory University. Sybil was clever, cynical, witty and extremely Southern—everything Jenny was not. Despite their differences, or perhaps because of them, they'd become friends.

It was thanks to Sybil that Jenny was at this party. Unlike the staid summer interns and GS-5 typists Jenny had gotten to know at the State Department, the folks over at HUD, where Sybil worked, were always throwing bashes. This party—the third Sybil had brought Jenny to—was being hosted by a group of guys from Dartmouth who were renting a town house from a Dartmouth alumnus who had packed up his family and moved to Maryland's Eastern Shore for the summer.

Jenny estimated that at least fifty people were at the party. By the looks of it, they were all college kids summering in D.C., accepting whatever temporary employment they could find for the privilege of living in the nation's capital for a couple of months. Bright, articulate people in their late teens and early twenties circulated through the house, clad in crisp summer cottons and sipping wine coolers. In the elegant first-floor living room with its Chippendale furnishings, its plush Persian rugs, framed oil paintings and ornately carved mantelpiece, Jenny could scarcely hear the strains of the rock music being played at high volume on the stereo in the finished basement.

From where she stood, just behind the open French doors separating the paneled dining room from the living room, she had a perfect view of the man Sybil had diagnosed as rich and blitzed. Jenny wasn't sure she'd concur in that assessment. The man did appear to be out of it, but she didn't think the glazed, unfocused condition of his eyes was a result of too much liquor. Nor did she ascribe to inebriation his posture—he was slumped deep into the cushions of a wing-back chair, with his legs stretched before him and a beer bottle dangling from one hand—or the disheveled state of his long, tawny hair.

His hair lent him the appearance of having just arrived from a particularly exhilarating cruise on a sailboat. The side part was crooked and the shiny locks, the color of coffee with lots of cream in it, dropped past the collar of his rumpled oxford shirt in back. A sail on the Potomac, Jenny imagined, with him at the helm, facing the wind, solitary and free ... For some reason it was remarkably easy to picture.

Unlikely, though. College kids with summer jobs spent their Tuesdays working, not sailing. In the evenings after work, they burned off their stress at parties like this. The man had probably mussed his hair by running his fingers through it too many times.

They were nice fingers, long and graceful. He had rolled the sleeves of his shirt up to his elbows, revealing forearms that were long and graceful, too. So were his legs. He appeared lean and lanky, too tall for the chair but not nearly wide enough for it.

It was his face, though, not his fingers or legs or hair, that caught Jenny's attention and held it. There was something stark about his features, something that put her in mind of polished marble—hard yet delicate, sensitive yet unforgiving. His eyes, glazed though they were, were the color of honey, and yet they had a coldness about them, an opaque, grainy quality—honey that had crystalized from too much refrigeration, Jenny decided. He had a firm, jutting jaw, a sharp nose and thin lips, all of which came together in a singularly attractive way, but she kept going back to his eyes, eyes inhabited by too many emotions, all of them frozen and mute.

"How do you know he's rich?" she whispered to Sybil, who remained beside her by the dining room doorway, nursing a wine cooler and sizing up the man.

"The shirt's a Ralph Lauren," Sybil explained in her savvy Southern accent. "Also, he's wearing deck shoes with no socks. That's always a giveaway."

Jenny had noticed the absence of socks; in fact, her gaze had lingered for several long seconds on the naked, bony ankles visible beneath the hems of his cuffed khaki trousers. She'd never have guessed his shirt was designer, though. She was amazed that Sybil could identify the brand from twenty feet away.

"As far as his being blitzed," Sybil continued tartly, "that's pretty obvious."

"I don't think he looks blitzed," Jenny argued. "I think he looks . . . troubled."

"Indeed. Troubled by demon alcohol. There are plenty of gents downstairs, Jenny, and I'd wager at least one of them is better looking than that boy. Come on down with me."

Jenny grinned and shook her head. Even if the family room in the basement was filled with contestants for the Mr. America pageant, she wouldn't have wanted to go downstairs, at least not before she'd talked to the man in the wing-back chair. If he slurred his words, if he donned a lamp shade or spilled his beer on her skirt, she would concede that he was drunk and dismiss him from her mind. But until she had absolute proof, she was determined to give him the benefit of the doubt.

"I'm going to introduce myself to him," she told Sybil.

"Bring a plastic bag with you," Sybil warned with a grin. "I'll be downstairs if y'all need me."

Jenny returned her grin, then entered the living room. She didn't make a habit of accosting strange men; while not shy, she wasn't overly forward, either. She knew that some men might consider an uninvited overture from a woman an act of aggression; she knew that other men might take one look at her short, girlish physique and her hot-lava hair and tell her to get lost. She was not a raving beauty; men didn't gasp for joy when she glanced their way. Usually she exercised caution at social gatherings, attempted to establish eye contact with a man, exchanged a few experimental smiles and then waited for him to approach her.

Tonight was different. The man in the wing-back chair hadn't once looked in her direction, but for some unfathomable reason she felt no qualms about marching across the room and imposing herself on him. If he rejected her, she wouldn't be crushed—yet something inside her felt certain that he wouldn't reject her. Some stubborn, self-confident part of her soul assured her that given a little time, she could thaw the icy crystals in his beautiful amber eyes.

She reached his chair. He didn't look up at her, didn't move.

"Hi," she said.

Slowly, as if he had to order each muscle into action individually, he twisted in his chair and tilted his head up. His eyes met hers and she sensed no overt hostility in them. On the other hand, he hardly seemed thrilled by the sight of her. A muscle twitched in his jaw, but he remained silent.

"My name is Jenny Perrin," she said.

He stared at her.

"I don't think you're drunk."

One corner of his mouth lifted slightly. "I'm not," he said, then raised the beer bottle to his lips.

Before he could drink, Jenny added, "You shouldn't have any more, though."

Surprised, he lowered the bottle. He appraised her five-foot-two-inch, one-hundred-one-pound body with a sweeping gaze, his expression one of suspicion laced with curiosity and begrudging amusement. "What are you, a bouncer?" he asked.

"No."

"One of those born-again teetotaler types?"

"No," she answered, wondering whether he was as irritated by her as his words implied, wondering why she didn't care if he was. "I'm just a busybody," she explained.

His amusement overcame his suspicion and he chuckled. She had hoped to thaw him, but to her surprise she was the one thawing, melting, feeling her insides turn to liquid at the sensuous sound of his soft laughter. All of a sudden she felt flushed and feverish and utterly smitten. If she were a teenager, she'd say she was experiencing a powerful, instantaneous crush on this nameless stranger.

She wasn't a teenager, however. She was twenty-one years old, and twenty-one-year-olds didn't get crushes. What they got, she realized with chagrin, was turned on.

"I'm sorry," she said, aware that her composure was on the verge of disintegrating. "I shouldn't have bothered you." She spun away, anxious to leave before he figured out why her cheeks had darkened to glow-in-the-dark red.

With a swiftness and accuracy that offered definitive evidence of his sobriety, he reached out and grabbed her arm. His fingers met easily around her narrow wrist, and she prayed he wouldn't detect her accelerated pulse. "Don't be sorry," he said. "I'm used to busybodies."

With a gentle tug, he urged her back to him. She was still standing, he was still seated, and she could have escaped from him the moment he released her. But she didn't. She stayed beside the chair, unconsciously rubbing her wrist where he'd briefly clasped it. His laughter had disarmed her but his touch gave her courage. "Would you like to dance?" she asked.

"I hate dancing."

What was she supposed to do now? Apparently he didn't want her to desert him, but she felt ridiculous hovering awkwardly above his chair, gazing down into his haunting eyes and panicking over their profound effect on her.

"Want to go outside?" he suggested.

"Okay." She was relieved that he'd taken the initiative just as her mind was going terminally blank. A few minutes in the fresh evening air might be just what she needed to clear her head and cool off.

He placed his bottle in a clean ashtray on the table at his side, a gesture that implied he'd grown up in classy surroundings where people knew how to avoid leaving water stains on the furniture. But of course he'd grown up in classy surroundings; he was wearing a Ralph Lauren shirt and no socks. Still, Jenny found it easier to envision him on a scrappy wood-hulled sailboat than in a mansion. He'd looked decidedly uncomfortable in the majestic wing-back chair.

As soon as he stood she suffered her own keen discomfort. He was nearly a foot taller than she. Ordinarily she didn't mind her diminutive size, but now she did.

He gave no indication that the drastic difference in their heights bothered him. With a wave of his hand he invited her to precede him out of the living room.

A cluster of people stood in the front hall, smoking cigarettes and arguing politics. Excusing herself repeatedly, Jenny inched through the crowd to the door and outside. This was something, she thought grimly: she was leaving a party with a gorgeous guy and she didn't even know his name. One of these days, she concluded with a rueful sigh, her trusting nature was going to get her in trouble.

But she couldn't bear the possibility that the world had no room in it for trust. Let people like Sybil be cynical. Jenny was an optimist. She was certain she had nothing to fear from this handsome stranger.

She waited until he had joined her on the brick front porch and the door had swung shut, cutting them off from the spirited debate in the front hall. Then she turned to him. "What's your name?" she asked.

He opened his mouth and then closed it, as if he actually had to mull over whether to answer what she considered a very reasonable question. If he decided not to, she would go right back inside, elbow her way past the smokers, head downstairs to the basement and dance herself into a sweat with a nice, uncomplicated man whose eyes weren't sending out an SOS.

"Lucas Benning," he said.

She rolled his name around in her mind and decided she liked it. He'd won himself a reprieve. "Should we take a walk?" she asked.

He shrugged and stepped off the porch. She joined him on the sidewalk and they began a leisurely stroll toward O Street. The block was picturesque, lined with charming town houses, leafy trees and decorative street lamps that cast pools of golden light onto the cobblestone roadway. The sky stretched rich and blue overhead, not quite dark enough to reveal the stars. The evening air was like velvet, thick and soft and warm.

Digging her hands into the pockets of her skirt, Jenny glanced up at Lucas and smiled tentatively. "Why don't you tell me something about yourself?" she asked.

He stumbled to a halt and gaped at her. Then he broke into a laugh, another low, throaty chuckle that had the same unfortunately arousing effect on her as his last laugh. "You really are a busybody, aren't you?"

She wished there was some way to explain that Lucas himself seemed to bring out the busybody in her. She didn't ordinarily interrogate strangers at parties. But the minute she'd seen the odd, desperate look in his eyes she'd felt an inexplicable compulsion to rescue him.

"Look," she said self-consciously, "if you want me to leave you alone, just say the word and I'll disappear."

He studied her for several seconds. Behind him a car bumped along the cobblestones; across the street a trio of youths whizzed down the sidewalk on skateboards. "What's the word?" he asked.

All right. He wanted her to leave. She'd tried and failed. Not everybody wanted to be rescued. "The word is 'Go,'" she told him.

He scrutinized her for another long moment. "I'll have to be careful so it doesn't slip out accidentally," he said. His lips skewed into a cockeyed smile and Jenny steeled herself against the unnerving surge of warmth it evoked inside her.

He resumed walking, and Jenny fell into step beside him. They turned the corner onto another tree-lined block of preserved historical houses and quaint street lamps. She didn't dare to look directly at him again, but a quick glimpse informed her that he, too, had buried his hands in his pockets. She recalled his tapered fingers, the way he'd held his beer bottle by the neck, the way his wrist bone had protruded. She noticed the masculine hair, a pale brown shade, growing over the sun-bronzed skin of his forearms.

To distract herself, she asked, "Where are you working?"

"On the Hill."

"The Capitol? How exciting!"

He shrugged nonchalantly.

Eager to spend her last summer before graduation in Washington, she had taken the civil service exam for summer employees and sent in a general application, agreeing to accept a job wherever an opening could be found. The State Department had contacted her, performed a security clearance and hired her as a floating clerk-typist to replace the regularly employed secretaries when they took their vacations. Some of the college kids she'd met were in the city on special grants to do research at the Library of Congress or the Smithsonian, and some with financial resources Jenny lacked were involved in volunteer work for political parties and the like.

But to work at the Capitol—that was where the glamour was. "What do you do there?" she asked Lucas.

"I'm a gofer," he said modestly. "I'm working in Senator Howard Milford's office."

"Senator Milford? Wow!"

He eyed her quizzically, and she realized she must be coming across like a hick. She refused to temper her enthusiasm, though. "My father got me the job," he elaborated, as if that was supposed to make it less thrilling.

"Does your father work in Washington?"

"Not directly." Lucas reflected for a minute, his gaze losing its focus again—or else focusing on something Jenny couldn't see. "He's a lawyer, representing clients who need access. He maintains contacts with a lot of people on the Hill. He does a fair amount of business here in town."

Lucas's voice had taken on a quality of . . . not quite disapproval but distaste, perhaps. It was considered fashionable to frown upon influence peddlers like his father. But most people were secretly jealous of their power.

Jenny wondered if Lucas was. She herself wasn't. Raw power had never held much appeal to her.

"How about you?" he asked. "Where are you working?"

"State."

"Oh, yeah?" He smiled inquisitively. "Do you get to read any juicy telexes?"

She smiled back and held up her hand. "I'm sworn to secrecy."

"Oh, come on, one little leak won't kill you."

She shook her head. "I can't." Then she relented with a laugh. "To tell the truth, I don't see much juicy stuff at all. I'm in the Western Europe division, which is about as unjuicy as you can get. It's all friendly communiqués."

"Not a single dirty little tidbit?" he goaded her.

"You want a dirty little tidbit?" She leaned toward him, as if about to confide an earthshaking secret. "One of the big policymakers in the Western Europe division—a deputy assistant secretary whose name you'd know if I ever mentioned it—is addicted to M&M Peanuts."

Lucas feigned shock. "No!"

"It's the truth. He goes through a 'Pounder' every couple of days."

"Is he fat?"

"If I described him to you you might figure out who he was."

Lucas laughed again. And then she saw it—a tinge of warmth in his eyes, an almost imperceptible change but one Jenny recognized because she'd been searching for it, hoping for it. A flicker of light, a hint of hope, a glimmer of spirit . . . she saw it and felt as if the universe had all of a sudden become a better place.

It made no sense. Why should this man mean anything special to her? Why should he have such a profound effect on her? Why was she willing to work so hard to find that spark of humor in him, that trace of warmth? Why, when there were plenty of other eligible young men in Washington, D.C., at least a score of them at the party Sybil had brought her to, did Lucas Benning matter?

Jenny didn't need a reason. She believed that *everyone* mattered, that the more people whose lives you could touch, the better a person you yourself would be, and that the people who were hardest to get through to were often the most important to reach.

For at least one precious moment on a quiet street in Georgetown, she'd reached Lucas Benning. Of course it mattered.

They continued around the block at an unhurried pace. "Where do you go to school?" he asked.

"Smith College. You?"

"Princeton. What are you studying?"

"I'm an English major," she told him. "I'm going to become a teacher."

"A teacher!" His laughter wasn't warm this time. It was mocking.

"What's wrong with being a teacher?"

His smile waned. "Nothing, really."

"So why did you laugh when I said it?"

"I don't know." He sounded contemplative. "I guess...it's just that everybody I know plans to make big bucks after graduation. Law school, business school, medical school—hustle, hustle. That's what it's all about, isn't it? That's what's out there waiting for us."

"You don't really believe that, do you?"

He eyed her speculatively. "I..." He considered a bit longer, then said, "I don't know." His tentative tone implied that he hadn't actually given the question much thought.

"What are you planning to do after graduation?" she asked.

"Law school," he muttered, sounding almost embarrassed.

She smiled to reassure him. "That's okay. I'll try not to hold it against you."

They turned the next corner. "A teacher, huh."

"Maybe it's an unusual choice in this day and age," she defended herself. "Especially for a woman. We're all supposed to be pursuing manly careers. But I've wanted to be a teacher my whole life."

"That's nice," he said quietly.

"Have you wanted to be a lawyer your whole life?"

His answer was a snort. Then: "So what are you doing in D.C.?"

The implication underlying his question was that only prelaw students would choose to take a summer job in Washington, America's premiere company town, where the company was government and the product was power. "I've only been to Washington once before,'' she told him. ''It was a family vacation when I was about eight. We spent two hours here, a half hour there—you know, the tourist route.'' She sighed happily. ''This is such a great city, Lucas. I just wanted to immerse myself in it for a summer. I mean, to be able to take in the Pei wing of the National Gallery on my lunch break, or to visit the Lincoln Memorial whenever I feel like it. Or to see the actual Declaration of Independence or the original Star-Spangled Banner. Or even these lovely old houses in Georgetown. They predate the Revolution, some of them.''

He shot her a bemused look. ''You're really into this, aren't you?''

She grinned, aware that she was once again coming across as unbearably corny. ''I'm probably more into it than all the high-power lawyers.''

''Ah, yes,'' he said dryly. ''We'll end up with all the money and the power, and you'll end up teaching idealism to a class full of dewy-eyed children.''

''That's where the *real* power is,'' she declared. ''You lawyers may make all the big bucks, but we teachers will be molding the minds of your kids.''

''We'll be so busy making big bucks we won't have time to have kids,'' he predicted.

They had reached the block where they'd started. The sparring smokers had migrated out onto the front porch; the orange butts of their cigarettes left traces in the gathering darkness and their voices were raised in animated debate. Every now and then someone opened the front door and a babble of voices, underlined by distant strains of some old Rolling Stones music, spilled out.

Lucas slowed to a stop and eyed the town house from the corner. ''Do you want to go back in?''

"Not if you don't want to dance," she said, hoping that he'd admit he'd been exaggerating when he'd told her he hated dancing.

He continued to scrutinize the house. "Do you live around here?"

"Thirty-sixth Street. How about you?"

"I've got an apartment in Capitol South," he said, ruminating. "Are you sharing your place?"

She nodded. "There are four of us. It's a two-bedroom apartment, though, so we aren't too crowded." She'd heard of summer sublets with three and four people sharing a single bedroom, sublets so overpopulated that some tenants had to sleep in the living room. "How about you?"

"The place is all mine," he said. At her wide-eyed look, he clarified, "Actually, it's my father's. He maintains an apartment down here for business. He's letting me stay there for the summer, as long as I'll put him up when he's in town."

"That's very generous of him," Jenny said, although she privately thought that it was also rather isolating. Part of the fun of spending the summer in D.C. was meeting new people.

Lucas stared at the house for a minute more, then shrugged and waved toward a silver BMW parked at the curb. "That's my car," he said. "Why don't we go to my place?"

"Your place?" A tiny alarm clanged inside her brain.

"Sure. We'd have it all to ourselves."

The alarm clanged louder. "Why do we need it all to ourselves?" she asked dubiously.

His smile appeared strained, as if he resented her for requiring him to spell out his intentions. "What do you think?"

"I'm not going to go to bed with you, if that's what you're suggesting."

Her bluntness took him aback. His gaze hardened and she noticed the muscle flexing in his jaw again as he mulled over his response. "Don't blame me for misunderstanding," he grumbled. "You came on to me, don't forget."

"Came on to you?" She cautioned herself not to lose her temper. She'd thought she had broken through to Lucas a little, maybe planted the seeds of a new friendship, maybe introduced a little warmth into his austere disposition. That he was good-looking, that his smile had aroused her, that she could imagine herself pursuing a relationship with him—eventually, if they spent more time together and got to know each other better—was irrelevant. With one sentence he'd exposed himself as a jerk. "You think I came on to you? All I did was say hello!"

"And leave the party with me."

"And take a walk around the block with you," she emphasized. "So?"

"So, that's the way these things are communicated."

"Well—" she was feeling progressively more disillusioned about Lucas, and more sorrowful about it "—let me make myself clear, mister. I do not care to go back to your place with you, nor do I have any desire to invite you back to my place."

It dawned on her that his impatience had vanished, replaced by what appeared to be genuine bafflement. "Then why did you come over and talk to me?" he asked, as if he could think of no other reason for a woman to be friendly to a man.

"Because you looked lonely, that's why," she snapped, furious with him for proving to be so shallow, and with herself for having been so dense. Furious because she would have liked to know him better, but never would. Furious because she truly preferred to give people the benefit of the doubt, open to them, trust them—and it hurt to find out that some people simply didn't deserve her trust.

Spinning on her heel, she stormed down the block to the town house and inside, refusing him a parting look.

Chapter Two

Lonely. Oh, God, he was lonely.

Slamming the door behind him, he dove headlong onto the leather couch in the living room. He lay there in the dark, inhaling the rich scent of the leather, listening to the silence that surrounded him. No pounding rock music, no voices, no laughter. Just the sound of loneliness.

He hadn't gone back to the party. After Jenny had stalked off in her self-righteous snit, he hadn't had the desire. He wasn't sure why he had even gone to the party in the first place. Taylor's sister Holly had phoned him at work to invite him, and he'd figured attending a party would be no worse than sitting around at home, watching the tube and drinking his father's bourbon. Taylor had told Holly and Luke to look after each other that summer, since they were both going to be in D.C. Luke had done his part by taking her out to dinner at L'Enfant Plaza, and Holly had done her part by informing him of this party being thrown by a group of guys she knew from Dartmouth.

He'd gone, figuring that if he didn't Holly would feel obligated to continue inviting him to things—and figuring, as well, that it wouldn't be a crime to check out some available females. Washington was supposed to be teeming with single women, but in the three weeks since he'd moved into his father's duplex across the street from Folger Park, he hadn't met anyone worth a second look.

Not that he'd knocked himself out trying.

For some reason, the notion of spending a couple of months in solitude appealed to him. He wasn't interested in racking up conquests. This was his last summer of freedom; already he could feel the noose tightening around his neck: *hustle, hustle*. He had no overwhelming urge to hustle for dates along with everything else.

Come autumn, he'd be facing law boards, law school applications, probably a few rejections—and his father's wrath, followed by an intense campaign of string pulling, if the rejections came from the more prestigious schools. James Benning had every intention of seeing his beloved son become a high-power attorney like himself, and ever since Luke's older brother Elliott had abdicated, Luke had found himself in the unexpected but longed-for position of beloved son.

He didn't want to go to law school, but he couldn't bear to disappoint his father. For the first time in his twenty-one years on the planet, Luke had gotten the old man to notice him. How could he ignore his father's wishes?

And yet . . . *law school*. The very words made him shudder.

As recently as four years ago, when he'd chosen to attend Princeton rather than his father's alma mater, Yale, his father hadn't cared what Luke might choose to do with his life. Elliott was attending Yale, Elliott was being groomed for law school, Elliott had been steered into the right classes, the right secret society, the right summer employment. Elliott had been the heir apparent and Luke had merely been "the other son."

The one advantage of being ignored, he realized in retrospect, was that in the days when Elliott had still been on the scene, nobody had interfered with Luke. He could go his own way—even if his way was convoluted and full of false turns—and dream his own dreams.

Not anymore. Luke was the number one son now. He had a duty to follow his father's direction and dream his father's dreams, and at times he came close to convincing himself his father's dreams could take the place of his own.

Even so, he couldn't help but admire Jenny Perrin's idealism. A schoolteacher, for crying out loud! This was the eighties. The only people who became schoolteachers were those who lacked the wherewithal to become something better.

But Jenny had seemed pleased by her choice and at peace with herself. She'd seemed overjoyed by the prospect of molding children's minds. It was her serenity and confidence, more than anything else, that had made Luke want to take her to bed.

Of course, her appearance hadn't hurt, either. She was a bit small, both in height and physique, but she didn't look dainty. He'd liked her narrow waist and slim hips, and her eyes were awfully pretty, wide and almond-shaped, sparkling with glints of green and silver. She had a nice smile, too, easy and natural, and while her chin was pointy it balanced her equally pointy nose. Her voice had a husky quality, a cross between Julie Harris and Lauren Bacall, only with a flat midwestern accent. As for her hair, that fiery stream of silk spilling down her back . . .

He still wanted to take her to bed. Despite her rejection, he wanted her.

Actually, now that he thought about it, she hadn't exactly rejected *him*. She'd rejected his invitation to have sex with him, but she had seemed reasonably accepting of him as a person. The highlight of the evening, the highlight of his stay in Washington so far, had been the stroll he'd taken with her around the block. For the first time in ages, he hadn't felt lonely.

That was the thing of it—not her appearance or even her serenity so much as the fact that she could look at him and understand his loneliness. How could he have been so crass as to have insinuated that she'd come on to him? How could he have tried to score with her?

He cursed. His voice was muffled by the plush upholstery, and he sat up and repeated the curse, letting the rarefied atmosphere of his father's luxurious duplex resound with that one profane syllable. His eyes took in the marble tables, the mirrored wall, the vertical blinds and objets d'art, the plush maroon carpeting. It was all so well coordinated, so tasteful, so impeccable.

He couldn't picture Jenny Perrin fitting into it, yet that didn't trouble him. The truth was, even though he was lounging on one of the couches in this starkly elegant room, he couldn't really picture himself fitting in, either.

Somehow, that made him feel a whole lot better.

"I NEED A PHONE NUMBER," Luke said to Stella the next morning. "Can you help me out?"

Stella lifted her gaze from the unopened envelopes piled on her desk and regarded him with a skeptical look. A heavyset woman in her mid-forties, Stella was an absolute marvel. She knew everything; she knew everyone; and if by chance there did happen to be something she didn't know, she could find it out in less time than it took a leak to travel from the Executive Office Building to the *Washington Post*. Senator Milford was humble enough to think his chief aide, Lee Pappelli, was running the show. Lee was arrogant enough to agree. But the truth of the matter was, they'd all be utterly lost without Stella. She was the engine and the wheels of the senator's staff, the backbone and the muscle, the wisdom and the know-how—the behind-the-scenes monarch reigning over this supposed enclave of democracy.

"Well, don't you look spiffy today," she said, appraising Luke's summer-weight beige suit, two-tone shirt, leather-trimmed suspenders and red power tie. "You have special plans or something?"

"I'd like to have special plans, but I won't if I can't find out this woman's telephone number," he told her. "She's a clerk-typist in the Western Europe division at State. A summer temp, so she won't be listed in the directory."

"And you want me to get her phone number for you."

He gave Stella his most ingratiating smile.

"Let me get this straight. We're talking about a young lady who chose not to give you her number herself," Stella reasoned, her grin mocking. "If she didn't give you her number, Luke, it just may be because she doesn't want you to have it."

"She probably doesn't," he conceded. "I behaved badly with her. But how am I going to apologize if I can't call her?"

Stella's grin grew wider. "And meanwhile, I've got all this mail to go through."

"I'll go through it for you," he volunteered.

She cackled and handed him the four-inch thick stack of envelopes. "You're on, doll. What's the girl's name?"

It took Luke several hours to open the letters, sort them and print out the appropriate computer-generated responses to the senator's correspondence from his constituents. Luke considered the time well spent, however, when he returned to Stella's desk. Her eyes on her PC monitor and her fingers flying across the keys, she didn't look at him. "There it is," she said, gesturing toward her message pad with her right elbow. "Invite me to the wedding."

Luke grinned. "I'll reserve a seat for you on the aisle," he promised, tearing the pink sheet of paper from the pad, folding it and stuffing it into his breast pocket. "I adore you, Stella."

"Yeah?" she said without a pause in her typing. "Maybe you ought to marry me instead of her."

"Get a divorce and I'll consider it," he shouted over his shoulder as he jogged down the hall to his windowless cubby of an office. That the room was gloomy and barely large enough to accommodate his desk and chair didn't bother him, since he spent much of his time on the move, in other staff offices or across the street in the Capitol building. What mattered right now was that his office had a door, which he promptly closed, and a telephone, which he promptly used to dial the number Stella had written down for him. He recited the extension to the operator and counted the seconds while his call was connected.

After the sixth second he heard a click, and then "Jennifer Perrin" in that alluringly husky voice of hers.

"Jenny?" he said, sounding more sure of himself than he felt. "Hi, this is Luke Benning."

A long silence. "Lucas?"

"Well ... yes. But please call me Luke."

Another long silence.

"From the party last night," he added.

"I know who you are."

Given her unenthusiastic reception to his call, he figured he was already doomed, which meant he had nothing to lose by forging ahead. "I was wondering whether you might be free for dinner this evening."

"Dinner?"

"Yes," he said, infusing his voice with a certainty he had to fake. "I'd like to see you, Jenny. And I'm only talking about dinner. I swear, I'm not going to ask you to spend the night with me or anything."

"Why not?"

He floundered. After last night's display of indignation, was she now playing coy and encouraging his advances? What the hell was she up to? "Hey, if you want to spend the night with me, that's fine, too," he offered. "Whatever you want."

Then he realized she was laughing. It was a low, throaty chuckle, and it eroded his doubts. "I think we'd better just stick to dinner," she said.

He wanted to let out a triumphant yell. He wanted to kick his heels, slap the ceiling, do all sorts of uncool things to celebrate. He wanted to race across the street to the Senate floor and enter the news into the Congressional Record. She had said yes to dinner.

Instead he said with masterful calm, "Dinner it is. What time should I pick you up?"

They decided on six-thirty. She gave him her address and then told him she had to get back to work. After saying goodbye, he hung up, punched the air with his fist and whispered, "Yeah!" Energized, he swung open his door, prepared to offer Stella his soul in gratitude.

Two steps before he reached Stella's desk he heard a voice emerging from Lee Pappelli's office. It was a smooth, assured baritone containing a well-practiced blend of humor and self-importance. Luke knew that voice; it was a voice that for nearly eighteen years he'd heard saying, "Oh, that's my other son," and now usually saying, "This is *my* boy, Luke."

Luke suffered a strange mix of emotions, prominent among them delight and dread. It had been this way ever since Elliott had vanished and his father had anointed Luke the favorite child. There was always the thrill of knowing that his father actually saw him, recognized him, took pride in him—maybe even loved him. And there was the uneasiness that came from wondering what kind of love it was, how long it would last, how hard Luke would have to work to keep earning it.

He waited in the alcove near Stella's desk, listening to his father exchanging a good-natured farewell with Senator Milford's aide as they emerged from the inner office. A handshake, a final quip from Luke's father and a final promise from Lee to look over an obscure clause in the latest revision of some farm-support bill, and then James Benning turned and faced his son.

Luke experienced another twinge of ambivalence. The broad smile his father beamed at him left him unsettled; he wasn't sure whether he'd done too much or not enough to merit it. He scarcely had time to brace himself for his father's crushing handclasp. "There's my boy!" James boomed as he appraised Luke. "You're looking a bit thin, son. Are you eating enough?"

From the day Luke was born his father had been complaining that he looked thin. Luke had inherited his mother's lanky build and fair coloring, whereas Elliott had taken after their father, more robust in stature and endowed with jet-black hair and dark brown eyes. The fact that Luke had a perfectly healthy physique never registered on James. All that mattered was how lean Luke was in comparison to his father.

"I'm eating fine, Dad," he said, managing a smile. "When did you get into town? Why didn't you tell me you were coming?"

"It's been hectic," his father explained, flashing another blinding grin. He slung his arm around Luke's shoulders and escorted him down the hall to the minuscule office Luke had been assigned. "I caught an early shuttle out of La-

Guardia. It was all last-minute. As it is, I've got to catch a shuttle back tonight."

"You won't be staying overnight?" Luke kept the master bedroom in the duplex in a constant state of readiness because his father frequently arrived in Washington without warning. He himself used the smallest of the three bedrooms.

"Not this trip," his father replied with a shake of his head. "But we'll have dinner together before I leave. The City Tavern, all right? I'll meet you there at—" he glanced at the thin gold Rolex adorning his wrist "—six o'clock. I've got to run, Luke. This damned farm-support package is giving a certain client of mine heartburn." He nudged Luke toward his office door and scowled. "I'm going to speak to Howard about getting you a larger office. This room isn't big enough to store a mop in. Six o'clock, the City Tavern."

Before Luke could beg his father not to speak to Senator Milford about the size of the office, James Benning was striding down the hall and away.

Typical. Luke sagged against the doorjamb and shook his head in awe at his father's audacity. Wasn't it just like him to blow into town, preempt his son's evening, wreck his plans and never give him a chance to sneak in a word edgewise?

On the other hand, Luke couldn't smother the reflexive filial gratitude he felt at his father's invitation. When it came to James Benning, love had its price, and no son desperate for his father's love would resort to haggling. Tonight the price would be having to break his date with Jenny.

She'd hate him. It was nothing short of a miracle that she had forgiven him for last night's stupidity. He couldn't expect two miracles from her. This was it—he'd cancel their date and she'd tell him to drop dead.

He stepped inside his office, closed the door, pulled the pink square of paper from his breast pocket and unfolded it. Reaching for the telephone receiver, he succumbed to an unexpected flare of anger at his father for being so high-handed. The nerve of him, appropriating Luke's life and organizing it down to the minute.

Yet hadn't he appropriated Luke's life the moment Elliott had disappeared? Hadn't he been organizing every minute of it ever since? Why should anything be different just because Luke happened to have met a cute redhead?

Sighing grimly, he pushed the buttons and recited Jenny's extension to the operator. After a moment she answered: "Jennifer Perrin."

He sighed again. "Jenny, it's Luke. I've got bad news."

"Oh, no," she said, although he could hear laughter in her voice. "You've decided you're going to try to get me into bed after all."

He felt an unwelcome tension in his groin. Her joke should have been funny but it wasn't, not when he kept thinking of her spectacular hair and compact body, her beautiful, perceptive eyes. "I wish," he muttered under his breath, then continued out loud, "I've just found out I can't make it for dinner tonight."

"Oh?"

"My father's in town. It was unexpected. He wants me to have dinner with him."

"Of course," she said simply.

Of course? "You aren't angry?" he asked.

"Why should I be angry? I think it's lovely that your father's in town. If my father was in Washington I'd rearrange my schedule to have dinner with him."

How many miracles was this woman good for? Luke dared to press his luck. "Are you free tomorrow by any chance?"

"Tomorrow?" She hesitated, then said, "I'm afraid not. I was planning to go to a concert."

"A concert."

"The Marine Band. They give free outdoor concerts in the summer, outside the Capitol building. They're supposed to be very good. Maybe you've heard about them."

He had, but he hadn't thought to attend their concerts. Who wanted to kill an evening listening to a military band play patriotic marches?

To his surprise, he did. "We could go to the concert together," he suggested. "We could have dinner first and then go afterward."

Again she hesitated. "It would be kind of tight. The concert starts at eight. I've got to leave work, go home and change my clothes. I'd barely have time to grab a sandwich and get down to the Capitol."

"We could have a picnic," he said. "We could meet on the Mall at six-thirty, eat and then head over to the Capitol for the concert afterward."

"All right," she said. "Let's do that."

A picnic, Luke thought in puzzlement after hanging up. How had he come up with that brainstorm? He never went on picnics. They weren't any more his style than Marine Band concerts.

Yet it seemed like the perfect evening to share with a woman like Jenny Perrin. A picnic and a band concert. Why not? If he enjoyed himself it would be a miracle—and more and more, Luke was coming to believe in miracles.

"Now, HERE," Sybil said as she pulled open the top drawer of her dresser, "is where I keep condoms. Please feel free to help yourself if you need one—or two..."

Jenny erupted in laughter. "I'm not bringing him back to our room," she declared for what felt like the zillionth time.

"Well, just in case," Sybil drawled, closing the drawer and coming up behind Jenny, who stood before the mirror above her own dresser and attempted to braid her hair neatly. She and Sybil had managed to remove from the room the most flagrant evidence that its school-term occupants were male. Gone from the walls were the lascivious pinup posters, the Yield traffic sign and the calligraphed sheet of ersatz parchment reading Abandon Hope, All Ye Who Enter. The stray sweat socks they'd exhumed from a corner of the closet floor had been stored in an unused drawer, along with the out-of-date schedule of Hoya games and the three poker chips they'd discovered among the dust balls under Sybil's bed. But they'd been unable to peel the Playboy Bunny decal from the mirror, and Jenny did her best to ignore it as she examined her reflection and fussed with her hair.

Sybil smoothed out the narrow shoulder straps of Jenny's tank-style cotton shift, then pulled her brush from her hands. "Let me do it in a French braid for you," she offered.

"Thank you."

"And don't pooh-pooh those condoms, honey. Better safe than sorry."

"I'm not—"

"Bringing him back here. So you've said. But I saw the boy and he's an eyeful. Rich and good-looking. A lot can happen."

"When you saw the boy you thought he was drunk," Jenny reminded her.

"And you told me I was wrong." Sybil skillfully wove Jenny's hair into a smooth, stylish plait. "You also told me he hit on you for an easy score."

"That won't happen tonight," Jenny said confidently. "We're going to be outdoors in a public place. And anyway..." She fastened two shiny gold hoops to her ears and grinned. "I trust him."

"Y'all are too trusting," Sybil commented. "Trust him all you want, but if he tells you he's had a vasectomy, you make sure you help yourself to my top-drawer supply." She stepped back and assessed Jenny with a critical eye. "You look great, Jen. And really, if things go well, I don't mind spending the night on the living room couch. I'd expect you to do the same for me if the occasion presented itself—which I'm sure it will," she added with a saucy smile.

"For your sake, if not mine," Jenny said, sharing her roommate's grin, "I hope it does." She grabbed her purse, stepped into her sandals and checked her hair in the mirror one last time. "You're an artist, Sybil. Thanks a million."

"Thank me in the morning," Sybil teased before chasing her out of the bedroom.

It was a few minutes past six when Jenny left the apartment, and she decided to walk to the Mall. While warm, the air had lost its midday humidity, and after a tiring day of typing memos, she believed a stroll would rejuvenate her. Besides, she still hadn't figured out the city's bus system. The metro seemed a bit less complicated, but there was no subway stop in Georgetown. As for the cabs, they were much too expensive.

Jenny liked walking, and she especially liked walking in downtown Washington. She was aware that the city contained its share of rundown neighborhoods, but it also contained buildings of great splendor, monuments, parks, upscale boutiques, cafés and majestic houses. The sidewalks teemed with pedestrians, vendors selling flowers, religious cultists, protestors soliciting signatures for petitions, women and men not much older than Jenny, carrying expensive leather briefcases and looking extremely important.

She wondered whether someday in the not too distant future Luke Benning would be one of those important-looking young movers and shakers strutting down M Street or Pennsylvania Avenue with a leather briefcase gripped in one hand. That was evidently what he was grooming himself for, and yet she couldn't see him happy at it. Sure, he was an eyeful, as Sybil had observed, but beneath his handsome veneer Jenny sensed a turbulence, a sadness, something she wanted to heal.

She'd always been that way, adopting stray cats and nursing ailing Boston ferns back to health. At school she befriended not just the strong students but the weak. Among her achievements at college she counted not only her years on the Dean's List but also her having talked an anorexic sophomore into seeking therapy and her having persuaded her freshman-year roommate not to quit school after she'd flunked Russian 100. Some of the girls at Chapin House had nicknamed her "Little Jenny Sunshine," but they used the moniker affectionately and Jenny didn't mind.

She didn't know whether Luke required rescuing, and if so, whether he wanted to be rescued. But when she'd seen him at the party the other night, she'd felt a powerful urge to try.

And, if nothing else, he *was* an eyeful.

At Lafayette Park she handed out two dollars' worth of loose change to the homeless people who resided on the park's benches across the street from the White House. Then she turned south, heading for the Mall. As usual it was teeming with tourists. She had learned to identify the tourists by their cameras, their airline bags, their wide-eyed expressions and their cranky, dog-tired children. Jenny was proud to think she was less a tourist than a resident. Even if she hadn't yet mastered the public transit system, she had come to think of Washington as her temporary home.

Reaching the Mall, she turned left. Luke had promised to meet her in front of the National Gallery of Art, and as she neared the regal white museum she spotted him sitting on the broad granite steps, gazing westward, searching the crowds. He had on a fresh-looking white shirt and casual khaki trousers, and his eyes squinted slightly as he stared in the direction of the descending sun. His bare forearms rested on his spread knees, and between his legs on the steps sat a huge wicker basket. He wasn't wearing socks.

Within a minute of her seeing him, he saw her. He stood, lifted the basket by its handle and descended the steps to the lawn, slowing only to let a sweaty jogger pass him on the unpaved path. "Hi," he greeted her, smiling tentatively.

He smelled of wild mint. He seemed to tower above her. His eyes were still that golden honey color, but today they were warm and sweet and translucent. Jenny had remembered him as good-looking, but somehow she'd forgotten the visceral impact he'd had on her at the party. For a fleeting instant she pictured Sybil pointing to the top drawer of her dresser.

No. Jenny was not going to need Sybil's supply. No matter how attractive she found Luke, she wasn't going to sleep with him tonight. She understood intuitively that if a relationship was to develop between them it would be based not on sex but on something much more profound. And if nothing profound developed, she certainly wasn't going to settle for sex.

She returned his smile and then lowered her eyes to the oversized picnic basket. "Are we going to be joined by some other people?"

He touched her elbow lightly, guiding her toward the Capitol building, and then let his hand fall as they strolled across the lawn. "No. Why do you ask?"

"That basket looks much too big."

He shrugged. "I wasn't sure what you'd like, so I asked them to pack it with an assortment of food."

"You asked *them*? Who's *them*?"

He shot her a quick, nervous look. "I ordered this from a caterer," he said, his voice edged with contrition.

She'd been expecting sandwiches and soda pop, not a catered feast. She was suddenly very glad she'd decided to wear a dress rather than the culottes she'd originally considered putting on after work. She was even more glad she'd dressed nicely when, upon deciding on a relatively out-of-the-way stretch of grass near the Capitol Reflecting Pool, Luke opened the basket to remove a red-checked linen tablecloth, two wineglasses and a chilled bottle of Chardonnay. He deftly uncorked the bottle, filled the goblets and handed them to Jenny to hold while he pulled from the basket doily-lined dishes of cold shrimp, Cajun chicken wings, sliced roast beef and Havarti, thick slabs of sourdough bread and wheat crackers, carrot sticks, celery stuffed with paté and florets of cauliflower and broccoli. And two red-checked linen napkins.

"Oh, my," Jenny said weakly.

"You don't like any of it, huh," Luke guessed, although his eyes were twinkling.

"I love all of it. I'm going to make a pig of myself." Handing back his glass of wine, she helped herself to a stalk of celery. "This is heavenly, Luke," she said after devouring it. "I can't believe you went to all this trouble."

"I didn't go to any trouble at all," he reminded her, uncapping a small tub of cocktail sauce and dipping a plump shrimp into it. "All I did was make a phone call and tell them to have something ready for a six-fifteen pickup."

She accepted the shrimp he'd prepared for her and tasted it. It was fresh and succulent. She sighed with delight. "You *are* rich, aren't you?" she blurted out.

He seemed startled. "What?"

She smiled bashfully. "I'm sorry. I'm afraid tact isn't my long suit."

"That's okay," he assured her. He fell silent, absorbing himself with the task of arranging a slice of roast beef on a piece of bread.

She'd made him uncomfortable. She nibbled on her shrimp thoughtfully, trying to decide how to repair the damage. "It was my friend Sybil who figured out you were rich," she explained. "She said rich guys don't wear socks."

He glanced at his naked ankles and laughed. Then he scrutinized her bare calves and her tiny feet crisscrossed by the leather straps of her sandals. "By that standard, you must be rich, too," he deduced.

"I'm not a guy."

He took a bite of his roast beef sandwich, chewed and swallowed. "All right. I'm rich. Or perhaps it would be more accurate to say I come from a wealthy background. My father does well, and his father before him did even better."

"Was your grandfather a power broker, too?"

"He had friends in high places," Luke said vaguely. "He was a banker, not a lawyer. He was one of those lucky bankers who played the Depression for all it was worth and wound up in clover. He wears socks, though."

"At his age, he probably needs them."

Luke laughed. "How about you? Do you come from a long line of schoolteachers?"

Smiling, she shook her head. "My parents run an insurance agency outside Chicago."

"Chicago, huh," he said with a nod. "You've got an accent."

"No," she corrected him. "Everyone else has an accent."

He laughed.

"Did you have a good visit with your father yesterday?" she asked.

His smile faded. "It was okay," he said, then cut himself off. He averted his eyes for a minute, gazing up toward the illuminated dome of the Capitol building, then turned back to Jenny. "We ate dinner at a private club in Georgetown. The City Tavern. It's one of my father's favorite places to eat when he's down here. And we sat there, eating and talking, and I kept thinking..." He drifted off again, curiously pensive.

"Thinking what?"

He looked directly, unflinchingly at her. "Thinking about how you were just a few blocks away."

Jenny's heart beat faster. She understood that Luke's words had been said not to ply her with blandishments but simply because they were the truth. She was touched—more than touched. She had thought about him last night, too, thought about how pleased she was that he'd called her, how much she was looking forward to seeing him the next day, how greatly she hoped he wouldn't spoil their budding friendship by trying to get her into the sack. But to realize that he was thinking about her the way she was thinking about him moved her deeply.

She wasn't going to get a crush on him. She wasn't going to romp with him through a crazy, meaningless two-month affair. And while she wasn't sure exactly what his objectives were, she trusted him enough to find out.

"I'm not looking for a summer romance, Luke," she warned him.

He continued to gaze steadily at her. "Neither am I," he said.

Simultaneously, without consciously intending to, they both lifted their wineglasses and drank.

Chapter Three

The concert, like the picnic, was unexpectedly refined. Seated on the steps in front of the Capitol, with an unobstructed view of the Mall and the sunset above the Potomac River, Jenny and Luke listened to the band perform not just marches but classical compositions, jazz, show tunes and a concerto for harp solo so delicate Jenny had to remind herself that the music was actually being performed by Marines.

As enchanted as she was by the band's artistry—and by Mother Nature's artistry in painting the dusk sky with streaks of pink and mauve—one part of Jenny's mind remained fixed on Luke. He sat to her left on the red-checked tablecloth, which he'd folded into a rectangle and spread across the hard stone step to cushion their seat. Several inches separated her hip and shoulder from his, yet she could feel the heat of his body all along the left side of hers, a heat far different from the warmth of the summer evening. She was conscious of his tawny hair brushing the collar of his shirt in back, the sharp lines of his jaw, nose and brow, the understated strength in his forearms, his bony wrists and patrician fingers, his lean, athletic legs. The subtle scent of his after-shave. The gentle radiance of his eyes. Sybil might have been able to discern the make of Luke's shirt from across a room, but Jenny was aware only of the human being inside the shirt.

They didn't touch. Just the slightest movement and her elbow would bump his, her hand would find his, yet she exercised restraint. She felt as if they'd exchanged a vow that evening, a promise that they wouldn't let their budding friendship degenerate into a meaningless sexual escapade. It was a promise she'd needed to establish, because for the first time in her life she understood what lust was all about. Luke Benning was without a doubt the sexiest man she'd ever met, and when she was with him she experienced a hunger that no amount of shrimp and stuffed celery could assuage.

She was rather old-fashioned about sex. She'd slept with only one man in her life, someone she'd dated for five years, throughout high school and on into college, and it was only after knowing Peter for four years that she'd finally gone to bed with him. The two thousand miles separating Smith College from the University of Texas, where he was a student, ultimately led to the demise of their relationship, but there had never been any question in Jenny's mind that she and Peter had loved each other before they'd become physically intimate—and afterward, as well.

That was how she believed things should be. Perhaps in time she would love Luke, and if so she would be thrilled to satisfy her raging curiosity about what lurked beneath his Ralph Lauren shirt and his smartly tailored trousers. But for now she considered it wise to maintain a buffer between him and herself.

The final piece the band performed was a rousing rendition of the Marine Corps anthem, and it brought the audience to its feet. Once the applause died down and the band members began to pack up, Luke lifted the tablecloth, folded it and placed it inside the picnic basket, which contained plenty of leftovers from their feast. He cupped his free hand around Jenny's shoulder as they descended the stairs, but she understood he was only trying to keep from losing her in the swarming crowd.

Once they'd crossed the street to the Reflecting Pool, they stopped beneath a street lamp. "Wasn't that glorious?" Jenny exclaimed, invigorated by the bouncy final number the band had played.

"Yes. It was really nice," Luke said, sounding surprised.

"And to think they give these concerts for free!"

"They aren't exactly free," he pointed out. "Your tax dollars and mine are paying for them."

"Well..." She refused to let him undermine her ebullient mood. "It pleases me to think that my tax dollars are being used for this instead of some military adventure halfway around the globe."

Gazing down at her, he smiled. "It's only nine o'clock," he said, "and we've still got half a bottle of Chardonnay. Would you like a glass of wine?"

Jenny nodded. The sky still held traces of waning light, and she was far from ready to say goodbye to Luke. She accompanied him to the site of their picnic, held the basket for him while he spread out the tablecloth, and then sat beside him and gazed first westward to the Washington Monument, now illuminated by white spotlights, and then eastward to the Capitol, its ornate dome and American flag also illuminated. She knew about greed and corruption in high places, about the overfed bureaucracy, the undue influence of lobbyists and PACs and all the rest of it. But sitting in the heart of the nation's capital, beside a shimmering pool of water, with inspiring monuments to liberty and democracy all around and the exhilarating harmonies of the band still echoing in her head, filled Jenny with reverence.

"What an incredible place," she murmured.

Luke wedged the cork back into the bottle and handed Jenny one of the two glasses he'd filled. "Where, the Reflecting Pool?"

"Washington," she clarified. "This city. It's so beautiful."

Luke eyed her warily, although a smile teased the corners of his lips. "You aren't going to recite the Pledge of Allegiance, are you?"

She chuckled. "I know I'm a cornball," she admitted without apology. "But if you ask me—you didn't, of course, but I'm going to say it anyway—if you ask me, the biggest problem with this country is that people aren't corny enough. They're all so busy hustling. That was your word, wasn't it? They're too busy hustling to stop and think about how magnificent this city is—not just this city but everything it stands for."

Luke stretched out his legs and leaned back, propping himself up on his elbows. "Do you want to know what goes on inside that magnificent building behind me?" he asked, angling his head toward the Capitol. "People talk too much without saying a damned thing. They cut deals. They focus on the next election instead of the next century. They worry about how to get onto *Nightline*, and then, if they're lucky enough to land a booking, they worry about how to handle Ted Koppel. That's what the Capitol stands for."

Jenny had seen enough cynicism in her peers not to be taken aback by Luke's claim. What did take her aback was the strange wistfulness in his voice, as if he honestly wished things were different. "If that's the way you feel, Luke, why on earth do you want to become a lawyer and join the hustle?"

"Who says I want to?" he let slip, then shot her a quick, tenuous smile and looked away.

She studied him for a moment. He eluded her scrutiny by gazing steadily at the Washington Monument towering above the Mall amid a circle of flags. She could exercise tact and refrain from questioning him on the little bombshell he'd just dropped, but that would be out of character. He knew she was a busybody, and he'd told her the night they'd met that he didn't mind.

Taking a deep breath, she asked, "Why are you planning to become a lawyer if you don't want to be one?"

He shifted his weight onto one elbow so he could free the other arm, which he used to lift his glass to his lips. He took a long sip of wine, then lowered the glass and continued to look at the monument. "Things aren't always so simple, Jenny," he said cryptically.

Most things had always seemed extremely simple to her—not advanced calculus or foreign languages, but the essential things: love, work, responsibility, hope, trust, knowing right from wrong. If a person didn't want to become a lawyer, he shouldn't become one. There were so many equally worthwhile professions to choose from, so much equally important work to be done. "You aren't just doing it for the money, are you?" she asked, praying Luke wasn't that shallow.

He let out a wry laugh. "You've already figured out I'm rich," he answered. "Making lots of money isn't an issue."

"Then why are you going to law school?"

At last he turned to look at her. His eyes were piercing, his smile poignant. She realized at once that she was nosing around in sensitive territory. Yet Luke could have told her to stop; he could have castigated her for her busybody tendencies and sent her on her way. "If you really want to know..." he began, then drifted off.

She urged him on with a solemn nod.

He contemplated her for a moment more, then said, "I've got to become a lawyer because my brother's in Alaska."

His brother? Alaska? Jenny frowned. "Is he in jail there? Have you got to go there and defend him or something?"

"No, he's not in jail. Last I heard he was working at a marina in Sitka."

"That must be exciting," Jenny said, meaning it. She loved exploring marinas and fantasizing about the millionaires who owned the yachts. And Alaska seemed wonderfully exotic.

"He's not doing it for excitement," Luke corrected her. "He's doing it because he didn't want to become a lawyer."

All right, maybe some things weren't so simple. "Are those the only two choices a person has? Either you become a lawyer or you work at a marina in Sitka?"

"In my family, it comes down to that, more or less." He took another long sip of wine, draining his glass, and then set it down and shifted his weight back to both his elbows. "Elliott's the firstborn. He was supposed to follow in my father's footsteps, become the next hotshot attorney, find his place in the loop and rub elbows with the power people. He was the oldest son. The crown was waiting for him. But ..." Luke shrugged. "He abdicated. And I'm next in line."

Jenny would have laughed at the absurdity of Luke's statement, except that he was apparently quite serious. "Just because you're rich doesn't mean you have to live like royalty," she pointed out. "I mean, primogeniture seems a bit archaic, doesn't it?"

"It doesn't matter what it *seems*," Luke argued somberly. "That's the way it is in my family. I'm the heir apparent now that Elliott's given up his place in line for the throne. I'm the one who has to follow in my father's foot-steps."

"Why? I mean, what's to keep you from doing what your brother did, giving up and getting a job at a marina in, say, Key West?"

Luke's eyes narrowed, suddenly darkening with emotion. "My father loves me," he said, his voice low and intense. "I'm not going to disappoint him."

This was definitely not simple. "If your father loved you," she said gently, "he wouldn't want you to go to law school if you didn't want to."

Luke responded to her observation by growing tense. His jaw stiffened, his lips pressed tightly together and his eyes lost a good measure of their warmth. Interpreting his reaction, Jenny acknowledged that she'd gone too far. Some things seemed so obvious to her—for instance, a father accepting a beloved child's aspirations without quibble—that she blurted them out without weighing how people might take them.

Luke clearly didn't take her remark well. "I've been presumptuous," she said contritely. "I'm sorry, Luke."

"Forget it."

"Maybe I should skip teaching and become a family therapist," she muttered. "I could recite all sorts of platitudes and spend my whole life making people angry with me."

"I'm not angry," he insisted, giving her a crooked smile. "If you want to make a career of reciting platitudes, you ought to consider running for Congress."

Whatever injury she'd inflicted, he seemed to have recovered. She was enormously relieved. "Tell me about Princeton," she requested. "I've never been there, but I've heard it's a beautiful campus."

"It is," Luke confirmed, his smile widening and his eyes regaining their earlier warmth. She suspected that his pleasure had less to do with Princeton than with her having changed the topic. If Luke's father's love truly depended on Luke's attending law school, it was a very sad situation, and Luke didn't need Jenny to point that out to him.

She listened to his descriptions of the ivy-covered fieldstone buildings with their sloping roofs and latticed windows, the stately shade trees and rolling lawns, the charm of the town surrounding the school. He made Princeton sound so pretty, she privately swore to herself that she'd visit the school someday, even if not as Luke's guest. She barely knew him, after all; she had no idea whether their fledgling relationship would survive the summer.

Still, it was a glorious dream: that she and Luke would continue to see each other, that they'd grow closer, that he'd forgive her for being so blunt and frank—that he'd even like her for it. That their friendship would evolve, that in time kissing him would feel right, that she would look into his eyes and see nothing but warmth, heat, love. That, come autumn, the love wouldn't evanesce into a fond memory but would endure, and she'd go to Princeton and he'd come to Smith, and he'd chuck the idea of becoming a lawyer and find out what he really wanted to do with his life, and they'd do it together.

Glorious but utterly absurd. She'd only just met him. She had no reason to be mapping out a future with him.

But optimism never hurt anybody, and Jenny was an optimist. So she secretly continued to enjoy her fantasy and didn't trouble herself with finding a reason for it.

"YALE, STANFORD and Harvard, of course," said Luke's father, lowering his silverware in order to tick the schools off on his fingertips as he named them. "Columbia, Penn..."

Luke stared at the top his father's head; a goodly number of silver strands laced through the black waves, but it was still as thick as an adolescent's. He wished he could see his father's face rather than his hair, though. He wished his father would look up, would talk *to* him instead of *at* him.

"Duke would be acceptable, I suppose," his father droned. "Chicago..."

"Dad."

His father ignored the interruption. "As far as the second-tier schools—although heaven knows you'd go to one of them only as a last resort—there are plenty to choose from right in the New York area: N.Y.U., Fordham, Saint John's—"

"Dad, please." *Look at me,* he silently implored. *Just look at me.*

Without meeting Luke's gaze, James Benning lifted his fork and knife and cut into the pink slab of prime rib on his plate. "You remind me of your mother," he said, his tone implying that this wasn't a compliment. "She's always complaining that it's impolite to discuss business at the dinner table. I say there's no such thing as a bad time to discuss business. It's July, son. You can't procrastinate when it comes to considering where to apply to law school. Now Yale is your first choice, of course. I can speak to some of the law school's trustees for you. And Roger Chase maintains close ties with Columbia—"

"Dad." Luke tried without success to keep his voice from revealing his impatience. His father raised his eyebrows in tacit disapproval of his son's impertinence. Luke offered an ameliorating smile. "I don't want you speaking to people about getting me into law school," he explained. "If I can't get into law school on my own, then maybe I don't belong there."

"That's a very noble sentiment," his father said in a condescending tone. He cut another forkful of roast beef and popped it into his mouth. "However, much as I hate to have to remind you at this late date, the first rule of survival in this world is: Use what you've got. What you are very privileged to have, son, is a father with a network that runs through the best law schools in the country. If you don't tap into that network you're a fool." He set down his fork and reached for his glass of wine. The gold and onyx cuff link at his wrist glinted beneath the sleeve of his jacket.

Luke felt as if he were spinning back in time. Suddenly he was thirteen years old, sitting in the somber walnut-paneled formal dining room at the house in Larchmont. His father sat at the head of the table in the room's one armchair—his throne. Luke's mother sat at the other end of the table, fair and fragile in her silk dress and pearls, with her ash-blond hair swept back into a knot at the nape of her neck, her eyelids permanently at half-mast and the pale, slender fingers of her left hand curled around her martini glass. Across from Luke sat Elliott, dark-haired and broad-shouldered, being lectured by their father about his performance on the links at the country club that day, or about the importance of rising to a leadership position on the debate team or the basketball team, or about the significance of the country's cultivating new Asian markets for American goods. Luke's mother remained silent throughout the meal, sipping her drink, and Luke attempted futilely to contribute to the discussion. He tried to offer an opinion and his father cut him off, bore down on Elliott and said, "But you see, the zone defense detracts from individual effort."

Look at me, Luke silently pleaded. *Look at me, Dad!*

His father never attended the soccer games Luke played. No matter how high Luke's grades were, his father never commented on them, except to say, "That's nice. Now, Elliott, what can we do about this B in trigonometry? Should I hire a tutor for you? We've got to raise it to an A if you expect to get into Yale.'' So many years later, Luke still felt the pain of it.

"And I can put in a word for you with Henry Carlisle in New Haven," his father was now saying. "If only you'd gone to Yale for your undergraduate schooling, you'd be a shoo-in for the law school."

Look at me, Dad! He was twenty-one years old, and he was still aching to be noticed. It was beginning to dawn on him that being the focus of his father's dreams didn't guarantee that his father would actually notice him. Being the number one son didn't entitle him to enter the discussion. It wasn't a discussion, anyway. It was a monologue.

If his father was looking at Luke, the old man certainly wasn't *seeing* him.

James helped himself to a fresh piece of bread. Luke poked his veal with the tines of his fork, trying to muster an appetite. The City Tavern served hearty fare, but he wasn't hungry.

He wanted astronaut ice cream.

He and Jenny had gone to the Air and Space Museum on Saturday. The place was jammed—it always was jammed—but they'd fought their way gallantly through the mobs. Everything seemed to thrill Jenny, from Lucky Lindy's *Spirit of Saint Louis* to the models of the space shuttle. She'd squealed with delight at the astronaut uniforms and gasped in astonishment at the realization that people had actually flown in the rickety old biplanes on display. Luke had been to the museum countless times before, but he'd never enjoyed it as much as he had viewing the exhibits through Jenny's eyes.

It was in the museum's cafeteria, where they'd gone to have a snack, that they'd discovered astronaut ice cream.

He'd tried to convince Jenny that, whatever the stuff was, it was bound to be vile, but she had insisted on buying a package for them to share.

He'd been right; it was vile. "This is what I'd imagine Styrofoam tastes like," he'd said.

"Only sweeter," she'd added. "It has a Styrofoam texture, but the flavor is kind of like sugary children's cereal."

Vile though it was, they'd devoured the entire contents of the package, grimacing and laughing through their self-inflicted torture. And two days later, seated across a linen-draped table from his father in the dining room of an exclusive private club on the southern edge of Georgetown, it was all Luke could imagine eating.

"You aren't paying attention," his father chided. "This is important, Luke. We're talking about your future."

My future, Luke thought glumly. It didn't sound much like his, though.

"Have you called your mother lately?" his father asked.

Luke eyed his wineglass, then reached for his ice water instead. "Yes, Dad," he said. "I talk to her twice a week."

"She's not in good shape," his father said blandly. "She's still eating too little and drinking too much. She misses Elliott."

Luke nodded. As recessive as his mother had always been, she'd become even more withdrawn after Elliott had done his vanishing act a year ago. He had sent his parents a Christmas card postmarked Helena, Montana, but other than that they heard nothing from him. He wrote to Luke at Princeton every month or so, but he insisted that Luke keep his whereabouts a secret from their parents, and Luke complied. "If Dad knows where I am," Elliott wrote, "he'll charter a jet and come after me. You know he will."

Luke believed Elliott was right. There were times when their father's pressure tactics became so annoying that Luke was almost tempted to pass along Elliott's address in Sitka, just so his father would let up on him and redirect his attention to his older son. But Luke would never betray Elliott. In spite of the years he'd spent envying him, he never blamed his brother for receiving the lion's share of their father's love. Indeed, now he could empathize with Elliott's need to run away.

He made a more concerted effort to look interested as his father droned on about his mother's drinking. But behind his cool amber eyes his mind drifted back to the Saturday he'd spent with Jenny. The museum had been so crowded he'd had to hold her hand in order not to lose her. Her hand was so tiny, it felt like a child's. Yet her body was definitely a woman's. He'd been aware of the small, firm swells of her breasts beneath her loose-fitting T-shirt, and the curves of her slim waist, her hips and her calves, visible below the knee-length hem of her denim skirt. He'd been aware of her lightly scented cologne, the feathery wisps of hair that had unraveled from her braid at her temples, the faint sprinkle of golden freckles over the narrow bridge of her nose.

His father waxed emphatic about how Yale was superior to Harvard, and Luke thought about what it would be like to kiss those freckles, and her smiling lips, and her breasts, what it would be like to run his hands over those supple legs and compact hips, what it would be like...

"So, are you making any friends down here?" his father asked.

Luke coughed and forced his thoughts back to the dinner table. "Yes, a few," he said evasively.

"Isn't your roommate's sister in town?"

"Holly," Luke informed him. "She's a summer intern at the Corcoran."

"Art galleries," James Benning sniffed. "And her brother wants to go into the restaurant business, of all things. He seemed like a sensible boy, but I don't know."

"He'll be good at it," Luke defended Taylor. "He's learned a lot about the business from his uncle, and he loves what he's doing." Taylor's uncle owned a three-star restaurant in Newport, and Taylor had spent his summers working there ever since he was a teenager.

"To each his own," his father muttered with another sniff. Loving what you were doing was all right for some people, apparently, but not for the second son of James Benning. "Well, you'd be wise to steer clear of Taylor's sister," he went on. "Another important rule of survival is: Never fool around with your best friend's sister." He grinned slyly and winked.

Luke returned his father's grin. "I'll remember that, Dad."

"And you've probably met plenty of other women down here, anyway. D.C. is rumored to be bursting at the seams with available women."

Luke opened his mouth to tell his father about Jenny, then shut it. He could predict what his father would say if Luke described her. Smith College was acceptable, but the daughter of insurance salespeople was bad, and red hair, even if determined by genetics and not L'Oréal, was déclassé. An English major was valid, but a schoolteacher was not. And someone who actually clapped her hands together and insisted on climbing inside a mock-up of the lunar module was sorely lacking in sophistication.

And Luke hadn't even gotten her into bed. Why was he wasting his time on a girl like her?

Because—Luke would say if he had the nerve—the time he'd spent with Jenny Perrin was time spent happily. Because when he thought about it, it seemed as if much of his life had been a waste of time until the moment she'd marched up to him at a party and said hello.

Because Jenny Perrin was a miracle worker. That was why.

Chapter Four

"I'm surprised you liked it," he remarked as he and Jenny left the church building, the interior of which had been gutted and converted into a flexible performance space. He had asked her if she wanted to see one of the Broadway hits whose touring companies were currently playing in town, but she'd suggested instead that they attend a new play at an experimental theater near Dupont Circle. Her theater-major roommate Sybil knew somebody affiliated with the theater, and Sybil had attended an earlier performance of the play and told Jenny it was worth seeing.

The play had been well acted but depressing. The plot had revolved around the fleecing of an elderly widow by a cabal of selfish, money-mad young people. Yet Jenny liked the show—and Luke was coming to realize that he liked anything and everything he did in her company.

Last night he'd taken her out for pizza, and afterward they'd returned to her apartment in time to watch *Hill Street Blues*. That the show was in reruns didn't bother her; she and Sybil and her two other roommates had all laughed and groaned and guessed what the next scene was going to be before it unfolded on the screen. They'd devoured a ton of popcorn and enough diet soda to float a navy, and they'd voted—with Luke abstaining—that Bobby Hill was the best-looking cop in the precinct.

It had been fun sitting on the lumpy old sofa in the living room, surrounded by four appealing young women yet feeling no compulsion to be cool or suave or seductive. Jenny's apartment mates had interrogated him on what it was like working for a senator—like Jenny, they were all working as temporary clerk-typists in assorted federal departments and agencies. Sybil had inquired as to whether during his three years at Princeton Luke might have come across one "Stephen Ray Fontiere, a renegade cousin of mine who chose to attend that Yankee school of yours," and Fran had politely requested some assistance in changing the ceiling light bulb in the kitchen, which none of the four women was tall enough to change without balancing precariously on a chair placed on top of the kitchen table.

They were a terrific group of women. Sybil was deliciously sultry, Kate had the sort of cheerleader personality for which the word "perky" had been coined and Fran was quiet and scholarly, almost Talmudic as she analyzed the television show.

In Luke's eyes, though, Jenny outshone the others. Maybe Kate was prettier in a classic sort of way, and Sybil unquestionably had a more curvaceous figure, and Fran's soft-spoken reflectiveness appealed to Luke's intellect. But Jenny... Jenny glowed. She exuded affection and trust. To be with her was to get caught up in her optimism, to experience an incomprehensible sense of well-being.

He felt comfortable with her in a way he rarely felt comfortable with anyone—let alone someone of the opposite sex. When he'd teased her about how she seemed to have the TV show memorized, she'd poked him in the ribs, and when he'd extended his arm along the back of the sofa, she'd promptly cuddled against him so there would be room for

Sybil to squeeze onto the cushions next to her. There had been nothing overtly romantic in her nearness—what with three chaperons in the room, Luke wasn't about to make a pass at her. The fact was, he hadn't wanted to. He'd been content simply to have her next to him, leaning into him, behaving as if this cozy evening of popcorn and TV was nothing out of the ordinary.

That was the way it was with Jenny. Her closeness—both physical and emotional—seemed natural and right. When he walked with her down Church Street tonight, as when they'd walked from the pizza place back to her apartment on Thirty-sixth Street last night, they held hands, and it meant nothing—and everything. He was still occasionally distracted by thoughts of making love to her, but more often his fantasies centered on simply being with her, talking to her, knowing he could tell her whatever was on his mind or in his heart and she would assure him that it was okay, that he was good, that he had nothing to fear.

"Don't you see?" she explained, ambling down the street with him, her mimeographed program clutched in her free hand. "All those venal characters, they didn't really want to be the way they were. You could sense the moral struggle in them. They were searching for a way to let their goodness rise to the surface."

Luke grinned. How typical of her to put a positive spin on such a grim, misanthropic theater piece. He'd love to hear her dissect *Macbeth* someday: "Lady Macbeth wasn't really an evil person. Women had so little power in those days. They had to funnel all their ambitions into their husbands. It's no wonder she got frustrated and cracked up..."

"The trouble with these people," she declared, referring to the play they'd just seen, "was that they'd lost the ability to listen to their inner voices. They'd forgotten how to trust their instincts."

"What makes you think their instincts weren't telling them to con the widow out of her life's savings?"

"Because they were miserable," Jenny explained simply. "Not just after they conned the widow but before. You could see their torment. They were doing something they didn't want to do because they'd lost faith in themselves. But faith is something you can regain any time you want. Faith is always there. I don't mean religious faith, but faith in yourself, in your ability to trust others and do good things."

"Cornball," Luke teased.

Jenny chuckled. "It's really sickening, isn't it? I wonder if there's a cure for corniness."

"I hope not."

They'd reached Dupont Circle. Cars and bicycles cruised down the avenues that converged at the circle like the spokes of a wheel. Elegant new high-rise condominiums towered over the fashionable neighborhood. A third of the way around the circle from the corner on which Luke and Jenny stood was a café with a dining patio; several dozen small round tables were arranged behind a decorative wrought iron fence, each table adorned with a flickering candle.

"Should we have a drink or an ice cream?" Luke asked, gesturing toward the patio.

"An ice cream," Jenny decided enthusiastically. She'd had a glass of beer with dinner, but Luke had spent enough time with her in the past week and a half to understand that Jenny was not much of a drinker.

The light turned green and they started across the street. The next arc of the circle contained a small plot of greenery—flowering shrubs and grass, a dogwood tree and a couple of carved concrete benches. A young man in a T-shirt, tattered jeans and torn canvas sneakers sat on one of the benches. His sunken cheeks were darkened by a several-days-old stubble of beard; his shoulder-length hair appeared not to have been brushed in ages; his fingers were grimy and his fingernails discolored. A bulging plastic garbage bag stood between his legs. He exuded the sour smell of unbathed flesh.

Luke instinctively tightened his hold on Jenny's hand. She wriggled free and stalked across the sidewalk to the man on the bench. For an instant, Luke was too stunned to chase after her. Then he did, panicked by the thought of what the vagrant might do to her.

By the time he'd reached her she was addressing the man in a low, earnest voice: "Have you eaten anything today?"

"I had sumpin," the man mumbled.

"Do you have a place to stay for the night?"

"Ain't gonna rain, lady. I'm all right here."

Luke wanted to scream at her to get away from the man. But he held his words, sensing that Jenny would be furious with him if he interfered. She rummaged in her purse, a colorful bag of woven cloth that she wore on a strap over her shoulder, pulled out some coins and pressed them into the vagrant's grubby hand. "If you're not hungry tonight, you can save this for tomorrow," she instructed him.

"Thank you, ma'am," said the man. "Thank you. God bless." He stuffed the coins into a pocket of his jeans and then looked away bashfully.

Jenny straightened up and turned to Luke. Relief rushed through him at the comprehension that the street person hadn't mugged her. In fact, the fellow had behaved with remarkable civility. Even so, she had taken a grave risk in approaching him, and as soon as they put some distance between themselves and the guy Luke intended to give her a stern sermon on the limits of mercy in the real world.

He took her hand and hiked with her around the circle to the sidewalk café. Except to request a table for two, he remained silent until the hostess had ushered them to one of the candle-lit tables, presented them with menus and departed.

"Jenny," he said, ignoring his menu, "that man could have hurt you."

She rolled her eyes at what she obviously considered an unnecessarily melodramatic view of things.

"I'm not kidding, Jenny. He's a bum. He could have done something awful to you."

"Why on earth would he have wanted to do anything to me?"

Luke could think of no good reason, but that wasn't the point. "If he's deranged enough to be spending his nights on a park bench in Dupont Circle, he's probably deranged enough to be capable of violence."

"That's ridiculous," Jenny argued, although her voice was devoid of criticism. "There are plenty of reasons why he might be spending the night on a park bench. Maybe he got evicted from his apartment. Maybe his home was gentrified out of existence," she said, waving at the luxurious new residential towers that bordered the Circle. "Maybe he's just down on his luck. He could be an alcoholic, or—"

"Exactly. Or a drug addict, ready to knife a naive young lady for the contents of her purse."

"Just because he hasn't bathed in a while doesn't mean he's a murderer," Jenny contended with a laugh.

"How are you going to feel if he takes that money you gave him and uses it to buy drugs?"

Jenny laughed again. Luke knew she wasn't laughing at him, though; her laughter was gentle, underlined with sympathy. "I only gave him seventy-five cents, and that won't go far if he's in the market for drugs. But why assume he's going to use that money to get high? Why assume the worst? Why not assume he's going to do something good with that seventy-five cents? There's always a possibility he'll spend it on a bagel or a piece of fruit. If I had walked past him without giving him any money, there would have been no chance of that good thing happening.''

She was crazy, arguably as deranged as the street person on the bench. But when Luke gazed into her wide hazel eyes and acknowledged the depth of her compassion, when he opened himself to the power of her convictions, he lost the will to refute her. What a wonderful thing it must be to go through life expecting the best and giving everyone the benefit of the doubt.

He permitted himself a slight smile. "Are you going to feel guilty eating a banana split knowing that a hungry person is bunking down for the night on a park bench a block away?"

"I wasn't planning to order a banana split," Jenny told him as she lifted her menu. "That would be much too filling. I was thinking of just a dish of ice cream."

"Not even a hot fudge sundae?"

She shook her head. "I'm still pretty stuffed from dinner."

Dinner had been sandwiches at a gourmet deli a few blocks south of the theater. Since they'd both been at work all day, Luke hadn't gotten to her apartment until six-fifteen, and curtain time at the theater had been eight o'clock. He'd consumed a side order of fries along with his sandwich and he was feeling a little hungry now, but he supposed a pita pocket of chicken salad was enough to fill someone of Jenny's diminutive size.

He ordered a sundae for himself and a dish of hazelnut ice cream for her. "Eat it slowly," he commanded once the waitress delivered their snacks.

Jenny eyed him curiously. "Why?"

"I'm not ready to take you home yet."

She grinned. "I'm not ready to go home." She tasted her ice cream and her grin widened. "Wow, this is great. I've never had hazelnut ice cream before. Taste it, Luke."

He took a taste, then insisted she taste his sundae. He was feeling expansive, delighted that she was in no hurry to bring their night to an end. He wanted to sit with her for hours, watching the flickering light of the candle dance across her face, watching the rare but welcome breezes toy with the coppery waves of her hair. She'd worn it loose, and it spread like a cape over her shoulders, emphasizing their narrowness. Her blouse was a gauzy white linen, the neckline and short sleeves trimmed with crocheted lace, and her skirt was the same white fabric with lace along the mid-calf hem. She looked like an angel, a nymph, a bride.

"You're beautiful," he murmured.

She had just closed her lips around her spoon, and a small drip of ice cream got trapped in the corner of her mouth. Staring at him, she slowly removed the spoon and ran her tongue over her lips to capture the drip. After an unnervingly long moment she lowered her eyes. "Maybe we ought to talk about this," she said.

"Talk about what?" All he'd done was to compliment her on her appearance, which was extremely deserving of a compliment. He hadn't mentioned the effect her beauty had on him, or the more disturbing effect of glimpsing the tantalizing pink tip of her tongue as it darted across her lips. Thanks to the strategically positioned table between them, the most blatant evidence of her effect on him was well hidden, and he saw no need to mention it.

"I know we've seen each other a few times. You've taken me out and spent money on me..."

Taken her out? For what, sandwiches? Pizza? A picnic and a free concert and a pass-the-hat experimental theater performance? Astronaut ice cream?

Before he could argue she continued. "And Sybil—who's much more worldly than me, or at least she says she is—anyway, she keeps telling me that sooner or later you're bound to demand something in return."

"Now wait a minute," he broke in. "If we're discussing what I think we're discussing, let me assure you I never *demand* anything. If it happens, fine, but if it doesn't I'm not an animal. I don't make demands like that. And I don't know why we're even discussing this particular subject, Jenny. All I said was that you're beautiful—"

"We're discussing it because it's there," she persisted, once more lifting her eyes to him. She reached across the table and cupped her hand over his. "I like you, Luke."

His heart began to pound and his brain instantly reverted to his earliest erotic daydreams of her, daydreams of her lips on his and her small body beneath him, above him, surrounding him.

"I'm just . . . kind of slow about these things," she said.

"No problem." His voice sounded oddly raspy to him.

"I mean, I have to love a person first. Can you understand that?"

She had to love a person first. His pulse began to slow, his abdominal muscles to relax, his respiration to become regular. He wasn't going to sleep with her tonight, that much was certain. He might never sleep with her. She had to love him first.

While he wouldn't call such a condition unthinkable, there were no guarantees that their friendship would ever deepen enough to qualify as love. Love took time; love was capricious and unpredictable. They would be together in Washington only six weeks longer. Whatever happened happened.

He should have been immune to her blunt honesty by now, but he wasn't used to a woman being so direct, so utterly devoid of pretense. He appreciated her candor, and he was determined to match it. "I don't want to play games with you, Jenny," he said. "I'm attracted to you. But I'm not going to pressure you. I'm not going to give lip service to love just so I can get you into bed. If you're slow about these things, you're slow about them. I can live with that."

Her hand tightened on his for a second, and when she relaxed her grip he rotated his wrist and wove his fingers through hers. They finished eating their ice cream that way, Luke wielding his spoon clumsily with his left hand, happy to sacrifice dexterity for the pleasure of holding her hand. He wouldn't let go of her, not to scrape the syrup from the bottom of his dish, not to wipe his face, not to pull his wallet from his hip pocket.

Even if what they had wasn't love, he wanted it. And he had no intention of letting go.

SHE WAS FALLING in love with him.

It was too soon, really. She'd known him less than two weeks. Just because he was intelligent, just because he was rivetingly handsome, just because he was thoughtful enough to shorten his pace to match hers as they strolled westward toward Georgetown in the balmy, starlit evening, just because her hand felt so secure in his... None of that could explain her certainty that she was destined to love Luke Benning.

It was always possible that he'd made his noble statements merely to soften her up, but she couldn't believe he was that duplicitous. It was also possible she was willing to label her feelings love because she was desperately attracted to him, but she knew the workings of her mind and heart too well to be able to fool herself. If she wanted to make love with him badly enough, she wouldn't resort to rationalizations.

She did want to make love with him, but even more she wanted to love him. She wanted to know all the warmth inside him, warmth he seemed to have spent too much of his life containing, disguising and ignoring. She wanted to savor the trust that was building between them, not to rush it but to let it blossom at its own leisurely pace. For the moment she wanted nothing more than to experience the love his fingers were making to hers as his hand enveloped hers.

"Do you have any plans for tomorrow?" he asked as they ventured into her neighborhood.

She peered up at him and smiled. "You tell me."

He returned her smile, and her heart quickened at the unique male beauty of his features. If it wasn't love she was experiencing, it was something equally exciting—and whatever it was, she was thrilled by it.

"We could drive down to Mount Vernon for the day if you'd like."

"Would you like that?" she asked, frowning slightly. Last Saturday they'd gone to the Air and Space Museum; Mount Vernon was like another museum. Just because she was enamored of all the historical tourist attractions Washington had to offer didn't mean Luke wanted to spend every weekend staring at artifacts and perusing explanatory plaques.

"I wouldn't have suggested it if I didn't want to do it," he assured her. They turned the corner onto her block. "I could even arrange for a picnic lunch, if you think you could stomach some more shrimp and chicken wings."

"I think you're plotting to make me fat," she scolded.

"Found out at last," he confessed, eyeing her petite figure and chuckling.

They drew to a halt at the foot of the stairs leading up to the front door of the brownstone where she lived. Still holding her hand, Luke turned her to face him. "All right," she said, scaling the first step so she was nearly standing eye to eye with him. "Make me fat, see if I care. We'll go to Mount Vernon and eat shrimp."

"I'll pick you up at eleven."

"Great."

Still he didn't release her. She didn't want him to. She concentrated on the shape and strength of his hand enfolding hers, the dry smoothness of his palm, the tapered length of his fingers, the light pressure of his thumb against her wrist. She wished he would take her other hand in his as well.

He did. He held her hands at her sides and moved closer, close enough to brush his lips over hers. It was barely a whisper of a kiss, yet it ignited tiny shocks of energy throughout her entire body. Reflexively she gasped.

"I'm sorry," he said, though he didn't look the least bit repentant.

She meant to tell him she forgave him. She meant to clarify that, while she was fairly traditional about love and lovemaking, there were really no hard and fast rules about a kiss between friends.

What she did was lean forward until their mouths were touching again.

She heard a barely audible groan coming from him—or perhaps from her. Their lips fused, moved, opened, and then their tongues found each other. Luke let go of her hands so he could gather her in his arms. He wrapped them around her slim waist, then slid one hand up her back and beneath her hair to the nape of her neck. His tongue explored the tender flesh of her lips, the sharp edges of her teeth, the dark sweetness beyond, moving in thorough, unhurried thrusts that sent fresh jolts of electrifying sensation through her flesh. Her thighs grew tense, her breasts burned at the luscious pressure of his chest against hers as he pulled her more intimately to himself.

Her hands had clenched into fists, and she willfully unfurled them and lifted them to touch him. Through the cotton broadcloth of his shirt she felt the bones and sinews of his shoulders, the supple muscles of his upper back. He angled his head slightly, and his tongue moved deeper, absorbing her breath and melting her soul. She ached everywhere, ached for Luke, ached so much she couldn't suppress the small agonized cry that tore free from her throat.

Pulling back from her, he sucked in a ragged breath. She buried her face in the warm hollow of his throat, too embarrassed to face him. What a hypocrite she was, giving him that prim little speech about sex and love and how slow she tended to be about such things, and then dissolving into a seething mass of uncontrolled passion in the wake of one kiss.

His fingers twirled through her hair. She listened to his erratic respiration, to the frenetic drumming of his heart against his ribs. Several minutes elapsed, and then he spoke in a rough, breathless whisper. "Jenny?"

"Yes?"

Gently he urged her away from him, gripping her shoulders and holding her steady so he could look at her. She imagined she must look appalling—flushed and glassy eyed, wanton and disheveled. His enchanting smile as he examined her proved it.

"That was incredible," he said.

"Yes."

"Whose turn is it to apologize?"

She managed a feeble smile of her own. "Mine, I think."

"Then we're even?"

"I suppose."

He brought one hand forward to her cheek. His fingers caressed her with such excruciating tenderness she let out a sigh. "My sentiments exactly," he murmured. He traced the pointy edge of her chin with his thumb, then let his hand drop. "I'd better leave."

"All right."

He took a step backward, and another, his eyes remaining on her. "I'll see you tomorrow," he said, at last pivoting on his heel and striding down the block to where he'd parked his car when he'd come to call for her earlier that evening.

"Good night," she whispered after him. The taste of his lips lingered on hers; the heat of his kiss continued to grip her body even after she watched him unlock the silver BMW, settle himself behind the wheel, rev the engine and maneuver out of the parking space. Not until he'd driven down the block and out of sight did she find the fortitude to go inside.

A small, neat pile of her things sat on the floor in front of the closed door to the bedroom she and Sybil shared: Jenny's pillow, her nightgown, her hairbrush and the dog-eared copy of *Pride and Prejudice* she was rereading in preparation for her senior honors thesis on Jane Austen. Jenny understood what the pile meant.

"Do you want to borrow my sleeping bag?" Fran asked.

Jenny spun around to see her solemn, bespectacled apartment mate standing in the doorway of the other bedroom. She glanced down at the articles Sybil had left for her, then accepted Fran's offer with a smile. "She put out my pillow but no blanket."

"The couch is kind of uncomfortable."

"If it's that bad I'll use the floor."

Fran shrugged. "Sybil, Kate and I went to a HUD party. All the guys Kate and I met there were dorks, but the guy Sybil brought back was pretty foxy-looking. Not that looks are everything, but he wasn't bad. How was your date with Luke?''

"It was...very nice," Jenny said vaguely, following Fran into the bedroom and taking the down-filled sleeping bag Fran pulled out of the closet. She wasn't in any condition to describe her evening to Fran, who would no doubt enjoy interpreting it with scholarly exactitude if Jenny gave her the chance.

After thanking Fran for the sleeping bag, she returned to the hall, where she spotted Kate emerging from the bathroom dressed in pajamas and a robe. Kate took note of the sleeping bag in Jenny's arms, then at Jenny's shut bedroom door, and then at Jenny herself. "Men," she said with a disdainful sniff.

Men, Jenny pondered fifteen minutes later as, washed and clad in her nightgown, she crawled into the sleeping bag on top of the lumpy living room couch. *Men.* Sybil was right now sleeping with a man she'd met just hours ago, and Jenny would be spending the night alone instead of with a man she was practically in love with.

Far from condemning Sybil, Jenny envied her. All her old-fashioned sentiments couldn't nullify the fact that her body still simmered with arousal. Every time she closed her eyes she imagined Luke's lips on hers, his arms around her, and her soul seemed to clench with yearning. Kissing him had been both spiritual and abundantly carnal. If only she had Sybil's nerve, she could be in his bed right now, kissing him again, allowing her body the full pleasure of his love.

But that was the problem: love. Did she really love him? Did he love her? Why rush when she wasn't sure? She'd know when it was time to know. Luke Benning was a decent man; he'd promised he would wait until she knew.

That alone was reason enough to love him. And to her surprise, the restless longing that had been tormenting her from the moment she'd seen him drive away was replaced by a transcendent peace, an understanding that she'd done the right thing, that everything was going to work out magnificently, that the future held splendid things for her and Luke.

With a smile, she nestled into the pillow and drifted off to sleep.

Chapter Five

"Did I mention that I spoke with Jack Halliford? Seems an uncle of his contributed heavily to an endowed chair at Duke a few years back. The Halliford name has clout down in Durham, if we should find it necessary."

Luke ground his teeth together to keep from railing at his father. He had already told the old man innumerable times that he didn't want any strings pulled to get him into law school, and the old man had steadfastly ignored him. Why bother protesting anymore? Let James Benning prattle on about his networks and connections. Maybe in time he'd run out of steam, and then Luke could make himself heard.

He cursed the traffic. What strange spasm of filial duty had compelled him to offer to drive his father to the airport? His father had arrived in the city yesterday, dined with Luke and returned to the duplex for the night, spent all day today massaging some muckamuck at the FDA on behalf of one his clients and then met with Luke for dinner at Duke Ziebert's prior to catching the shuttle back to LaGuardia. Luke had had to listen to him babble about law school all last night. He'd been subjected to more law school babble over breakfast and still more over dinner. And like a fool, he had volunteered to drive his father to the airport, thereby opening himself to yet another half-hour discourse on the topic.

"Your mother said you called her during the day on Monday," his father remarked, offering Luke a glimmer of hope that they were done discussing law school for now.

"That's right," he confirmed. "There was an unexpected roll call on the Senate floor and I found myself with some time to kill, so I gave her a ring."

"That was good of you. It made her happy."

Perhaps it had, but it had made Luke uneasy. He would have understood if his mother had wanted to talk about Elliott's prolonged absence. But she hadn't seemed particularly interested in Elliott at all. "It's *you* I'm worried about," she'd told Luke.

He'd been flabbergasted. It wasn't like his mother to contradict anything his father said, and his father had told him she was upset about Elliott.

"Luke, are you still there?"

"Yes, Mom, I'm still here. I'm calling because Dad said—"

"'Dad said,'" she'd echoed in a surprisingly caustic tone. "Your dad said things and scared Elliott away. I'm worried that he's going to scare you away next."

"He hasn't scared me away," Luke had insisted.

"The man..." She'd sounded tentative to Luke, almost diffident. In the Benning family it was considered heretical to voice criticism of James. "He's like a bull in a china shop, Luke. He just stampedes through life, knocking over everything in his path..."

"Mom, what are you talking about?"

"I'm talking about you. I'm afraid he's going to stampede you the way he stampeded Elliott."

Luke was afraid of that, too. More and more, he was afraid of that. But he'd never admit it, certainly not to his mother, even if she was demonstrating an awareness he hadn't known she'd possessed. "He's a strong man," Luke had said, "but I'm not exactly a weakling."

He'd heard a faint giggle through the receiver, the nervous sort of laughter his mother succumbed to when she was feeling the first flush of a vodka-induced languor. And indeed, she probably wouldn't have had the nerve to say such things to him if she hadn't been drinking. "Your father goes on and on," she'd said. "Every day. It's 'When Luke does this,' or 'When Luke becomes that.' He's got your whole life planned out."

"That's his style."

"He just . . . he railroads everyone."

"You're mixing your metaphors, Mom," Luke had said, anxious to inject some humor into the conversation.

"I don't want to lose you, Luke," she'd murmured, sounding pathetically sad. "I should have protected Elliott but I didn't, and now I've lost him. And I'm too old and tired to protect you—"

"You aren't old and tired," Luke had argued, wishing he could convince himself as well as her. "And anyway, I don't need your protection. I'm all right. I can handle him."

"He says you aren't eating enough."

"I'm eating plenty," Luke had assured her. "I've got to get off, Mom. They've just opened the doors to the Senate chamber."

He hadn't eaten plenty that night, he admitted silently as he followed the signs to the main terminal building and braked to a halt outside the Eastern Airlines entry. His father had wolfed down a well-aged Angus sirloin and chattered ad nausem about the tough Con-Law prof he'd had at Yale and the strategies one needed for scoring high on the boards. Luke had sipped his iced tea, picked at his marinated chicken and wished he was somewhere else.

With Jenny. He'd wished he was with Jenny.

"No need to come in with me," his father said as he swung open the passenger-side door and reached into the back seat for his briefcase. "The next shuttle should be leaving in about fifteen minutes. Oh, has Howard done anything about switching your office yet?"

Luke sighed. Senator Milford couldn't switch his office; there was no other office empty and available anywhere in the Hart Building. Luke didn't care. The office he had now suited him fine.

Apparently James was able to sense his son's indifference. "You may think the size of your office is a trivial issue," he explained. "But people make judgments on you based on your office. Now, supposing you have to hold a meeting in that broom closet of yours, and—"

"A meeting? Dad, I'm an errand boy!"

"Bad attitude," his father chided. "You're a member of a senator's staff, and don't you forget it." A quick glance at his Rolex and he swung out of the car. "I'd better go if I'm going to catch this flight."

Yes, go. Please, just go.

"See you later, son." His father shut the door and strode to the building's entry. Luke watched until James had vanished inside, then released his tension with a shudder.

What kind of son was he, to want his father to make a fast exit?

What kind of father was James Benning, not even to thank his son for giving him a lift to the airport?

What kind of person could have health, a top-drawer education, tolerably good looks, a prosperous family, his own late-model BMW, a father who doted on him—what kind of person could have as much going for him as Luke did and still feel as if everything in his life was a sham?

Not everything. Jenny was in his life, and she was real, true, genuine. Buoyed by the thought, he ignited the engine and steered away from the terminal, heading for Georgetown.

HER ROBE TIED around her waist and her wet hair brushed smooth over her shoulders, Jenny had just turned off the bathroom light when she heard the doorbell. Kate was playing one of her Tom Petty tapes at top volume in the bedroom she and Fran shared, so they couldn't have heard the bell, and Sybil hadn't yet returned home from her dinner date with her beau from HUD. In fact, it could be Sybil at the door right now. She might have forgotten her key. Jenny could think of no one else who would ring their bell at nearly ten o'clock on a weeknight.

Tightening the sash of her robe, she padded barefoot through the empty living room to the front hall. She peeked through the peephole and saw not her roommate but Luke.

She didn't care that she'd just stepped out of the shower, that she was wearing her nightgown, that she hadn't had a chance to blow-dry her hair. Throwing open the door, she greeted him with a smile of pure delight. "Luke! Hello! What a surprise!"

"Hi."

Her smile faded as his grim expression registered on her. He was dressed in his business clothes, but he'd removed the jacket of the lightweight gray suit, loosened the knot of his silk rep tie and unfastened the collar button of his wilted cotton shirt. He looked rumpled and fatigued and deeply troubled.

"Come in," she said at once.

"No, I shouldn't have come," he muttered, although he put up only halfhearted resistance when she took his hand

and pulled him over the threshold. "I should have called. You're about to go to bed."

"I was about to dry my hair, but that can wait. What happened? What's wrong?"

For a long moment he only gazed down into her face. She watched as the muscles in his jaw relaxed, as the crystalline hardness in his eyes softened, as one corner of his mouth twitched upward in a noble attempt at a smile. "Oh, Jenny..." He sighed. "Just being here, I feel better already."

Warmed by the compliment, she steered him into the living room and urged him onto the couch. "Do you want anything? Something to drink?" she asked.

He shook his head, grasped her hand and pulled her down onto the couch next to him. "Just your company." He continued to hold her hand, drawing it onto his lap. His thumb sketched an abstract pattern against her palm.

In another context she might have found his light caress arousing, but not tonight. Luke had come here seeking friendship, not passion. In the four times they'd seen each other since the night they'd attended the theater together, they had never gone further than a few kisses good-night. Admittedly they were pretty spectacular kisses, but Luke seemed to be waiting for a sign from Jenny before he attempted anything more intimate.

Sometimes she thought she was ready for more. Ironically those times were not when Luke was kissing her but rather when he was talking to her. When they were kissing she felt hunger and thirst, want and need, but not love. It was when they were talking that she felt most certain that she loved him. When Luke described the soccer team he'd played on in prep school or the bizarre recipes his best friend Taylor liked to test on him at Princeton or some new intrigue shaping up in the back halls of Congress, when he strolled hand in hand with her through the Museum of American History and free-associated about all the cultural artifacts on display, when he argued with her over the death penalty—he was for it, she adamantly opposed—those were the times she loved him. It didn't matter that they disagreed about the death penalty. What mattered was that he was smart and verbal, he challenged her and he respected her opinions.

He'd come to talk tonight, and Jenny knew intuitively that her desire for him would be aroused not by the nearness of his body or the warmth of his hand around hers but by his words, his trust, his willingness to confide in her.

She sat quietly beside him, waiting for him to speak. After a while he did. "I just dropped my father off at the airport."

He had told her his father would be spending a couple of days in D.C. "Did you have a good visit with him?" she asked.

He grimaced. "I don't know.... Oh, Jenny, it's so hard to be with him sometimes. I used to dream—when I was a kid, I used to dream he and I would have times like this, special times when it was just the two of us, no Elliott getting in the way, just my old man and me. And now, at last, we're having those special times and—'' He let out a long, doleful breath. "Oh, God," he groaned, squeezing his eyes shut. "I don't want to be a lawyer."

From anyone else such a statement would have seemed unexceptional. But from Luke it was the most agonizing confession, each word wrenched from his soul, a devastating truth he had suppressed for as long as he could. He appeared haggard and pale, as if he'd uttered a blasphemy and was now awaiting divine punishment.

She rose onto her knees on the couch cushion and tucked her hand under his chin. "Look at me, Luke," she commanded gently, turning his face to her.

Slowly his eyes came into focus on her. She had no difficulty reading the torment in them.

"This is not such a big deal," she said.

"Right," he grunted.

"Luke, *lots* of people don't want to be lawyers."

"Lots of people don't have James Benning for a father," he countered. "As a matter of fact, only two people *do* have James Benning for a father, and one of them moved four thousand miles away just to get out from under him." He grimaced again, as if he were suffering the worst sort of pain—which, Jenny had to admit, he probably was. "Oh, Jenny," he whispered. "I wanted this. I wanted it so badly. I wanted him to fuss over me the way he fussed over Elliott. And now I've finally gotten what I wanted . . . and it's destroying me."

"It's not destroying you," she murmured. "You've grappled with it for a while, and now you've finally figured out what's right for you. That's not destruction."

"But my father—"

"Your father can't live your life for you, and you can't live yours for him."

"Right," he grunted again, putting a wildly sarcastic spin on the word. When he next spoke his voice was soft, almost plaintive. "I want him to love me, Jenny. Is that such a terrible thing?"

It was the most natural thing in the world, but Jenny couldn't figure out what it had to do with Luke's choice of career. If his father loved him he would accept him and give him the emotional support he needed. Jenny's father loved her, and the only real demand he'd ever made on her was to do the best she could and take pride in her efforts. When she'd wanted to play in the Little League as a child, he'd fought long and hard to get the local league to admit girls onto the team. When she'd wanted to take an afterschool job at one of the fast-food joints in town, he'd expressed his reservations about the effect it might have on her school-work, but he'd let her take the job. When she'd gotten accepted to Smith College, he hadn't balked at the fact that it was expensive and far from home. Instead he and her mother had hung a sign in the window of their agency proclaiming, "Jenny's Going to Smith!" and filed a zillion complicated forms so she would qualify for financial aid.

Even when she'd been among a group of kids rounded up at a high school graduation party and escorted to the local police station because they'd been drinking beer, her father hadn't stopped loving her. He'd been furious, he'd grounded her for two weeks, but he hadn't stopped loving her.

She was his only child. He was her father. It was all very simple.

But what had Luke once said? *Things aren't always so simple.*

"You've got to do what's right for yourself," she told him. Perhaps his relationship with his father was more complicated than hers with her father, but this much was obvious. Luke was going to have to live with himself for the rest of his life. He had to listen to his heart and choose his own path. He couldn't sacrifice his future and his happi-ness to please his father.

"He'll kill me," Luke said glumly.

She laughed at his exaggeration. "He may be disap-pointed, Luke, but he'll get over it."

"You don't know him."

"I wish I did." If only she could meet the man, she could reassure herself that Luke was, in fact, blowing this situation way out of proportion. She would view Luke's father more objectively than Luke himself could. She'd see that he wasn't the monster Luke had made him out to be, and she'd be able to convince Luke that, whatever hurdles he and his father faced, they weren't insurmountable.

She would prove to Luke that his father wasn't going to kill him or destroy him. Then he could lighten up on himself and face the future with joy.

Excited by the idea, she squeezed his hand. "Let me meet him, okay? The next time he's in town."

"No," Luke said swiftly.

Surprised, she sank down into the cushions and stared at Luke. "Why not?"

"You'd hate him."

"I would not."

"He's..." Luke struggled with his words. He ran the fingers of his free hand repeatedly through his hair, as if trying to work out his anxiety. "Jenny, he can be a mean SOB when he wants to be. You don't know him, you don't understand him and you'll wind up hating him. I don't see any good coming of that."

She smiled and squeezed Luke's hand once more, this time for comfort. "First of all, I've never hated anyone— with the possible exception of Adolf Hitler and Idi Amin, neither of whom I've met. I'm sure your father isn't in their class, Luke. He helped to make you the person you are. How can I hate him?"

"Trust me. It's possible." But in spite of his words, he allowed himself a small grin.

"We'll talk. We'll get to know each other. We'll swap knock-knock jokes. I'll debate the death penalty with him. It could be fun."

"Sure. About as fun as getting hit by a truck."

"Don't be such a pessimist," Jenny scolded. "I'd like to meet your father. I can't believe he's as bad as you say."

"That's your problem," said Luke. "You can't believe panhandlers on the street might be drug addicts, and you can't believe my father can be a first-class bastard if he thinks the occasion calls for it." He rotated his wrist so his hand was on top of hers, and folded his long fingers around her delicate ones. "He's my father—as you said, he helped to make me the person I am—so I've got to love him, and I've got to do whatever it takes to win his love. But that's him and me. That's blood. It's family. You don't have to get involved, Jenny. There's no need for it."

She almost objected that there *was* a need. She needed to meet his father because she cared for Luke, because he was important to her, because she would understand him better if she knew what he was fighting.

"I want to," she said quietly, beseechingly. "Please."

Luke shook his head. He tightened his grip on her hand. He opened his mouth, and she braced herself for his refusal.

"All right," he said.

"FORGIVE ME if I'm having a little trouble with this," Sybil drawled. "Why are you meeting his father if you haven't even slept with him?"

Laughing, Jenny sat on the edge of her bed and buckled her sandals onto her feet. "What does one thing have to do with another?"

"Well, meeting Luke's father implies a certain seriousness, doesn't it?"

"Not necessarily," Jenny replied, although deep down she suspected that Sybil might be right. To meet a boyfriend's father when said father happened to be in town didn't automatically connote something significant. But to meet Luke's father was quite another thing. It was serious enough for her to have chosen the gauzy lace-trimmed linen skirt and blouse she'd worn the night she and Luke had gone to the theater, the night she'd admitted to herself that she was falling in love with him. Maybe it would bring her good luck tonight.

She crossed to the dresser, lifted her brush and attacked her hair. She knew she looked woefully young for her age, small and slight and horribly fresh-faced. If only she could do something a bit sophisticated with her hair...

Sybil read her mind. She rose from her own bed, glided across the room and took the brush from Jenny's hand. After stroking it through the long red tresses for a moment, she twisted the hair and piled it on top of Jenny's head. Jenny studied her reflection in the mirror and wrinkled her nose. "It isn't me," she confessed.

"It certainly isn't." Sybil let go of the haphazard knot and Jenny's hair tumbled loose down her back. "How about if I do it in a French braid?"

"I'll be forever in your debt," Jenny said dramatically, though she was grinning. "I wish I could make a French braid."

"It's easy to do them on someone else," Sybil explained. "Doing them on yourself is downright torturous. So tell me," she said, brushing the hair back from Jenny's temples, "you've known Luke for over a month now. You've visited every major tourist attraction in town with him. You've eaten with him, you've watched the tube with him, you've taken drives in the country with him, and one of your phone conversations with him ran forty-seven minutes; Fran was timing it. You've even gone to Chinatown with him and eaten marinated duck's feet, and if that isn't a sign that this relationship is serious, I'm sure I don't know what is."

"Those duck's feet were disgusting," Jenny recalled with a smile.

"And now you're going to have dinner with him and his father at his father's private club," she continued. "And you still haven't bedded the man. I don't get it."

"There's nothing to get," Jenny assured her. "I think the relationship is serious, too." It was the first time she'd actually admitted such a possibility out loud, and hearing herself put the idea into words only made its inherent truth resonate more profoundly inside her.

"Then what is it? Are y'all saving yourself for marriage?"

Jenny guffawed and shook her head.

"Be still," Sybil scolded, tightening her grip on the braid she was weaving down the back of Jenny's scalp. "Then what is it? The man is a prime cut, Jenny. And don't tell me he isn't interested in you that way, because I've seen the two of you together. I've seen the way he looks at you, honey, and it's most certainly not the way a man looks at his maiden aunt."

Jenny let out a long breath. She wasn't sure she could explain to herself her failure to sleep with Luke, let alone explain it to Sybil. She wasn't a prude or a moralist. Her desire for him was stronger than ever, and she knew all she had to do was wink and he'd whisk her off to bed.

She gazed at her reflection, her hazel eyes suddenly solemn, her chin proudly raised. "You know what it is, Sybil?" she said, once again putting her feelings into words for the first time. "If I sleep with Luke, that's it. I'll be his forever. And I don't think I'd mind that. It's just such a big decision." A tear surprised her, leaking through her lashes and skittering down her cheek. "I love him, Sybil."

"Damn," Sybil muttered. "You know what my mama says? Love's a quagmire. If the mud doesn't get you, the copperheads will. Either way, you're doomed.'' She clipped a barrette around the end of Jenny's braid and took a step back to appraise her. ''You're also coiffed. If you want a word of advice—''

''I don't,'' Jenny said emphatically.

Undeterred, Sybil went on. ''Don't let Luke's daddy catch on that you're in love with his son. If you do he'll despise you.''

''He won't despise me,'' Jenny asserted. ''We're going to have a grand old time debating the death penalty. And he's going to adore my braid.''

''You're forever in my debt,'' Sybil reminded her.

''Forever and ever,'' Jenny dutifully confirmed.

There was a tap at the door, followed by Kate's voice: ''Jenny? Luke is here.''

''Knock him dead,'' Sybil whispered, handing Jenny her purse. ''The father, not the son.''

''Got it,'' Jenny whispered back as she waltzed to the door and opened it. Maybe it was the attractively shaped braid, maybe Sybil's generous encouragement, or maybe it was the peace of mind she felt in the wake of her acknowledgement that she was in love...but whatever it was, as she headed down the hall to meet Luke, she felt absolutely no misgivings. Tonight was going to be wonderful.

TONIGHT WAS going to be disastrous, Luke thought as Jenny sauntered down the hall to him. She was wearing the beautiful white skirt and blouse that had put him in mind of nymphs and brides the last time he'd seen her in it, and her hair was pulled back from her face in a sleek, stylish braid. She had on her gold hoop earrings and her college ring, and she looked radiant.

This time, however, he thought not of nymphs and brides but rather of a lamb being led to slaughter.

"Are you absolutely sure you want to go through with this?" he asked, extending his arm to her.

"A dinner at a private Georgetown club? You bet," she joked, hooking her hand around the bend in his elbow and letting him usher her out of the apartment.

"Seriously, Jenny, I could tell my father something came up at the last minute and you couldn't make it."

She sent him a luminous smile. "Relax, Luke," she murmured.

He wished he could. But he knew, he just knew this evening was going to be a mistake. Things were strained enough between him and his father without having Jenny in the picture. His father had been down to Washington two other times since she'd said she wanted to meet him, and Luke had twice considered arranging a dinner threesome like tonight's. Twice he'd thought better of it.

He had only been delaying the inevitable, he acknowledged. Sooner or later Jenny and his father were bound to meet each other—not only because Jenny had her heart set on it but also because Luke intended to keep her as a friend for a long, long time.

Still, he would have preferred to put off introducing her to his family until he and his father had gotten a few things straightened out. During his father's last two trips to Washington, Luke had dropped all sorts of hints about how he wasn't keen on attending law school. His father had alternately pretended not to hear him or else refuted him. "Law school is the foundation," he'd pontificated. "It's the basis for all that follows. This isn't open to discussion, Luke. You'll get the law degree under your belt, and then you can start picking and choosing. But first things first. We'll get you into Yale…" And on and on, as if Luke hadn't even spoken.

His mother's warning echoed in his head: *He's going to stampede you the way he stampeded Elliott*. The way he'd stampeded her, as well. She had escaped into liquor, Elliott into the icy mists of Sitka. But Luke, if he could find the courage within himself, was not going to escape. He was going to stand and fight.

He only wished Jenny didn't have to witness the battle. It was likely to be brutal, and she might get caught in the cross fire.

"What a lovely evening it is!" she exclaimed as they descended the steps to the sidewalk. Obviously brutality was the farthest thing from her mind. "Why don't we walk to the restaurant?"

He glimpsed his BMW, parked halfway down the street. He had intended to drive over to the restaurant, and then, after dinner, he and his father would drop Jenny off and from her place travel directly back to the duplex in Capitol South. But now that she'd mentioned it, he realized that he wanted to walk. A little exercise in the balmy evening air might dissipate some of his tension. And that way he'd have to walk Jenny home after dinner, which would give him a few minutes alone with her before he had to resign himself to his father's company for the night.

Jenny talked during the entire stroll. He didn't pay close attention to her words—she was rambling on about the excitement generated in Western Europe division when someone stole the candy supply of the State Department's M&M Peanuts addict that morning—and he understood that she didn't mind his distracted state. She was talking to put him at ease, and her soft, sandpapery voice did seem to allay his anxiety. He concentrated on its pitch and timbre, on the light pressure of her fingers curving around the sleeve of his jacket, and on her attempts to lengthen her stride as he shortened his. He wrapped himself up in the comfort of having her with him.

Maybe this evening wouldn't be a complete disaster. Maybe only a partial one. Luke would take whatever he could get.

They entered the City Tavern through the unobtrusive door of the Federal-style brick building on M Street and Jenny gazed around, wide-eyed. Luke almost cautioned her not to act awed or say anything corny, on the chance that such behavior would bring his father's scorn down on her. But he held his words. Let Jenny be herself. If his father didn't like her, that was his problem.

If he heaped scorn upon her, though, that would be Jenny's problem. And Luke's, because he didn't think he could bear seeing her insulted by anyone, especially his father.

"It isn't too late to back out," he whispered as a doorman in gold-braided livery approached them. "Are you sure you want to go through with this?"

She chuckled. "You make it sound like I'm going in for elective surgery," she teased. "It's only dinner, and you should know by now that I'm a swell eater."

"Right." He sighed, admiring her bravery and simultaneously regretting it.

He gave his name to the doorman, who led them into the dining room. Luke scanned the room and saw no sign of his father. He wished the old man had gotten to the club first; sitting at the table with Jenny gave him an unwelcome chance to relapse into nervousness as the soothing effect of their stroll wore off.

They took their seats at a reserved table at the center of the room. "I like this place already," Jenny declared, gazing around her in appreciation of the dining room's faded luxury. She admired the heavy china and the thick, soft linen of the napkins. "Don't worry about a thing," she confided under her breath. "I know which one is the salad fork. They teach that kind of thing at Smith."

In spite of his qualms, Luke laughed. Once again he conceded that Jenny was capable of miracles. Surely it was miraculous that she could make him smile at a time like this.

His laughter trailed off as the familiar sound of his father's voice filtered into his consciousness. Twisting in his seat, he spotted his father jovially greeting the doorman. "That's him," Luke muttered.

Jenny scrutinized the tall, robust middle-aged man in the impeccably tailored suit. Her gaze ran from his thick mane of black hair sprinkled with silver to his bold, square face, his broad shoulders, the leather briefcase he toted in his right hand, the diamond ring on his right ring finger. Turning to Luke, she whispered, "You don't look anything like him."

"I take after my mother," he whispered back. "He's never forgiven me for that."

The doorman pointed out Luke's table, and James Benning nodded, murmured something to the doorman and walked to the table unescorted. Luke stood to shake his father's hand, then took a deep breath for fortitude and said, "Dad, this is Jennifer Perrin. Jenny, my father, James Benning."

"Jennifer," his father said, oozing charm as he took Jenny's hand. "What a pleasure."

"Please call me Jenny," she said with a sweet, guileless smile.

Luke watched as his father settled into his chair and gave the young woman at the table a sharp, swift assessment. Although James's smile never flagged, Luke discerned the calculating hardness of his father's eyes and cringed inwardly. "Luke's been telling me about you," his father said.

Jenny's smile was so sincere compared to his father's. Her eyes were so bright and trusting. Still, she didn't seem the least bit cowed by his father's subtly imperious attitude. "Luke's told me a lot about you, too, Mr. Benning."

"Uh-oh," said James with a falsely hearty laugh. "I'd better watch my step. I think we'll skip cocktails and go with a bottle of wine," he resolved, turning to the waiter who had materialized at the table to take their drink orders. "The Chateau Maucaillou, '78."

"Yes, sir." The waiter gave a slight, deferential bow and left the table.

Jenny's eyes grew round as she regarded Luke's father. "You didn't even look at the wine list."

Luke cringed again. This was it: the first evidence that James Benning had intimidated her with his unctuous superiority. "Well, dear," he said with a supercilious smile, "I eat here quite often and I know what I like. So, I'm happy to say, does the sommelier, who makes it a point to keep certain bottles of wine on hand for me."

Oh, yes, you're wonderful, Luke thought bitterly. *And the foundation of it all is a law degree.*

To Luke's dismay, Jenny seemed truly delighted. "That's neat!" she said. "Does the chef keep certain dishes on hand for you, too?"

"He does try."

"Wow." So naive, so vulnerable to a hawk like James Benning. "I'd love to be a regular at a classy private club like this," she admitted. "Back home, the only place I was ever a regular was McDonald's—behind the counter."

"You worked at McDonald's?" Luke's father asked.

"After school when I was in high school."

"How enterprising," he said dryly. Luke could tell that his father had all but dismissed Jenny in his mind. He shifted slightly in his seat, as if to shut her out of the conversation, and addressed Luke: "Did I tell you I had lunch with Roger Chase last Friday? We had a most enlightening discussion regarding the effects of affirmative action on Columbia Law's admissions policies—"

"Dad," Luke interrupted. "I'd rather not talk about that now."

"You'd rather not talk about it ever," his father chided. He paused when the waiter appeared at their table with the wine bottle, which James examined thoroughly before nodding his approval. The waiter uncorked it and poured a taste for James. Another lordly nod from James, and the other wineglasses were filled.

Jenny lifted her glass. "Let's drink a toast," she suggested.

Corny, thought Luke. He adored her corniness, but he knew his father would find it silly and knock her down another notch in his esteem. Given how confident Jenny was, she might not give a damn what Luke's father thought of her, but Luke gave a damn. He knew that his father could cut her to ribbons if the mood struck him, and he wanted to spare her that hurt if he could.

"A toast," James echoed with a scarcely disguised smirk. "And why not?" He lifted his glass. "Here's to my son's future. And to yours, Jenny." There was nothing subtle about the way he'd stressed that their futures were two separate entities. Luke glanced at Jenny, wondering whether she'd caught his father's implication. She was smiling.

He thought of innocent lambs. He thought of the fog-shrouded coast of Alaska. He thought of his mother saying, "He's got your whole life planned out." He thought of a wiry teenager on the soccer team, scoring a point and searching the stands in vain for his father. He thought of a dinner party at which two young boys were marched into the dining room in their pajamas to say hello to their parents' guests. "This is Elliott," the father said, pulling the bigger boy to his side. "A chip off the old block, isn't he? Bound for glory, just like his dad. Oh, and that's—" with a wave toward the small, pale boy "—my other son."

Look at me, Dad! he wanted to scream.

But it was too late. His father and Jenny had become engrossed in a heated debate about...oh, God, about lawyers.

"To be totally frank, Mr. Benning," she was saying, "I think one of the main reasons things are so fouled up these days is that we've got too many lawyers involved in too many aspects of our lives. Don't take this personally—I mean, we *do* need lawyers, of course—but really, when you take a bunch of people whose minds have been trained to think in a certain circumscribed way and whose language has become polluted with all that contrived legalistic jargon, and you ask them to figure out a way to deal with, say, the homeless...well, you know they aren't going to approach the problem with sympathy. They aren't going to look at street people and say, 'There but for the grace of God go I.' They're going to immerse themselves in mumbo jumbo and wrangle over all sorts of grand-sounding but ineffective legislation, and the lawyers will get their two hundred dollars an hour and the homeless will wind up with zilch."

"If the homeless wind up with zilch," James retorted, veiling his indignation behind a malevolent smile, "it's because they deserve zilch. Those with legitimate problems have resources at their disposal—"

"What resources? Many of them were released from mental institutions. Many of them were evicted from their homes due to gentrification."

"A mere function of the market," he contended. "If they're able-bodied, they can get a job that will cover the cost of housing elsewhere."

"Sure, or they could go to law school," Jenny observed, her smile remaining steadfastly earnest. "A mother doesn't need a law degree to know if her baby is hungry. But what happens if you train her as a lawyer? When her baby starts crying she might start searching the literature for precedents."

James looked at Luke. "A feisty little one, isn't she?" he muttered.

Luke scowled at his father's condescending attitude. He considered defending Jenny, then decided not to. To defend her would be, in its own way, equally condescending. Besides, she seemed to be doing all right defending herself.

James fingered one of the menus the waiter had left on the table, but his eyes shuttled back and forth between Luke and Jenny. "Luke tells me you want to be a teacher," he said.

"That's right," Jenny confirmed, still smiling.

Luke wanted to bask in the warmth of that smile, in her decency and goodness and her high-minded convictions. But he couldn't shake the understanding that his father was setting her up somehow, tossing her into the air like a clay pigeon so he could shoot her down for the sport of it.

"You like dealing with children, I take it."

"I'd make a pretty rotten teacher if I didn't," she replied with a laugh.

"Well, I'm sure your passionate arguments will prove quite effective with the primary school set, Jenny. Young children lack the wit and experience to poke holes in your theories. You might find yourself more equally matched in that environment." With that, he lifted his menu and occupied himself with its listings.

Jenny sat motionless in her chair, obviously stunned. Luke knew his father too well to be stunned; he himself had been cut down to size many times by the man. "Dad," he said quietly. "That was rude."

His father eyed him over the top of his menu. "Oh, was it?" he asked disingenuously. "I thought Jenny and I were just having a little philosophical disagreement. I certainly don't think it's rude that she's impugning our profession."

"*Your* profession," Luke erupted. "*Yours*, Dad, not mine."

"It's only a matter of time—"

"No, it's not a matter of time." Luke felt as if the sky was opening above him, as if the dense clouds of fear and anxiety and wanting had suddenly parted, letting the hot, bright sunlight through. He could not ransom his father's love at the cost of his future. He could not be the number one son at the cost of his soul. What he wanted—his father's unconditional love—was beyond his reach. Nothing he could do would ever change that fact. "I won't be going to law school, Dad," he announced, no longer willing to pretend he could win his father's affection by sacrificing his own happiness. "Not next year, not ever. I will not go."

His father labored mightily to keep his face devoid of emotion, but Luke could see the hardening in his eyes, the tensing of his jaw as he regarded his son. "This is not open to discussion, Lucas."

"There's nothing to discuss," Luke agreed. Already his declaration was having a salutary effect on him. The last clouds were drifting away. He wanted to stand tall, lift his head and breathe in the fresh sun-scented air. "I will not go."

His father opened his mouth and then shut it. He glowered at Jenny for a minute, then scrutinized Luke and nodded, as if fitting the pieces together. "Your head has been turned by a pretty coed," he muttered.

"My eyes have been opened by a wise woman," Luke countered, looking at Jenny.

She seemed distraught. "I'm sorry," she mumbled. "This isn't an argument I should be a part of."

"Oh, but you *are* a part of it, aren't you?" James accused in his lustrous baritone. "You've seduced my son, and now he thinks teaching is the highest aspiration in the world."

"Dad—"

"Teaching!" Ignoring Luke, James favored Jenny with a withering look. "Heaven only knows what reality you're living in, missy, but it isn't Luke's. You have no right to interfere in his life, no right to plant the seeds of discontent in him. He met you a few weeks ago, am I correct? And in those few weeks he's suddenly started to question his destiny. Forgive me for sensing a cause-and-effect relationship here."

Jenny clutched the arms of her chair but refused to quail before Luke's father. "Mr. Benning, I never—"

"My son's smitten with you, and although I wouldn't have taken you for his type, I won't deny that you're an appealing young girl. However, there's no reason to assume you have his interests at heart. I do. I'm his father. I know what's best for him. You want to be a teacher, you want to play with finger paints for nine months a year and extort an exorbitant salary from the taxpayers—be my guest. I would not be so presumptuous as to tell you that's the wrong profession for you. In turn, I would urge you to keep your opinions of Luke's chosen profession to yourself."

"It's *not* my chosen profession," Luke interjected.

"Mr. Benning, I've never done what you're accusing me of doing," Jenny overrode him, her voice trembling slightly.

"Luke is my friend and I care about him. I would never tell him what to do."

"Jenny," Luke silenced her, covering her hand with his. Her knuckles felt icy against his warm palm. It pained him to see her so upset just when he was feeling better than he had in years. He gave her a long, meaningful look, then addressed his father. "Jenny has never told me what to do," he said. "All she's ever done was to listen to me, which is more than I can say for you."

"I will not have you talking back to me."

"She's listened and she's reassured me I wasn't crazy. She's given me more in these past few weeks than I've gotten in a lifetime with you."

"What?" Luke's father snapped. "What has she given you, besides perhaps some excitement between the sheets?" James was usually irreproachably courteous, but right now he was fighting too hard for his son's soul to bother with courtesy. "For God's sake, Luke, she's just a girlfriend, a summer playmate. How on earth can you take seriously all her claptrap about lawyers? Where's your perspective, boy?"

"I've only just found it," Luke answered, tightening his hold on Jenny. "And I'm not about to abandon it. Come on, Jenny, let's get out of here. I seem to have lost my appetite." He rose to his feet.

Jenny hesitated for a moment before letting him help her out of her chair as well. She gazed miserably at Luke's father, who remained in his seat, thunderstruck. "I'm so sorry, Mr. Benning..."

Luke wanted to tell her to save her breath. She owed his father no apology; quite the contrary, he ought to be begging her forgiveness. But Luke wouldn't stifle her. He understood that she was apologizing not for her opinions, not for her influence over Luke, but for having inadvertently spoiled the dinner party. She hadn't realized that expressing a sentiment contrary to James Benning's was tantamount to a declaration of war, and that when James Benning went to war he honored no protocol, no Geneva Convention—nothing but victory at any cost.

And if Luke had explained all this to her beforehand? She probably would have spoken her mind anyway. That was the way Jenny was.

Not wishing to offer his father the opportunity to fire another salvo, Luke stalked through the dining room with Jenny. He continued through the foyer and out the door at such a rapid clip she had to run to keep up with him. Not until they were half a block down M Street did he break stride.

He took a long breath, let it out slowly, and turned to look at Jenny. She was weeping.

"Oh, Jenny, I'm sorry," he whispered, folding his arms around her. She'd fought so valiantly inside the restaurant; it never occurred to Luke that she'd fall apart the minute the battle ended.

She nestled into his chest, shivering against him. "I didn't know..." She sniffled and began again. "I didn't know he had so much anger in him."

"Anger? He's got plenty of anger for anyone who dares to cross him."

"No, his anger is much more general than that," she argued. "He's such a bitter man, so discontent. It's really sad, Luke. I feel so badly for him."

"Badly for *him*?" Luke let out a hoot. "Hey, come on, Jenny, he insulted you! He called you a summer playmate!"

"Even worse, he called me a coed," she muttered, lifting her head and peering up at Luke, a crooked smile breaking across her lips as she blinked away her tears. "I hate that expression. And missy, that's another one."

"He has a way with words sometimes."

"I do feel sorry for him," she said, her smile waning. "He must be very troubled to drive both his sons away from him."

Luke wanted to assert that whatever trouble James was suffering was self-inflicted. He wanted to encourage Jenny to save her compassion for those who deserved it.

But that was part of her beauty, of course; she had compassion for *everyone*, even the most loathsome, offensive human beings. Her heart was big enough to embrace Luke's father.

"I love you, Jenny," Luke murmured, touching his lips briefly to hers.

"I love you, too."

He stroked his hands over her tearstained cheeks, wiping the lingering dampness away. His heart ached from all the love he felt for her. He wanted only to stand here with her, ignoring the pedestrians swarming past them on the busy boulevard, ignoring the traffic and the noise. He wanted just to hold her and revel in their love.

But he couldn't. "I'd better take you home," he said reluctantly. "Then I'll have to go back and deal with my father."

"Now?" she asked. "Maybe you ought to let him cool off for a while."

"How long? He's spending the night at the duplex. I'm going to have to face him sooner or later."

"Later," Jenny said. "Not tonight." Her eyes blazed into his with certainty; her arms closed snugly around his waist. "Tonight you'll stay with me."

Chapter Six

"Marry me," said Luke.

Staring up into his warm honey-brown eyes, Jenny was sorely tempted to say yes. Nothing, nothing in her life had ever been as good as this. And considering that her life had, by and large, been filled to bursting with good things, that was saying a lot.

He had a beautiful body, long and lean and sinewy. His back was smooth. Even now, luxuriating in the tranquil aftermath of their lovemaking, she couldn't stop running her hands over its supple contours, stroking down his spine to his waist and back up again to the bony ridge of his shoulders. His chest was smooth, too, his nipples small and taut. He had let her touch them, let her touch him everywhere. He'd invited her boldness and trust, and in spite of her relative inexperience, she'd accepted the invitation.

He'd touched her, too—not just her body but her soul. Simply looking at him now, basking in the strength of his smile and savoring the weight of his body on top of hers, sent echoes of pleasure through her flesh.

He had propped himself up on his elbows so he could view her face. She felt the hard surface of his abdomen against her belly, the delicious pressure of his hips against hers. "How about it, Jenny?" he asked. "Should we get married?'' His smile remained, but his voice had a certain gravity to it.

Afraid to take him too seriously, she said, ''If we did, your father and I would probably set a new world record for awful in-law relationships.''

Luke chuckled. ''My mother would like you. Elliott would, too, if he ever got to meet you.''

''We could go to Sitka and visit him,'' she suggested. ''We could sail through the Panama Canal and then up to Alaska on our honeymoon.''

''If that's the kind of honeymoon you want, you'd better marry a rich lawyer.''

She pretended to mull over his advice for a moment, then joined his laughter. ''Forget it. We'll meet Elliott halfway. Where would that put us? Someplace in Idaho, maybe? I've always had my heart set on an Idaho honeymoon.''

''Idaho it is.'' He sealed their agreement with a kiss, one that began playfully but quickly intensified until their tongues were dueling and her hands were clinging to his shoulders, until she was twisting restlessly beneath him and he was hard again, moving against her. Shuddering, he pulled back and sucked in a ragged breath. ''I want you,'' he groaned.

''I want you, too,'' she murmured, sliding one hand up into his hair and urging his face back to hers for another kiss.

He resisted. ''I've got to go raid Sybil's stash,'' he said, wrestling out of her embrace and rising from the bed. When they'd arrived at Jenny's apartment, Sybil had immediately comprehended the situation and evacuated the room, taking her pillow, her nightgown and a few toiletries with her and, on her way out, reminding Jenny that she was welcome to dip into the top dresser drawer should the need arise.

"I like Sybil," Luke said now as he returned to the bed, carrying the box. At Jenny's questioning look, he added, "I'll buy her a new supply tomorrow."

Jenny laughed. Luke brought passion and tenderness to sex, but he also brought humor to it, which was particularly amazing after the rancor of his falling-out with his father earlier that evening. Or maybe it wasn't amazing. Maybe his confrontation with his father was directly responsible for his humor now, for his passion. After all the tension, this was his release. It was his escape.

She didn't doubt that he'd been speaking truthfully when he'd said he loved her. But she couldn't ignore the possibility that what was going on here in her bed had as much to do with Luke's father and his future as it had to do with Jenny, that the ecstasy he found with her was somehow magnified by the anguish that had preceded it.

Luke took her mouth with his again, and she let his kiss sweep all conscious thought from her mind. She closed her eyes, concentrating on the sliding motion of his tongue against hers and on the play of his fingertips against her cheek, her throat, her breast. She sighed as his thumb found her nipple and rubbed it, as his hand ventured lower, below her ribs, below her waist, down into the soft curls of hair between her legs. Her hand mimicked his, gliding down his body, past his much broader rib cage, the well-toned muscles of his abdomen and lower. She closed her fingers around him and stroked. At his gasp, she smiled, partly in delight at the power she exerted over him and partly in astonishment at her own powerlessness as he moved his fingers against her.

She recalled the way he had felt inside her the first time they'd made love. "I don't want to hurt you," he'd whispered when he'd realized how small she was. But he hadn't hurt her. He'd felt wonderful.

And as he rose fully on top of her, as his legs nudged hers apart and his body surged deep within her, he felt wonderful again. Better than wonderful. He felt like life itself, energy and light, desire and need, fear and the exhilaration of overcoming fear. She held him, loved him, rose to meet his fierce thrusts until the painfully sweet sensations broke free and pulsed through her, taking her somewhere she'd never been before, somewhere she hadn't known existed.

Until tonight. Until Luke shared it with her.

"MARRY ME," he said again, a long time later.

They were breathing normally at last, resting side by side in the shadowy bedroom, facing each other on the pillow with their hands clasped between them. The sun had set, throwing the room into near darkness, but Jenny was still able to make out the details of Luke's face just inches from hers.

He wasn't smiling.

"Is this some kind of plot?" she teased. "You think if you make love to me enough times I'll say yes to anything?"

"That's an interesting idea." He gently wedged his knee between her thighs. "Will it work?"

She almost dared him to try it and see. She fantasized about making love with him over and over until they were too exhausted to continue. She fantasized about marrying him. That was all it was, of course—a fantasy. She couldn't possibly take him seriously.

Her stomach made a faint growl, just loud enough to remind her that she hadn't eaten anything since lunch. Reality was intruding; she had to set aside the fantasies. "I love you, Luke," she said, gazing steadily at him. "But we're so young. We have to finish college, at least, don't you think?"

"We can still finish college if we're married."

"If you're in New Jersey and I'm in Massachusetts, it's not going to be much of a marriage."

"Where's your optimism?" he asked, a hint of accusation filtering through his voice. "You don't think we could work it out?"

"I think we could," she assured him. "I think we can. But I have to finish college first. And I'll need a master's degree if I want to teach. I have a ton of educational loans to pay off—"

"In that case, I retract the proposal," Luke said wryly. "I don't want to get stuck paying off your loans."

She was relieved by the return, however vague, of his sense of humor. Smiling, she lifted his hand to her lips and kissed it. "I'm not saying no, Luke. I'm saying maybe yes. But we need time. You know I'm right."

"You're always right," he muttered, mirroring her smile. "I'm going to have to think this thing through a little more. I don't know if I can stand being married to someone who's always right."

"Oh, you can stand it just fine," she joked. "Trust me, Luke—I'm right about this. As always." Then she cuddled up to him, cushioning her head on his shoulder and closing her eyes again.

He wanted to marry her. He really wanted to.

His life was in a state of upheaval right now. His professional future had just been thrown into turmoil, his father was furious with him, his brother lived halfway around the world... In his position she wouldn't know what to do or where to turn.

Luke knew where to turn: to Jenny. He knew what to do: hold on to her, anyway he could. Her love was the only constant, the one thing he could rely on in his turbulent universe.

She did love him. As she'd said to Sybil that very evening, if she made love with Luke she would be his forever. That premonition seemed as true now as it had been when she'd spoken it.

She and Luke were too young. So many things were waiting to happen to them, so much growing remained to be done. She couldn't marry him, not yet.

But she was his. She couldn't deny it. She was his.

TWO DAYS LATER he left Washington.

His father was gone when he returned to the duplex the following morning to shower and change his clothes before work. Not a sign of the old man, not a trace, not even a dirty cup in the kitchen sink. The swanky modern furnishings looked colder and more stark than ever. Moving through the duplex to the upstairs bedroom he'd been using, Luke felt like a trespasser.

The call came at work: not his father, not his mother, not even Elliott. "Luke," his grandfather proclaimed, "you'd better come home." No explanation offered; none needed.

"I'll get there as soon as I can," he promised.

August had begun, and the halls of Congress were emptying as senators and representatives left town. Lee Pappelli could have found tasks to keep Luke occupied—just because Congress was in recess didn't mean Senator Milford stopped receiving constituent mail and no longer needed up-to-date research on the bills coming up for a vote during the fall session. But when Luke explained that he had some family problems to attend to, Lee thanked him for a productive June and July, wished him well and sent him on his way. The busywork Luke had been doing could be handled by any literate human being. Surely some other lobbyist was waiting in the wings, ready to finger Howard Milford for a job for his kid.

Saying goodbye to his summer job was easy enough. Saying goodbye to Jenny, however, would be agony. Luke met her at the C Street exit from her building after work and they walked together to the Mall, where they bought hot dogs and sodas from a street vendor. Among the many things he'd learned from Jenny this summer was how to simplify a picnic.

"I have to go home," he told her.

They sat on a bench near the Freer Gallery. The air was hot and muggy, sour with the smell of auto exhausts. Yet in her loose, sleeveless cotton shift with its delicate pattern of yellow and green flowers, and with her hair braided back from her face, Jenny looked cool and refreshed. Sipping her soda through a straw, she studied him intently, her eyes reflecting the green in her dress. "Is it bad?" she finally asked.

"I think so. My grandfather called."

"It's my fault, isn't it?" she concluded mournfully.

"No, Jenny, it's not." In spite of the heat he wrapped his arm snugly around her. "You've saved my life. You've made me see the light. Don't ever apologize."

"But your father—"

"My father is angry with me. It's something I'm going to have to deal with." He ought to have felt some trepidation about returning to the family estate in Larchmont and going head-to-head with his father, but he didn't. He no longer had to prostrate himself before the old man. He no longer had to go begging for love. Jenny loved him for who he was, not for who she wanted him to be. She gave her love freely, without stipulations or riders.

After all these years, Luke finally understood what love was all about. He loved his father, but the only love he would accept from his father in return was unconditional love. He would always, always long for his father's love, but he would no longer barter his soul for it. Love wasn't a bargaining chip. It was nonnegotiable.

"I wish I could come with you," Jenny said.

He let out a short laugh. "And do what? Deflect the bullets? Taste my food for poison?"

She remained solemn. "I could give you moral support."

"You can give me moral support even if you're in Washington."

"And you can come back to Washington after you work things out with your father," she added, brightening.

"*If* I work things out with him."

"Is there a chance you won't?"

He issued another brief, humorless laugh. "I don't know. He's already blown it with Elliott. Maybe he'll be more willing to compromise with me. I don't know." He shook his head. "Who am I kidding? I've known the guy for twenty-one years. I'm not going to be able to work things out with him in a few days." Giving Jenny's shoulders a squeeze, he added, "But I'm not going to run away like Elliott. I'm going to stick around and see it through."

She rested her head on his shoulder. "You'll make your peace with your father," she insisted. "I've got faith in you, Luke. Everything's going to turn out just fine."

If he let himself, he could almost believe her. Rising from the bench, discarding their napkins and cans in a trash bin and then strolling along one of the unpaved paths across the Mall with her, he could very nearly believe that things would work out.

At least this much would work out, he vowed to himself. At least he and Jenny would have each other. He would keep in close touch with her, and they would date long-distance during their final year of college, and then, wherever she decided to go to graduate school, he'd go there, too. Perhaps he would go to graduate school—not law school but a decent Ph.D. program. He would devote himself this year to his studies instead of preparing for the law boards, and then he would earn himself a doctorate. He and Jenny would move into a married-students dorm. They could graduate as Mr. and Mrs. Benning, or Dr. and Mrs. or— why not?—Dr. and Dr.

Or else he'd take a job. With a degree from Princeton he ought to be able to find some sort of reputable employment, something that paid well enough to cover his new bride's education loans. Once he was with Jenny, the particulars would fall into place.

They continued to walk, passing joggers and tourists and other young couples out for the evening. Jenny's braid began to unravel, leaking wavy tendrils that softened the angles of her face. "I think it's a good thing that you're going," she remarked. "Not that I want you to leave, Luke, I'm going to miss you. But it's good for you to go and get things settled."

The sun was sinking toward the Virginia horizon, glazing the sky with gold.

"Your father will have had a little time to cool off and think about things, too," she went on. "He'll probably feel more comfortable hearing you out when he's at home. A public dining room isn't the right place to sort out a family disagreement."

Luke didn't bother to point out that James Benning was used to doing the bulk of his wheeling and dealing in public places, or that he considered the City Tavern one of his homes away from home. Jenny's pep talk encouraged him. He wouldn't interrupt.

"Under all his bluff and bluster, Luke, your father is a good man. I'm sure of it. I know he doesn't like me. He's coming from a different place than I am. But I think he's basically good inside."

"I love you," Luke whispered into her hair. After his father had browbeaten and insulted her, after he'd behaved so uncivilly to her, she still saw the good in him. More than anything, more even than the splendors they had shared in her bed last night, Luke loved her for her unshakable faith in others.

"Look at the sunset," she said, halting on the grass and gazing toward the west. The Washington Monument rose in a proud silhouette against the sky, which was streaked with pink and dark blue and gold. "It's so beautiful. There's so much beauty in this world, Luke."

Any world that had Jenny in it had to be beautiful, he thought. Whatever the outcome of his showdown with his father, Luke knew he would survive, even triumph. His world had Jenny in it; he needed nothing else.

HE HAD NEVER GUESSED that merely returning to Princeton to finish his undergraduate work would constitute a major victory. His homecoming had gone much worse than he'd anticipated. At times he'd found it almost impossible to hang on to the optimism Jenny had instilled in him.

By the time he'd pulled onto the broad circular driveway in front of his parents' stately home in Larchmont, some forty-eight hours after he'd stormed out of the City Tavern with Jenny, his father had all but declared him dead. "After everything I've done to you, you turned your back on me!" he shouted. "You're a selfish ingrate. You're as bad as your brother. Even worse. I don't want to see you again."

Perhaps all the old man needed was a longer cooling-off period, but in the meantime the bill for Luke's senior-year tuition had come due. James refused to pay it. "Not another cent," his father railed. Luke took refuge in his bedroom, but even there he was unable to escape his father's raging, which reached his ears through the closed door, through the walls and floorboards. After a couple of days he moved out, accepting his grandfather's reluctant offer of hospitality.

His mother sneaked him a thousand dollars from a household account, and his grandfather, who believed Luke had made the wrong choice but admired his nerve, gave him another two thousand dollars. He sold the BMW for a bargain-basement seven thousand dollars, applied for a loan and took the bus down to Princeton two weeks before the fall term began so he could find himself a part-time job near campus. Upon hearing what Luke had done, Elliott forwarded a check for two hundred and seventy-five dollars. "It's all I can spare," he wrote. "You've got more guts than me, kid. Go for it."

He landed a job working the graveyard shift three nights a week at a convenience store a few blocks from the campus. Never before had he had to budget every penny—and every minute—but he didn't mind his straitened circumstances. Sometimes he would bolster himself with the thought that hard work built character. At one-thirty in the morning, when the convenience store was empty of customers but still open, Luke could get a great deal of studying accomplished while getting paid four-eighty an hour. If he was chronically exhausted, if he was a little ragged at the edges, so be it. He was going to get his damned degree—with honors, if he could manage it—and thumb his nose at his father.

He had two secret weapons. One was his best friend Taylor, who sent him to his night shift behind the counter with portable gourmet feasts—overstuffed sandwiches, reheatable meat pies, slices of mocha cheesecake. "Hey, man, if you've got to stay awake till two in the morning, you may as well have some fettuccini Alfredo to keep you company," Taylor would say as he packed various concoctions in microwavable containers for his friend.

Luke's other secret weapon was Jenny. He would have liked to talk to her every night, but he couldn't afford to run up exorbitant phone bills. So he called her every Saturday morning, and she called him every Tuesday evening. "I miss you," he'd tell her. "If only I hadn't had to sell my car, I could come up and visit you."

"I could come down to Princeton," she would offer.

"It's two buses. You have to change at the Port Authority terminal. It would probably take seven or eight hours—"

"Maybe I can find someone else who's driving down," she'd suggest. "I'll put a sign on the ride board."

But no one ever responded to her sign requesting a ride to Princeton. As September slipped away, Luke began to give serious consideration to taking the two buses north to visit Jenny. But that meant sacrificing eight hours he might have spent working at the convenience store, earning the money to pay for the bus ticket and the long-distance phone calls. Being poor was a drag.

Still, they did have their phone calls. A long-distance connection with Jenny wasn't the same as holding her, caressing her small, perfect breasts, driving his tongue against hers and feeling her so warm around him, so responsive. But he would take what he could get: her husky, sexy voice and her bubbly words. She described to him the seminar she was taking at the UMass School of Education, her progress on her honors thesis on Jane Austen, and the goings-on at Chapin House, her campus dormitory. She shared her telephone with two other girls on her hall, but they had learned not to answer it when it rang on Saturday morning at ten, nor to tie it up on Tuesday evening at seven-thirty. The telephone belonged to Jenny at those two times, Jenny and Luke.

One Monday evening in October, while Luke was manning the computerized cash register at the convenience store, Taylor sauntered in. Luke's mouth began to water on cue, and he suffered a keen disappointment when Taylor emerged from behind a magazine rack to reveal that his hands were empty.

"Where's my dinner?" Luke demanded.

Taylor lifted a bag of taco chips from one of the racks and tossed it at him. "Here, a buck twenty-five. I'll treat you."

"Don't do me any favors," Luke grunted. His first week on the job, he'd consumed enough junk food to last him the rest of his life.

Taylor feigned indignation. "And here I came with the express purpose of offering to do you a favor."

"What favor?"

"I just broke up with Nancy," Taylor announced.

"Oh, yeah? Too bad." Nancy was not the first girl Taylor had courted since the fall term began. Taylor had dated her for all of two weeks. Luke didn't think the occasion called for black crepe and tears.

Neither, apparently, did Taylor. He considerately stepped aside so Luke could ring up a customer's purchase. Once the customer left the store, Taylor sidled back to the counter. "Anyway, I suddenly discover I'm free this weekend, and I was thinking, hey, I bet the leaves look great in western Massachusetts at this time of year."

Luke stopped straightening out the candy bar display and looked at Taylor.

"The deal goes like this," Taylor explained. "You fill my gas tank with premium unleaded, you pay the tolls and you tell this Smithie sweetheart of yours to set me up with a friend of hers for the weekend, okay? Just someone to keep me company. I'm not asking for a hot romance, but I'm not going to sit all by myself for the weekend while you and Jenny lock yourselves into her room and make up for lost time.''

"This weekend?"

Taylor gave a cocky shrug. "By next weekend I expect to have a new local girlfriend. This is your window of opportunity, Luke. Don't let it slip away."

"I won't. You're the best, Taylor!"

"You say that now," Taylor muttered ominously. "Wait till you realize how much it costs to fill my gas tank."

Luke telephoned Jenny from the store. He shoved coin after coin into the pay phone only to get a busy signal the first three times he tried. Finally, at ten o'clock, he heard the phone ringing on the other end.

"Hello?" said an unfamiliar voice.

"Is Jenny Perrin there?"

"I think she's asleep," the woman said.

"Wake her up," Luke pleaded. "This is Luke."

"Oh, of course. Luke," she said in a tone of voice that implied she had heard Luke's name mentioned enough times to be bored by it. It was similar to the tone of voice Taylor frequently used when Luke mentioned Jenny.

After a minute, and another quarter in the slot, Luke heard Jenny, her voice hoarse with drowsiness. "Luke?"

"I've got a ride up to Smith this weekend," he told her.

"Oh, Luke! That's great!"

They talked briefly, and Luke promised to call her again on Thursday evening, once he knew what was going on. Then he started to make plans. He rearranged his schedule at the store so he'd have Friday night off. He pored over maps, plotting the shortest route to Northampton. He raided his dwindling bank account for cash. He organized his schoolwork so he'd have only some reading to do on the weekend. He washed three loads of dirty laundry.

He dreamed. He dreamed of sleeping with Jenny and talking with Jenny. He dreamed of receiving her generous love. He dreamed of reassuring her that he hadn't been kidding around when he'd broached the subject of marriage last summer, that while she'd been correct in pointing out that marriage would have to wait until they were done with their schooling, he was prepared to wait. He dreamed of running his fingers through that glorious red hair of hers, gazing into those glorious hazel eyes and knowing, for the first time since he'd said goodbye to her in Washington, the immeasurable joy of trusting a person in heart and soul and having that trust returned.

As promised, on Thursday evening he telephoned her from his dorm to confirm the arrangements for the visit. Taylor hovered in the background, shouting, "Find out who she's setting me up with. Make sure it's someone pretty. I've heard rumors about these Smithies—"

"If Jenny is representative, you have nothing to worry about," Luke responded as he dialed her number. "She's gorgeous."

"Well, of course she's gorgeous," Taylor scoffed. "She's perfect, isn't she?"

Luke waved at him to shut up, then hunched over the phone, listening to it ring. It was answered by the same woman who'd answered the last time Luke called.

"Hi," he said, trying to picture the woman, the room in which the phone was kept, the hallway leading to Jenny's room. Tomorrow night he would finally see it all. This was his last chance to imagine it. "May I speak to Jenny Perrin, please?"

There was a long silence, and then, "Jenny isn't here."

Luke scowled. Jenny was always in her dorm when she expected him to call. In fact, he was surprised she hadn't answered the phone herself. She always answered on the first ring when he telephoned her at the appointed time on Saturday mornings. "I told her I'd call her tonight," he said. "Where is she?"

"Who is this?" the woman asked.

His scowl intensified. He decided he loathed the woman on the other end. "This is Luke Benning," he said with forced patience. "Please put Jenny on."

Another, longer silence. "She's not here."

"Where is she?"

"She's gone."

His heart began to race. His throat went dry. It must be a joke. That was it, a bad joke. Jenny was much too sincere to resort to a tasteless practical joke like this, but maybe her friends at Chapin House had cooked it up. Maybe Jenny was as much a butt of it as Luke was.

His loathing expanded to include anyone who was a part of this sick gag. "Look, it isn't funny," he said angrily. "Would you just—"

"She's gone, Luke," the woman said. Abruptly his anger faded, his resentment vanished. He had heard the quiver in her voice, the frightened, frightening hush. He had heard the way she'd spoken his name, not as an enemy but as someone sad and upset. "I'm sorry," she said. "Jenny's gone."

"Where did she go?" he asked carefully, swallowing again and again in an effort to keep his voice from breaking.

"She's gone, okay?"

"How can I reach her?"

"You can't," the woman said.

"What happened? Oh, God. Did something happen to her?"

The woman took a deep breath. "I'm sorry, Luke, okay? She doesn't want to talk to you. She doesn't want to hear from you. She's gone, and that's it."

"She said that?" He was going to choke. He was going to curse. He was going to explode. "She said that? She doesn't want to hear from me?"

"Yes."

"When? When did she say that?"

"I'm trying to be straight with you, Luke, okay? She doesn't want to see you. She doesn't want anything to do with you. So do everyone a favor and stay away."

The phone went dead.

Luke stared at the receiver in his hand. *She doesn't want anything to do with you.*

He felt dizzy.

"What happened?" Taylor asked quietly.

Ignoring him, Luke hung up and dialed Jenny's number again. This time it was answered at once by the same woman who'd just hung up on him. "I want to speak to Jenny," he demanded.

"She's gone," the woman retorted. "Get it through your head, guy. She's gone, and she wants you out of her life. Don't call again, okay?"

He heard the click of the connection being severed.

Taylor approached him from behind. "Luke? What's going on?"

He dropped the receiver, spun around and stormed past Taylor and out of the room. Later, when he calmed down enough to think, he'd figure out what to do. He'd work out a strategy. He'd make sense of it.

Maybe it *was* just a horrible joke and Jenny was right this minute returning from the library to await his call. Maybe her friend had confused this message with another one; maybe the woman was supposed to say those coldhearted words to someone else's boyfriend. Maybe it was all a nightmare and he'd wake up.

But even as he told himself such things he knew they weren't true. He knew that if he ever tried to call Jenny again, he'd speak to the same woman, and she'd tell him the same thing.

She doesn't want anything to do with you... She wants you out of her life... Don't call again... She's gone...

It wasn't a joke. A nightmare, yes, but one from which he would never escape.

He tore down the dorm stairs, through the door and out into the crisp autumn night. He raced across the leaf-strewn grass, inhaling the brisk, apple-scented air, avoiding the pools of light thrown down upon the lawn by the street lamps. He ran to the shadows, let the darkness swallow him, and understood that trust and love were empty promises and nothing more.

Wandering into the night, alone and bereft, he felt his faith slip away.

Four Silhouette Special Edition romances FREE! *Plus*

Special Editions bring you all the heartbreak and ecstasy of involving and often complex relationships as they are lived today.

And to introduce to you this highly powerful contemporary series, we'll send you four Special Edition romances, a cuddly teddy plus a mystery gift; absolutely FREE when you complete and return this card.

We'll also reserve a subscription for you to our Reader Service, which means that you'll enjoy...

▶ **Six wonderful novels** – sent direct to you every month.
▶ **Free postage and packing** – we pay all the extras.
▶ **Free regular newsletter** – packed with competitions, author news and much more.
▶ **Special Offers** – selected only for our subscribers.

Claim your **FREE** gifts overleaf

FREE BOOKS CERTIFICATE

YES! Please send me my four free Silhouette Special Editions together with my **FREE GIFTS**. Please also reserve a special Reader Service Subscription for me. If I decide to subscribe, I will receive six new titles every month for just £9.90 postage and packing free. If I decide not to subscribe I shall write to you within 10 days. The free books and gifts will be mine to keep in any case. I understand that I am under no obligation whatsoever - I may cancel or suspend my subscription at any time simply by writing to you .

NAME _____

ADDRESS _____

_____

_____

POSTCODE _____

SIGNATURE _____

I am over 18 years of age.   **IOSISE**

A MYSTERY GIFT – POST TODAY!

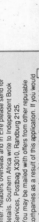

We all love mysteries so as well as the FREE books and cuddly teddy, there's an intriguing FREE gift specially for you.

Reader Service
FREEPOST
P.O. Box 236
Croydon
CR9 9EL

PART TWO
July, 1991

Chapter Seven

At eleven-thirty on Wednesday morning, with only five jurors picked, the judge called a recess so that Stewart Shaw, the defense attorney, could get his tooth filled.

Jenny didn't mind the early adjournment; jury selection could be finished quickly the following morning, leaving plenty of time for opening arguments. She liked the way the panel was shaping up: two young single women who were bound to know what life was like out there in the real world of dating, a middle-aged man who had two daughters in high school; a prim-looking grandmother; a social worker. Jenny had had to use only one of her peremptory challenges so far.

She shifted her gaze from the prospective jurors to the defense table, where Matthew Sullivan sat beside his attorney, brooding. In his suit and tie Sullivan looked like a kid who'd raided his father's closet: his face was youthful, his cheeks smooth, his dark hair neatly barbered, his eyes glistening with feigned innocence and indignation. *Hey, I'm just a guy,* he seemed to be saying. *I was only doing what comes naturally. Give me a break.*

She would love to give him a break. She would love to break his nose, his jaw, his neck, his ribs, his back and then, working her way down...

Never mind. She was a prosecutor; she'd break him with the best weapon available to her—the law. She would try him, convict him and send him to jail. She wouldn't dwell on the fact that this was her first major trial and a tough one at that. She'd asked for it, all but begged for it, and now it was hers.

She was going to win. She refused to consider any other outcome.

She shrugged her shoulders to loosen them, closed her pen and slid her notes into her briefcase. Standing, she grinned at Stewart, who like her was shuffling papers into his attaché case. "Don't let the dentist shoot you with too much novocaine," she warned. "It's bad form to drool during voir dire."

"Actually, I was figuring I'd come in tomorrow with an ice pack against my cheek," Stewart joked back. "That's our strategy—cultivate the jury's sympathy. If I groan and clutch my jaw enough times they'll vote to acquit."

Jenny rolled her eyes. Behind Stewart, Matthew Sullivan glowered at her. She smiled back. She wasn't going to let him think he could intimidate her.

After bidding Stewart goodbye, she lifted her briefcase and strode up the aisle. The hallway outside the courtroom bustled with human traffic. Lawyers, cops, reporters, court officers and suspects milled about, a physical manifestation of the clutter and confusion of the legal process.

Just as Matthew Sullivan couldn't intimidate Jenny, neither could this chaos. In truth, she found it invigorating. She'd done her time in the trenches in Framingham, handling DWI's and controlled-substance cases. She'd earned the right to be here in Superior Court, trying jerks like Sullivan.

Glancing at her watch, she proceeded down the hall to the elevator and rode downstairs to the D.A.'s office on the second floor. As she swept into the front room the receptionist arched her eyebrows in surprise. "You're back early," she said, skimming the neat piles of pink notepaper for Jenny's messages.

"Stewart Shaw lost a filling over breakfast," Jenny explained as she flipped through her messages. "He had a noon appointment to get it fixed. No big deal. I've got plenty to keep me busy." Slipping the messages into the pocket of her blazer, she headed down the hall to the office she shared with Willy Taggart. Actually, it was less an office than a twelve-foot-square space enclosed by movable partitions, and she was relieved to discover she had it to herself. She liked Willy and she exerted herself to be tolerant of his habitual sloppiness, but sometimes when they were both at their desks, she felt almost oppressed by his nearness.

Willy was currently busy with a case involving a car-theft ring; he would probably be gone all day. Jenny gingerly lifted a browning apple core from his desk and tossed it into the trash can, then wiped her fingers on a tissue and discarded it. She pulled her phone messages out of her pocket and flipped through them again. One was from a parole officer in Cambridge, one from a detective on the Somerville police force, one from her instructor at the gym in Framingham reminding her that her class had been moved up to five-thirty that evening, and one was a mystery message: "Nine-thirty-five. Friend—no name, said he'd try again later."

Messages like that gave her the creeps. What "friend" wouldn't leave his name? Her reaction—suspicion mixed with a hefty dose of anxiety—was normal, but she hated feeling uneasy. Even more, she hated the comprehension that as long as she lived she would feel just as uneasy whenever she got a weird message from a "friend."

Sighing, she crumpled the pink slip and tossed it into the trash can with the apple core. Then she circled her desk, dropped onto her chair, wiggled her feet out of her spectator pumps and lifted the phone receiver. While she was spinning her Rolodex to the Somerville Police Department's number, she heard a light rap on the edge of the partition wall and glanced up to see her boss hovering in the doorway.

"How'd it go?" he asked.

She smiled. Balding and good-natured, District Attorney Steven Blair tended to fuss over Jenny. Once at a party, when a few drinks had loosened his tongue, he'd confessed that he couldn't help worrying about someone as petite and pretty as she was. "Is it my fault that you look like a little girl?" he'd asked, to which she'd replied, "No, but it's your fault that you act like an overbearing macho man." Ever since that party, he'd tried not to be so obviously protective of her.

"It went fine," she answered now.

"So how come you're back early?"

She told him about the defense attorney's dental woes.

"So you aren't having any problems with the case?"

"Not a one."

Steve fidgeted with his tie and gave Jenny a comprehensive inspection, checking for evidence that things might not have gone as smoothly as she'd claimed. "Was Sullivan in court?"

"Uh-huh. Looking extremely surly and self-righteous. I can't wait to nail the bastard."

"I love it when you talk dirty." Steve let go of his tie and rapped his knuckles against the partition once more. "So, you'll let me know if you're having any trouble?"

"Goodbye, Steve," she said pointedly, then swiveled in her chair to answer the receptionist's buzz on her telephone. She pressed the intercom button and said, "Yes?"

"There's someone here to see you. He hasn't got an appointment. He said he's an old friend of yours. His name is Lucas Benning."

Lucas Benning.

She felt her cheeks go very cold and then very hot, burning with color. She eyed the trash can where she'd tossed the mystery message. It must have been from him.

"Of course," she said into the phone as she shoved her feet back into her shoes and straightened her spine. "He *is* an old friend. Send him in." After hanging up the phone she raised her hands to her hair and patted the flyaway red strands in a futile attempt to neaten her appearance. Yanking the center drawer of her desk open, she searched for the pocket mirror she kept there. She located it, pulled it out and studied her reflection.

Acceptable. Not great, but acceptable.

"What's up?" Steve asked.

She had forgotten he was still loitering in her doorway. "Isn't there somewhere else you have to be?" she asked.

"Hey, come on," he teased. "You don't fix your hair for just any old visitor."

"As a matter of fact, I do. Go away, Steve."

"You look pale."

"I'm fine."

Too late. Her visitor had reached the doorway, and Steve spun around to inspect the tall, lanky man with unfashionably long straw-colored hair and warm, amber-brown eyes. He was clad in a crisp cotton shirt with the sleeves rolled up, tailored cotton trousers and leather deck shoes—no socks. He gave Steve a brief look before peering around the partition. The instant he made eye contact with Jenny, the corners of his thin lips skewed upward in a marvelously familiar smile.

Luke.

She returned his stare—and his smile. Her heart seemed to beat stronger, her cheeks flushed again, her breath lodged in her throat, and a sudden aching warmth spread down from her breasts to her hips.

The very first time Luke Benning had gazed into her eyes, she'd experienced the same symptoms—the blushing, the breathlessness, the vibrant desire humming through her nervous system. But now, after so many years, so many changes...she wasn't supposed to feel this way. Not anymore.

She wasn't *really* feeling it, she convinced herself, quickly recovering from the disconcerting sensation. What she had felt was merely a memory. She was no longer the Jenny Perrin who had fallen in love with Luke one idyllic summer seven years ago. She no longer believed what that innocent child had believed. She no longer wanted what she'd wanted then. Everything was different, including Jenny. Especially Jenny.

She wasn't sorry to see Luke, though. She was shocked, dazed, puzzled—and genuinely pleased. Her smile expanding, she rose from her desk and glided across the office to him. Her impulse was to throw her arms around him in a joyous hug, but she opted for discretion and limited herself to extending her right hand. "Luke! What a surprise!"

He took her hand in his, but instead of shaking it he simply held it for a minute, closing his long, graceful fingers around hers. Then he released her. "Hello, Jenny," he said.

His voice was low and hesitant. She peered up at him, knowing she ought to say something but having absolutely no idea where to begin. Should she comment on the beautiful warmth in his eyes, the contagious charm of his smile?

Should she inquire about how he'd found her—and why? There was so much to say, so much she wanted to hear, so much catching up to do.

Steve abruptly cleared his throat, and Jenny introduced the two men. "This is my boss, Steven Blair," she told Luke. "Steve, Luke Benning."

"An old friend, I understand," Steve said, giving Luke the obligatory handshake as he sized him up. Apparently he decided Luke didn't pose much of a threat to Jenny, because he gave her a wave and vanished down the hall.

She turned back to Luke. His presence seemed to fill the enclosed area, charging the atmosphere, illuminating it. Had he always had this effect on her? She could no longer remember.

Seven years. Seven years since she'd met him, nearly as long since she'd last spoken to him. Just thinking about it had a disorienting effect on her, but not an upsetting one. She was truly delighted that, for whatever reason, Luke had gone to the effort of locating her. He had been a good friend to her. She had missed his friendship.

"You look terrific," she said.

"So do you." He appraised her, his eyes as perceptive as they were warm. "You cut your hair."

"I chopped it off in law school," she told him. "I thought it would make me look more mature."

"Law school," he repeated, yielding to an incredulous laugh as his gaze circled the room. "I can't believe it, Jenny. You're a *lawyer*."

She laughed, too. Sometimes, when she got to reminiscing about the way she used to be, she herself found it hard to believe she'd wound up as she had. "It *is* funny, isn't it?"

He continued to scrutinize her, taking note of her beige linen suit, her paisley blouse, her stockings and conservative shoes. She didn't need his bemused expression to remind her of how much her appearance had transformed since that summer in Washington, when she'd worn loose, formless shifts, leather sandals, dangling earrings and unstyled hair, when her carefree style had matched her carefree nature. Now she was a few pounds thinner—a loss she could ill afford—and her lips occasionally had a pinched look about them. Her complexion was no longer naturally lustrous, and a few weeks ago she had discovered a silver hair sprouting from her part.

Luke, on the other hand, looked as handsome as he'd looked then. His body was lean and athletic. He hadn't gained a frown line over the years; he hadn't lost a single hair. His taste in clothing hadn't changed, but something about him *had*—for the better. He seemed more relaxed now than he'd been when she'd known him, more together. Jenny's decision to clear out of his life apparently hadn't done him any lasting harm.

Maybe it had done him good.

"I probably shouldn't have sprung myself on you like this," Luke was saying, and she forced her thoughts back to the present. "I telephoned your office, but the receptionist said you were going to be in court until one o'clock. It took me less time to get here than I thought it would. And obviously you got out of court before one."

She continued to stare at him, dumbfounded yet happy. Maybe she should have felt shy or embarrassed or ill-at-ease. But she'd never felt those things with Luke before, not even the first night they'd met, when she'd approached him without hesitation and announced that she was a busybody. "Where did you come from?" she asked. "I mean, are you living in the Boston area?"

"I'm spending the summer on Cape Cod," he explained. "I saw you on TV two nights ago, on the local news."

She nodded. Yesterday her associates had praised her for her polished delivery of the office's position, and one of her neighbors had told her she'd looked gorgeous and ought to forget about law and go into show biz. She herself had thought she'd looked spindly and sounded officious, but she had found the news report as a whole accurate and insightful.

"They said on the news that you were with the Middlesex County District Attorney's office," Luke explained modestly. "So I tracked you down. I hope you don't mind."

"Oh, no, not at all. I'm glad you did. I'm stunned..." She laughed again. "I'm more than stunned. But so glad, Luke." Impulsively she gathered his hand back in hers and gave it a squeeze. "You really look wonderful. Life must be agreeing with you. What are you doing? What are you up to these days? Where do you live when you aren't on the Cape?" As the initial shock of seeing Luke receded, curiosity took its place and her questions came tumbling out, one on top of another. She wanted to know everything instantly. She had cared so much about Luke and worried so much about his future. Now that the future had arrived, she could see that life had worked out well for him, and she wanted to know every detail, every development, every step he'd taken along the way.

Luke glanced past her for a moment, then focused on her upturned face. "Can we—could we go somewhere, maybe have a drink or some lunch?"

She looked at her watch, at the unreturned phone messages on her desk. "Sure. Let's get some lunch," she said.

Ten minutes later they were sitting across from each other in a cozy booth in a restaurant not far from the courthouse. It was a casual place—checkerboard tablecloths, tiled floors, a Tiffany-style lamp shedding dim light onto the table. A waitress took their drink orders—a Sam Adams for

Luke and a club soda for Jenny—and left them with menus. Luke ignored his. "Are you sure this is okay?" he asked.

"What's okay? This restaurant?"

"My being here."

The contentment she'd detected in him in her office was still there, but she also sensed doubt, confusion, wariness. Perhaps he hadn't expected her to be so enthusiastic about his abrupt reappearance in her life. If she had ever considered the possibility that she might see Luke again, she wouldn't have expected herself to be enthusiastic about it, either. But that was because, on those rare occasions when she allowed herself to think about him at all, she'd thought of him as a lover, not as a friend.

She didn't regret the demise of their love affair, but now that she thought about it, she *did* regret the loss of his friendship.

This reunion was a joyous event, not a time for rueful apologies. "Of course it's okay. Now tell me everything," she urged him. "You're spending the summer on Cape Cod?"

He nodded. "I'm staying with my friend Taylor Bryant. Remember him? He was my roommate at Princeton. He lives in Harwich Port now."

"Taylor Bryant," she repeated. The name sounded familiar. Taylor had had a car…. Jenny was supposed to find Taylor a date for the weekend. He was going to drive Luke to Smith College because Luke had sold his BMW.

God. It was all so long ago.

"He owns a restaurant," Luke went on.

"Wow. A restaurant?"

"The Haven, in Dennis. Continental style, with an emphasis on seafood."

"It sounds fantastic. I wish I knew someone who owned a restaurant. I'd have a good excuse to pig out all the time."

Luke's eyes narrowed on her for a minute. "You've lost weight."

She smiled. So much for the preliminary courtesies. Luke had progressed to blunt honesty, and she was oddly relieved. "Yes," she admitted. "One of my big challenges these days—other than putting bad guys behind bars—is to try and get my weight back up to a hundred."

"Maybe we should order some food," Luke suggested, reaching for his menu.

"Later." She pulled the menu from his hand and set it back on the table. "Let's talk. Tell me everything, Luke. I want the story of your life."

His expression reflected a series of emotions—astonishment, amusement and something dark, tinged with distrust, hinting at anger. "Should I start with the day you disappeared?" he asked.

Fair enough. As far as he was concerned, she *had* disappeared; she couldn't deny it and she couldn't change it. And seven years later, she couldn't convince herself that disappearing from his life had been the wrong thing to do.

"How about starting with when you finished Princeton?" she said quietly.

He continued to scrutinize her, looking alternately mystified and skeptical. He measured her with his gaze, weighed her words, attempted to fathom her thoughts. When his silence continued beyond a minute, she asked, "Did you go to law school?"

"No."

"So what are you doing these days?"

"I'm a teacher."

"A teacher! Really?" Spontaneously she clapped her hands with delight. She had never abandoned her belief that teaching was one of the most inspiring, important professions a person could choose. She herself would not be able to handle it, but it thrilled her to learn that Luke had dedicated himself to such vital work. "Tell me all about it," she implored him. "What do you teach? Where do you teach? Is it fun? Do you find it rewarding?"

Her barrage of questions provoked a grin from him. He remained silent while the waitress delivered their drinks, then took a sip of his beer and leaned back in his seat. "I teach social studies in a public high school on Long Island. American and European history and an elective on the Third World. I also coach the soccer team."

"Do you enjoy it?"

"I love it." His smile grew almost wistful when he added, "You were right, Jenny. All that stuff you used to spout about molding kids' minds—it's true. Some of the students are obnoxious, but all you need is a few good ones each year to make everything worthwhile. And I've had more than a few. I love it."

She felt warm again, not in the disturbingly sensual way she'd felt when she'd first seen him standing in her office doorway but emotionally, spiritually warm with happiness for Luke. He'd discovered the right path for himself, after all. He'd figured out what he was meant to do with his life. If she had helped him to find his way she was glad, but what gratified her most was knowing he'd listened to his heart and made the right choice.

"That's wonderful," she murmured, wishing she could gather his hand in hers and give it another affectionate squeeze. She rarely felt the urge to touch people, but with Luke she had to suppress what seemed like a wholly natural reflex. It used to be so easy for her to clasp his hand, to mold her fingers around his elbow, to nudge him or tap his shoulder or nestle in the curve of his arm. In nearly seven years she hadn't felt relaxed enough with anyone, man or woman, to indulge in that sort of friendly physical contact.

To this day she experienced a twinge of discomfort when her instructor at the gym gripped her shoulders or positioned her leg so she wouldn't strain the muscles.

Heaven only knew whether Luke still liked to be touched, but even if he did, he certainly wouldn't want to be touched by Jenny. That he'd gone to some effort to find her implied that he didn't despise her, but she couldn't shake the understanding she had that he didn't trust her, either.

"So you finished college and became a teacher," she summed up.

"Not directly."

"Tell me," she coaxed him.

He eyed her, smiled, and shook his head at her insistent nosiness. "When I graduated from Princeton I was broke. I had debts. I took a job writing an in-house newsletter at a chemical company in New Jersey, and I volunteered to coach in a local soccer league. A lot of the coaches were teachers, and I made friends with them." He drank some beer, then continued, "I liked working with the kids. They were teenagers, facing all the temptations—drugs, alcohol, sex. Some of them came from broken homes—they lived with their mothers and didn't see their fathers, so I was the adult male they turned to. Not that I'm the greatest role model in the world—"

"You're a magnificent role model," Jenny declared.

He shrugged modestly. "I was better than nothing. I was able to help some of the kids, give them some guidance. I'd like to think I made a difference in their lives." He drifted off for a minute, reminiscing. "So, after I paid off my Princeton loan I took out another loan and went back to school to get a master's degree in education. And maybe someday I'll finish paying off that loan, too," he concluded with a smile.

"You can't be in debt," Jenny teased. "You're not wearing socks. That's supposed to mean you're rich."

"Your theory, not mine," he reminded her. Then he shrugged again and confessed, "The truth is, I've just come in to an inheritance, so...yeah, after years of barely scraping by, I'm rich again."

"An inheritance?" Her happiness at his good fortune gave way to sympathy. "Oh, Luke, who died? Not your father..."

"My grandfather. He was eighty-nine. It wasn't exactly unexpected." He drummed his fingers on the table, sorting his thoughts. "If my father passed away I would most certainly *not* come into an inheritance."

"He still hasn't made peace with you?"

"I've given up on him," Luke answered, his light tone failing to conceal his lingering bitterness. After a swallow of beer, he brightened. "Remember Elliott?"

"Your brother in Alaska."

"He's married, now. He lives in New Paltz, New York, less than an hour from my parents. His wife is an anthropology professor at the state university. They've got two kids."

"Really? How lovely! Did he ever go to law school?"

Luke shook his head. "He's a house husband. He's raising the kids while my sister-in-law teaches. It infuriates my father to think of Elliott at home, changing diapers and clipping coupons."

A vision of Luke's arrogant, censorious father flashed across Jenny's mind. "I can imagine," she said with a dry laugh.

"My mother's doing well. I don't know if I ever told you, but for a while she had a drinking problem. She's on the wagon now. She lives for her grandchildren. Spoils them rotten. She's never been happier."

"Do you have any children?" Jenny asked. Given the way his eyes had lit up when he'd talked about his brother's children, it seemed like a reasonable thing to ask. For all she knew, he could be married and a father. A lot could happen in seven years.

He seemed startled by her question. "Do *I* have children? No. Do you?"

"No."

He lowered his eyes to her hands, which were folded on the table in front of her, and took note of her ringless fingers. "You haven't ... hooked up with anyone," he half asked.

"No." She would prefer not to discuss her personal life with Luke, but she recognized the impossibility of avoiding the subject. Sooner or later he would demand to know, and she would tell him. The longer she could put it off, though, the better. "So," she said, deliberately changing the subject, "things are still stormy between you and your father."

He drank some more beer, gazing across the table, contemplating her. "My father will never forgive me," he finally said, his voice heavy with resignation rather than bitterness. "He can't forgive me for not going to law school. He can't forgive me for being able to make it on my own. He can't forgive me for managing to survive without his money or his manipulation."

"Can you talk to him, at least?"

"We talk only when we have to." He turned the beer bottle around and around, as if to give his hand something to do. "On Thanksgiving we all go to Larchmont. My father sits sulking in his study until dinner is served, and then he takes his seat at the head of the table and continues sulking in front of us. He ignores everyone except my niece. He's trying to persuade her to become a high-power lawyer like him."

"How old is she?"

"Four."

"Well, she's got a little time to think about it," Jenny pointed out. Luke shared her smile.

The waitress returned and asked if they were ready to order. Jenny gave the menu a perfunctory glance, but none of the listings jogged her appetite. Before she could speak, Luke ordered a cheese pizza for them to share.

"That was presumptuous of you," she chided once the waitress was gone. She wasn't really angry, but she bristled whenever people tried to exert that kind of control over her.

"You like pizza," he countered. "I remember."

His allusion to their past made her even less hungry. She sipped her soda and wondered why. More than just his mention of the meals they'd shared so long ago, she was reacting to something about his presence itself, something about the smooth motions of his hands and his clean male aroma and the constant radiance of his eyes. She was reacting to the fact that the last man she had ever trusted was sitting less than three feet away from her and she wanted to trust him again—but she no longer knew how.

She braced herself for the likelihood that he would continue to delve into the past—specifically, her past. Exercising sensitivity, he refrained. Instead he critiqued the restaurant's decor, giving credit to Taylor for the knowledge he'd recently acquired about restaurants. Then he critiqued his beer. "Sam Adams is such a good beer, and it's next to impossible to find outside New England," he complained. "If they don't start selling it on Long Island soon, I might have to move permanently to the Cape."

"Have you been going to the beach much?"

"Taylor's house is right on the beach, so yes, I get my feet in the sand just about every day. I went sailing with Taylor yesterday. He's got a boat."

Jenny recalled her first impression of Luke—that he looked as if he belonged on a sailboat. She smiled. "That must have been fun."

"We argued the whole time," Luke confessed.

"About what?"

"About you." He drained his glass, his eyes never leaving her. "He didn't think I should track you down."

"He was wrong," she said decisively. "If you wanted to track me down you should have. I'm really glad you did, Luke." *I've missed you,* she almost added. She hadn't been aware of missing him until now, but then, there was so much missing from her life, so much she'd gotten used to doing without. Maybe she shouldn't be glad Luke had tracked her down; maybe acknowledging the pockets of emptiness in her life wasn't such a good thing.

The waitress delivered their pizza, sliced into steaming wedges. She placed a slice on a plate for each of them, nodded when Luke requested another beer and cleared away the empty bottle.

Luke took a bite of his pizza and swallowed, his gaze never leaving Jenny. "I think it's your turn," he said.

"The story of my life, you mean?"

"You were the one who was supposed to be a teacher," he reminded her. "How did you wind up a lawyer?"

She tasted her pizza. It was delicious, but she had trouble swallowing it. "Well," she said vaguely, "things change."

"So I've noticed."

She washed down the food with a cooling sip of soda. Talking to Luke used to be easy. It still was, except for this. She was pretty sure she knew what he wanted to hear, but maybe, just maybe she was wrong. Maybe he no longer gave a damn about her reason for cutting herself off from him. He seemed strong and well adjusted; maybe he had no desire to rehash an unpleasant incident that ought to have been forgotten by now. Maybe all he really wanted to know was what he'd asked: how she had wound up a lawyer.

"I didn't go straight to law school," she said, wincing inwardly at what an understatement that was. "I worked for a while in my parents' office, mostly clerical stuff. Eventually it dawned on me that this was where I belonged. I'm not the kind of lawyer your father wanted you to be. I'm not in it for the money or the power. I'm in it to see that justice is done."

"What happened to molding kids' minds?" he asked, sounding less accusing than baffled. "You used to say it had been your lifelong dream to become a teacher."

"Another lifetime, I guess." She sighed.

He waited for her to elaborate. When she didn't, he asked, "What lifetime are you in now?"

Behind his whimsical words lurked his real questions: What was it that changed her life? Who was Jenny Perrin now? Why wasn't she the person he'd known seven years ago?

He deserved answers. She had to tell him.

Setting down her fork, she bravely met his gaze. If it was ever possible for her to trust a man again, she imagined that Luke Benning would be the man she would trust. "I dropped out for a while," she began, slowly and calmly. "Not just from Smith College but from the world." Afraid she wasn't making sense, she took a deep breath and began again. "The reason I disappeared was that I..." Again she faltered. Again she dug deep for the courage she needed. This was Luke. It shouldn't be so difficult to tell him. "You were supposed to visit me at school that week."

"I remember." He sounded ambivalent, both eager to hear her explanation and apprehensive about what it might be.

"Well, I became a statistic that week. I became a crime victim." Okay, she could do it. She could talk about it with Luke. She was in control. "I was attacked by a classmate," she explained. "I was hurt. Badly."

"Oh, God." His jaw dropped and his eyes hardened in rage—not at Jenny but at a world that allowed such an appalling thing to happen. "What kind of crime?"

"I was assaulted. I was beaten up. I was smashed to bits." She heard the exasperation creeping into her voice and didn't bother to stifle it. What difference did the details make? She didn't want to go into it.

Clearly sensing her tension, he backed off. "Why didn't you tell me?" he asked gently, comfortingly. "I mean, at the time it happened. Why didn't anyone let me know?"

She let out a bleak laugh. "I was a mess. Not just physically—emotionally. I cracked up, Luke. I went insane. Here was this classmate I'd known for weeks, someone I talked to and considered a friend, someone I *trusted*. I couldn't believe a friend would hurt me that way. I just...I fell apart."

"Jenny." He scooped her hand up in his. The contrast of his warm, enveloping fingers made her realize how icy her own fingers had become.

"I had a nervous breakdown. My parents came to Northampton and brought me home, and I spent the rest of the year trying to recuperate. I couldn't go back to Smith. Even after a year I couldn't bring myself to go back."

"Of course not."

"I wound up taking my senior year at Lake Forest University, which isn't far from my parents' house. I lived at home and continued therapy. It was a long, slow process."

"Are you all better now?" he asked.

Her eyes met his. She wished she could say yes. More than anything, she wished she could assure him that she had recovered completely. But the sweet, dark sorrow in his eyes told her he already knew that if she said such things she would be lying. "I'm probably as 'better' as I'll ever be," she conceded. "There are scars. But I'm okay."

"And you became a lawyer to fight for justice," he murmured, making the obvious connection.

"It was a good choice for me," she said. "Better even than therapy. I forced myself to come back to Massachusetts for law school. I had to prove to myself that I could face it. So I went to Boston University. I got my law degree two years ago and joined Steve Blair's staff."

"And now you put the bad guys behind bars."

"That's the basic idea," she confirmed. The circulation began to return to her fingers, and she felt a healthy, welcome pang of hunger. Telling Luke these things wasn't so bad after all. "I've been taking self-defense courses for a few years, too. I've got muscles, Luke. And I went back to visit the Smith campus. I didn't fall apart. I'm doing fine."

"Yes," he said uncertainly.

"I am," she emphasized, smiling. "Please don't pity me."

"I don't pity you." He released her hand and shifted in his seat, cocking his head as he appraised her. "But I still don't understand..." His brow dipped slightly as he contemplated everything she had told him. "I can accept that you went through a traumatic experience, Jenny, but I can't accept why you couldn't tell me. I called you at school and one of your friends told me you didn't want to hear from me ever again. You just shut me out. *I* didn't do anything to you, Jenny, but you had your friend tell me to get lost."

She closed her eyes. She had revealed so much to him. What she'd said was the truth. But the rest of it...

No, that was hers alone. That was private. That was where the scars were most gruesome, most permanent. Luke didn't have to know about it.

"I never meant to hurt you," she said contritely. "I'm sorry if I did. When it happened..." She shook her head, as if conscious that even her best explanation might not be good enough. "I was crazy, Luke. I couldn't think rationally about how you'd feel or what you'd want to know. Don't take offense if I say you weren't my top priority at the time." She pressed her lips together, aware that she was skirting very close to the line between truth and lies. She *had* been thinking of Luke at the time—maybe not rationally, but he had been very much a part of her thoughts, and her decision to leave him had been quite deliberate.

"Of course," he quickly agreed. "You had more important things to deal with. But once you were out of danger... would it have been so hard just to get some word to me? I tried so hard to find you. I badgered the girls in your dorm with phone calls. I even tracked down your old pal Sybil, from Emory. She didn't know anything. I wrote letters. I sent them to the Dean of Students at Smith and asked her to forward them to your home. I didn't know where you were, but I thought your parents might. And if they didn't, maybe we could have joined forces to locate you. I didn't know whether you were dead or alive, Jenny," he muttered, staring past her. "You could have least sent me a note saying you weren't dead."

She remembered the letters. She remembered her mother handing them to her, one less than two weeks after she'd left school, one at Thanksgiving and one at Christmas. She'd handed each one back to her mother unopened. "Throw it out," she'd said. Her mother had suggested that Jenny might consider simply letting the young man know what had happened, and Jenny had screamed, "Never! Never!" and become hysterical.

"I never saw your letters," she whispered. She felt ghastly lying to him, sick about it. But maybe she was deluding herself to think she could still be friends with Luke. Even if they could be friends, it would never be the honest friendship they'd once had. Jenny had learned in the past seven years that self-protection was as important as candor.

Luke probed her with his eyes. Had he guessed that she was lying? Only about the letters, though; the rest was the truth. He had to believe her.

After a pregnant minute, he sighed. "You did get better," he pointed out. "Didn't you ever—" He averted his gaze, as if to deflect the pain her answer might bring. "Have you ever thought about me? Have you ever considered just letting me know?"

"I had no idea where you were," she said. "So much time had passed. You would have been done at Princeton, maybe attending law school somewhere . . . probably in love with someone else."

"Jenny—"

"You might have been married, and a letter from me would have stirred up trouble for you. Yes, Luke, I *have* thought about you. But it was a long time. Life goes on. For all I knew, you'd forgotten about me."

"Forgotten about you? Jenny, how could you think I'd forget about you?" He pressed his lips together and wrestled with his anger. "I'm sorry," he said softly. "I'm in no position to judge you. I can't imagine how I would have behaved if something that terrible had happened to me."

But it wouldn't have happened to him, she thought with an unexpected surge of bitterness. He might become a crime victim; even tall, strong, athletic men were crime victims. But he would never have suffered as Jenny had. He might have been in pain, he might have been left with scars, he might even have gone temporarily insane, as she had. But his loss could never have been as great as hers.

She had lost hope. She'd lost the ability to trust. She had been brutalized not by some deranged stranger, some thief or addict desperate for money or alienated from society, but by someone she'd liked, someone she'd wanted to help, someone she'd counted as a friend.

She had been savaged not just by her friend but by her own senseless yearning to believe the best of everyone.

And in the process she had lost a large part of her soul.

Chapter Eight

Midnight found Luke sitting motionless on the wooden steps leading down to the beach, his arms resting on his knees and his gaze absorbing the moonlit vista of sea and sand and dune grass. His trouser legs were rolled up to mid-calf and his bare feet were dusted with a pale film of sand. The wind tangled through his hair, and a stubble of beard darkened his chin. He'd been on the beach steps for hours, waiting for the shore breezes to sweep the clutter from his brain, waiting for his emotions to sort themselves out. Waiting for the universe to make sense.

He heard footsteps behind him, alerting him to the fact that Taylor had gotten home from work. Taylor's shoes resounded first on the wooden planks of the deck and then on the boardwalk connecting the deck to the stairs. Without turning to greet his friend, Luke slid to one side of the step he was sitting on, leaving room for Taylor to join him.

Taylor accepted Luke's unspoken invitation and lowered himself onto the step. He removed his loafers and socks, then tugged his tie free of its knot and unbuttoned his collar button. "Warm night, isn't it?" he said.

Luke nodded. His gaze remained on the beach, on the silver tufts of foam glistening along the edges of the waves, on the reflection of the full moon splintering across the surface of the water.

"How are you?" Taylor asked. No need to loosen up with banter about the restaurant, no need to open the dialogue with a report on the customers or the latest gossip concerning the dessert chef's infatuation with a busboy ten years her junior. Tonight there could be only one reason for Luke to sit in solitude on the steps at this unseemly hour, and Taylor knew what it was.

"I'm all right," said Luke.

"You want to talk?"

Luke tugged a long spike of grass until it tore free. "About what?" he asked, shooting Taylor a humorless grin.

Taylor didn't smile back. "I thought you might come over to the restaurant tonight. I was watching for you."

"Nah." Luke twirled the reed between his fingers. "I needed some time to think."

Now it was Taylor's turn to nod. He gave Luke a chance to elaborate, and when Luke remained silent he asked, "What's she like?"

"She's okay," Luke said. He heard her alluringly husky voice running through his head: *There are scars, but I'm okay.* "God," he whispered, for not the first time since he'd walked her back to the Superior Court Building, since he'd shaken her hand and mumbled something about keeping in touch and then climbed into his Hyundai hatchback and driven away. His voice trembled slightly with rage. "God, Taylor, it was all—the whole thing was so damned senseless."

"Not to say I told you so," Taylor muttered, "but you shouldn't have gone chasing after her."

"Chasing after her wasn't the senseless part," Luke argued. "It was good to see her. She's still smart and funny, and she's still got the most beautiful hair—shorter than it used to be, but it's still that same incredible color. And her voice, and her eyes..."

"Oh, swell," Taylor groaned. "Adolescent lust time."

"Forget about lust," Luke retorted. "We were adults. We shook hands. It was all very civilized."

"How charming."

"I mean, it was nice. We were friendly." Not passionate, though. Luke had absorbed everything about Jenny, the nuances, the inflections, the way she'd moved her head, the occasional, unexpected shimmer of tears in her eyes, the instant of indecision in her face before she'd taken his hand in welcome. Her pleasure at seeing him had seemed authentic, but he'd sensed a definite barrier—one of Jenny's construction—standing between them.

He was willing to respect that barrier. He wasn't looking for a replay of the summer of '84. He'd sought Jenny out of curiosity, nothing more.

"Did you talk about the good old days?" Taylor asked.

"Yes." Luke's voice dropped to a whisper again. More than Jenny's appearance, more than her choice of career, more even than the invisible wall that separated her from him, his mind lingered on what she'd told him about the good old days, which had been about as far from good as he could imagine. He had been sitting outside for most of the evening, thinking about the horror Jenny had endured, grieving for her, grieving for everything that had been destroyed thanks to a single irrational act of violence. Jenny had been strong enough to recover, and Luke, to his eternal amazement, had also been strong enough to survive the sorrow of losing her.

Oh, yes, they were both okay. They were both fine. No pity necessary for either of them.

"So?" Taylor nudged him. "By my reckoning, she still owes me a weekend with a gorgeous Smithie. I assume she came up with some excuse for having gone AWOL that weekend.''

"She did,'' Luke snapped, effectively stifling Taylor's flippant tone. "She was attacked, just days before we were supposed to visit.''

"Attacked?''

"Yes, attacked—as in crime. She was beaten up by some thug. Pretty badly injured, from what I gather.''

"Jeez.''

"And then she had a nervous breakdown.''

Taylor cursed. Luke couldn't blame him. He himself had been doing a lot of cursing since he'd said goodbye to Jenny eleven hours ago. "Bummer,'' Taylor grunted. "Is she okay?''

"Now? Yes. She says she is, anyway.'' Luke thought for a minute. "I don't know.''

"What kind of attack?''

"I really don't know,'' Luke admitted, turning his thoughts over and over in his head, examining them compulsively, searching for some new insight that would illuminate everything for him. "It was a classmate of hers, she said.''

"A classmate? I thought Smith College was all women.''

"Women can be thugs, too,'' Luke pointed out, although he'd also found it hard to believe that someone intelligent and hardworking enough to get into such a selective college could be pathologically violent. "I think men are allowed to take classes at Smith, guys from Amherst and Hampshire and UMass. Maybe it was a man. She didn't say.''

"Well, like, was she shot? Was she stabbed? Was she—''

"I don't know,'' Luke groaned, unable to smother his frustration at how little he *did* know. "How could I ask her for specifics like that? If she'd wanted to go into the details

she would have. For me to ask would have been . . . I don't
know, voyeuristic."

"She broke your heart. You have a right to ask."

"She didn't mean to break my heart," Luke reminded his
friend, just as Jenny had reminded him. "She was a basket
case at the time. As she put it, I wasn't her top priority."

Taylor raked his hair back from his sun-tanned face.
"Nervous breakdown, huh," he murmured, his tone for-
giving.

"I can believe it," Luke admitted. He couldn't help but
believe it, and it was the part of her story that caused him
the greatest pain. "She was such an optimist, Taylor. You
never got to meet her, but if you had you would know what
I mean. She trusted everyone. She trusted panhandlers on
the street. She trusted my father, for crying out loud. And
then something like this happened to her. It must have destroyed her value system. It must have demolished her entire view of the world. I feel—I feel bad for her, Taylor."

Taylor gave his friend a long, searching look. "Do you
still love her?" he asked, not bothering to disguise his apprehension.

"No," Luke said decisively. "She's changed. She isn't the
same person I fell in love with that summer."

"Then what? You're angry? Bitter? What?"

"Sad." Speaking the word forced Luke to recognize its
inherent truth. "I feel very sad, and sorry that it happened.
Damn . . ." He sighed. "She says she's okay, Taylor, but she's
not. I know it. There's something different about her, and
it isn't good."

"She's been through hell. She's had a breakdown. What
do you expect?"

"It's not what I *expect*," Luke maintained. "It's what I
want. I don't have to be in love with her to worry about the

change in her. I don't have to love her to wish there was something I could do to help."

"What do you think she wants?"

"From me? Probably to be left alone," Luke muttered, then discarded that obvious answer. "No. If she'd wanted me to leave her alone she would have said so. One thing that hasn't changed about her, she isn't coy. She looks you in the eye and tells you what she's thinking." He engaged in a quick mental review of the time he'd spent with Jenny that day and couldn't come up with a single word or gesture of hers implying that she resented him for tracking her down. "I'm not going to leave her alone," he resolved.

"Great. Maybe I should call her up and warn her."

Luke ignored the sardonic undertone in Taylor's words. He felt determined, heartened, infused with hope. "Jenny saved my life, you know," he remarked, as much to himself as to Taylor. "I was a mess when she met me. I was floundering. I didn't know which way I was going, and she swooped down on me and took me in hand and showed me the way. She saved my life. The least I can do is save hers."

"Really, Luke, don't you think you ought to let well enough alone? The lady fell apart, and somehow she pulled herself back together. Maybe you should leave it be. She's functioning, right? She's brainy, she's attractive and she's got a high-profile job as an assistant D.A. Maybe the *most* you can do is congratulate her on her spectacular recovery and kiss her goodbye."

"That's just it, though," Luke argued. "I don't think she's recovered. On the surface, maybe, but deep down…" He couldn't expect Taylor to understand, but he doggedly tried to explain anyway. "I knew her before," he said. "I knew what she was. Something is missing inside her, Taylor, something isn't quite right. If only I could make it better, whatever it is…"

"And then what?"

"And then," Luke insisted, "I *would* kiss her goodbye. I'm not looking to relive my past, Taylor. God knows my present is a lot better than my past. If I were interested in a romance it wouldn't be with Jenny. I just want to help her out."

Taylor appraised him skeptically. "So help me, pal, if she sets you up for another fall . . ."

Luke shook his head. "She can't. I'm a hell of a lot stronger now than I was seven years ago."

Taylor stared at him a moment longer and his doubt melted. "That you are, Lucas. That you are. I just hope you're strong enough to realize that some people don't want to be saved." He stood, gathered up his shoes and socks, and scaled the steps to the boardwalk. "Do me a favor and don't try to save her life at three o'clock tomorrow afternoon. My broker has a property to show me over in West Yarmouth, fully operational. The owner wants to retire and he wants to sell the place as a working establishment. You might want to come along."

"Three o'clock. Sure." Rising from the step, Luke dusted the sand from his slacks and followed Taylor into the house. He would be able to sleep now. He was imbued with a sense of purpose and commitment. Whatever had left him so unsettled about Jenny, he was going to fix it. He was going to slay her demons, just as she'd once slain his. He was going to heal her.

It had nothing to do with love, he assured himself as he secured the deck door behind him. It had nothing to do with the fact that, despite the anguish she'd been through, despite the scars she claimed to have, Jenny was still the most exciting, spirited, enchanting woman he'd ever known. It had nothing to do with his failure, in seven years, to forge a relationship with another woman comparable to what he'd had with her.

She wasn't the Jenny Perrin he had loved. Her hair was short and her naïveté was gone. It wasn't love.

It was only fairness, he swore to himself. One good turn deserving another. It was only a matter of compassion, something Luke had had too little of until Jenny had entered his life and unlocked his heart.

BY THE TIME he arrived at the courtroom the following morning, the remainder of the jury had already been impaneled. Luke slipped inconspicuously into a vacant seat at the rear of the courtroom and peered through the thicket of heads in front of him, searching for Jenny. She must have been sitting, because he couldn't see her.

The judge signaled the defense attorney, a debonair middle-aged man in an expensive-looking gray suit. He stood, nodded deferentially to the judge and then stepped around the defense table to address the jurors. "Ladies and gentlemen of the jury, the first thing I always like to remind a jury in a criminal trial is the law of the land, and that is that a person is innocent unless the prosecutor can prove his guilt beyond a reasonable doubt. What that means is that if there is the slightest shred of doubt in your minds as to whether Matthew Sullivan is guilty of the charge of rape that has been brought against him, you *must* find him not guilty.

"However, there won't be a shred of doubt in your mind. By the end of this trial, you will be positive that my client is innocent."

He went on in a smooth, urbane tone, reminding the jury that Matthew Sullivan could be their brother, their nephew, their cousin or their son. The attorney talked about the way young ladies didn't always know what they wanted, and the way they sent out mixed signals. He talked about how Trisha

Vincent and Matthew Sullivan had dated each other, and how Trisha's love had apparently induced her to go further sexually than she might have intended, but that didn't mean Matthew had raped her. The attorney talked about college life and about how long Trisha and Matthew had known each other, about how heartbroken his client was at having his former girlfriend bring such a charge against him.

"This trial is not about a crime. It is about a confused young girl and a decent, law-abiding young man. I know that once you've heard all the testimony you will recognize that what we have here is a lovers' spat blown way out of proportion."

The lawyer returned to his table and sat. Luke again craned his neck, and this time he was rewarded by the sight of Jenny rising from her chair and stepping forward. At first he could see her only from the back—her proud posture, her neatly arranged hair, her stylish belted blazer over a conservatively cut skirt. "Your Honor," she said in a crisp, assured voice as she acknowledged the judge. Then, turning to the jury, "Ladies and gentlemen, this trial is not about a lovers' spat. It's about a single word. That word is 'no.'

"The facts in this case are uncontested. Testimony will bear out that Trisha Vincent and Matthew Sullivan were classmates at Tufts University and that they dated. It will bear out that on the night of October fourteenth Ms. Vincent and Mr. Sullivan went to a movie and then returned to Mr. Sullivan's dormitory room. It will bear out that Mr. Sullivan tried to seduce Ms. Vincent, and that she said no.

"The law states that if a man forces a woman to engage in a sexual act against her will, he is a committing the crime of rape. Trisha Vincent clearly expressed her will. She said no. What Matthew Sullivan did was rape her."

Then Jenny returned to the prosecution table and sat down.

Luke let out a slow breath. He had been expecting a longer opening argument from Jenny, an eloquent recitation on a par with the defense attorney's. That she was so brief and direct took him by surprise, the way one might be stunned by a quick slap when one was expecting a verbal dressing-down. Her ploy was startling—and incredibly effective.

Damn, but she was good at this.

He wondered why he should be surprised. Perhaps it was because he hadn't totally relinquished his memory of the gentle, kindhearted woman he used to know. To be a successful litigator required an edge, a certain ruthlessness that Jenny hadn't displayed before.

Maybe it wasn't ruthlessness. Maybe it was the same passion for justice she'd exhibited when he'd known her seven years ago. Maybe she was just as committed to helping others today as she'd been then, except that instead of helping street bums she was now helping crime victims. Maybe she was the same old Jenny after all.

No. The woman Luke had known in Washington could brighten the universe with her smile. This new woman couldn't even brighten her own eyes with a smile. During lunch the previous day, he'd noticed the enigmatic shadows darkening her pretty hazel eyes even when she'd been laughing. She was still dedicated and principled and brimming with empathy, but she seemed leery, self-protective, distrustful.

And anyway, he assured himself, if she was the same person he'd known in Washington, he might wind up falling in love with her again. He had no intention of doing that. Too much time had passed, too much scar tissue had formed. He wasn't interested in getting romantically involved with her.

He steered his attention back to the proceedings at the front of the courtroom. The first prosecution witness, the physician at the school clinic who had examined Trisha Vincent after the alleged rape, was being sworn in.

Luke watched intently. Jenny's examination of the witness was straightforward and concise. No histrionics, no subterfuge, no playing to the balcony. Once again he was forced to reassess her, weighing her past and present. She'd always been refreshingly direct then, he recalled. She'd never resorted to game playing. If she had wanted to know something, she had asked. Her approach to people had been neither demanding nor cajoling but so frank and forthright a person couldn't help but answer honestly.

That much hadn't changed, at least.

Luke's attention flagged slightly when the defense attorney began his cross-examination. The man was obviously a seasoned professional, but his technique didn't strike Luke as particularly gutsy or dynamic. He often glanced at the jury in a collaborative way, as if to imply, "You don't believe this, do you?" as he picked through the doctor's testimony, hunting for exploitable chinks and flaws. In his effort to woo the jury, the man exuded intelligence and molasses-sweet charm.

Jenny hadn't exuded anything. She was what she was, neat and contained, nothing sticky or drippy or overly sweet about her. Undoubtedly Luke was biased, but he thought her brisk, laconic approach was much more compelling.

As soon as the physician was done testifying, the judge admonished the jury to avoid reading the newspapers or watching newscasts on television and then adjourned for the day. Luke checked his watch: ten minutes to one. He stood aside as a small stream of people filed up the center aisle and out of the courtroom. When an artist passed by, Luke glimpsed the pastel sketch of Jenny on the top of her pad. It was almost a caricature—the profile rendering showed Jenny's sharp little chin thrust forward pugnaciously and her gaze cool and relentless. For some reason, the stern demeanor captured in the sketch struck Luke as sexy.

The crowd thinned, and he turned to see Jenny hunched over her table, scribbling something onto a lined legal pad. She closed her pen with an efficient snap, slid the pad into her briefcase and straightened up. After exchanging a few words and a handshake with the doctor who had testified, she pivoted—and spotted Luke.

As she had yesterday, she appeared first shocked by the sight of him and then delighted. Swinging her briefcase from the table, she hurried up the aisle to him. "What are you doing here?" she asked.

Almost, he thought as he peered down at her. Her smile was natural and luminous—it almost brightened her eyes. If only...

If only what? If only her eyes lit up he would gather her into his arms and kiss her?

Where did that bizarre thought come from? He had promised Taylor he wasn't going to fall for her again, and it was a wise promise. He and Jenny were friends, that was all. Friends.

In answer to her question, he shrugged. "What am I doing here? I'm a citizen viewing a public trial."

"You aren't a citizen of the Commonwealth," she reminded him, beckoning him to follow her out of the courtroom.

"Oh, is there a state residency requirement for watching a trial?"

Jenny detected the teasing in his tone and chuckled. "If I had a choice between watching a Middlesex Superior Court trial and lolling about on the beach on Cape Cod, I don't think anyone would find me within fifty miles of the courthouse."

Luke nearly countered that she *had* had a choice. She could have chosen to become a teacher, with her summers relatively free for beachcombing. But the bustling sixth-floor hallway didn't seem like the appropriate setting to probe Jenny's psyche for clues as to what had led her to this place, this profession. After seeing her perform in court, he couldn't dismiss the possibility that she'd made the right choice.

"You were fantastic in there," he said.

She scoffed at what she apparently believed was a gross exaggeration. "Fantastic?"

"Brilliant," he insisted. "How do you think it went?"

"I was adequate."

They started down the hallway, Luke careful to shorten his pace so she wouldn't have to jog to keep up with him. "I've got to admit, one thing you did stymied me. You know those questions the defense attorney asked the doctor about why she accepted the girl's story that she'd been raped, when there were no obvious injuries. Isn't that conjecture? I thought the doctor was only supposed to testify on medical evidence."

"Well, yes," Jenny confirmed. "But I've found it's better to save your objections until you really need them. You object too much over trivia and the jury gets suspicious. They think you're panicking about the strength of your case. They sit there, wondering, 'Why doesn't she want us to hear this?' I always try to save my objections until I absolutely need them."

He regarded her as they waited for the elevator. The doors slid open and they stepped inside. Once they were descending, he murmured, "You really are good at this, aren't you?"

Jenny laughed. "You really are good for my ego. I wish you were on the jury."

"I would have been disqualified—old friend of the prosecutor."

The elevator door opened and they emerged onto the second floor. Instead of heading to her office, Jenny halted and studied Luke with the same bemusement with which he'd studied her. "Why *did* you come?" she asked.

"To see you at work," he admitted honestly. "I'm still having a little trouble thinking of you as an attorney. I'm having less trouble now that I've seen it with my own eyes, but..."

"I'm glad you were there," she said abruptly, then glanced away. "Maybe, if I had known you were watching, I would have done even better." Her gaze shuttled from the elevator door to her briefcase, avoiding Luke. "I wish we could spend some more time together this afternoon, but I've got a ton of work to do."

"The court recessed early again, didn't it?"

"They usually recess by one o'clock," she explained. "That gives everyone time to prep and oversee our other cases. And eat lunch, if we've got a minute to spare—which I don't, I'm afraid."

"That's all right. I've got to get back to the Cape, anyway. Taylor wants me to look at a restaurant in Yarmouth he's thinking of buying."

"Oh." She lifted her eyes to him. "Will you come again?"

"To see you do your Clarence Darrow impersonation? Sure."

"Not Clarence Darrow. He was a defense attorney," she pointed out.

"But he was a great lawyer, and so are you. Yes, I'll definitely come again." He hesitated, then succumbed to impulse and bowed to kiss her cheek. Just a quick, light kiss, the kind of kiss given in friendship. A kiss because he was proud of her and awed by her and—no matter how fantastic a lawyer she was—worried about her.

Yes, he would come again, and again, until he broke down the wall she'd built around herself and found out what was behind it.

Chapter Nine

How odd. He'd kissed her cheek and she'd survived.

She wandered down the hall to her office, distracted and disoriented. It had been such a long time before she'd allowed her own parents to kiss her cheek. The few friends who knew about her breakdown respected the buffer she diligently maintained between herself and others.

Yet Luke's kiss hadn't bothered her. It hadn't caused her stomach to clench, hadn't made her blood pressure rise, hadn't made her want to shove him away or run for cover. As a matter of fact, it had felt kind of...nice.

Maybe she was undergoing some sort of emotional transformation. Change might well be something she needed, but it was destabilizing. She wasn't sure she was strong enough to handle it. Maybe in another year...or another decade...

She sighed and shook her head. Too much self-analysis, she reproached herself, too much self-consciousness. After a while it could exhaust a person.

She entered the D.A.'s office and collected her messages from the receptionist. No mysterious ones, she noticed with relief as she thumbed through the slips of paper. After becoming so discombobulated by Luke's innocuous kiss, she didn't think she could handle one of those spooky "no message" messages at the moment.

Swinging around the partition, she entered the cubicle she shared with Willy Taggart. He sat in his chair, or more accurately, reclined in it, with his spine nearly parallel to the floor and his feet propped up on his desk, pinning down a loose stack of papers. His jacket dangled precariously from the back of the chair and his shirtsleeves were rolled up; he had one pen in his hand and another wedged behind his ear. A bag of potato chips lay open on his blotter, and he simultaneously munched on them and leafed through a folder of notes balanced on his thighs.

At Jenny's entrance, he glanced up from the dossier and grinned. Swinging his feet down, he straightened in his chair but didn't bother standing. He and Jenny were equals, and they'd known each other since their days trying misdemeanors in Framingham. Etiquette wasn't necessary.

"What's up?" she asked pleasantly as she strode directly to her own tidy desk.

"I'm learning more than I ever wanted to know about chop shops. You wouldn't believe how sophisticated these operations are. I'll tell you, the folks running them make a hell of a lot more money than we do." He waved toward a brown paper bag resting atop his in-basket. "That's for you," he said.

"For me?" Jenny set down her briefcase and phone messages and crossed to his desk. Opening the bag, she inspected its contents: a cellophane-wrapped submarine sandwich, a container of milk, a banana and an oversized chocolate-chip cookie. "What's this?"

"Lunch. My treat."

"Oh." Confused, she shaped a tentative smile. "Thank you, Willy."

"But?" he prompted her.

"Well—" she carried the bag to her own desk, frowning at its contents "—you know I usually just have a cup of yogurt for lunch."

"Steve assigned me to a new case: fattening you up."

Jenny rolled her eyes.

"He says he thinks you're looking thin. Here, you can have the rest of these, too," he said, shoving the bag of chips toward her.

It was a white package with the brand name written across it in thick block letters: Cape Cod Potato Chips. Cape Cod. She immediately thought of Luke.

Uncannily Willy switched to a new subject: "Steve also mentioned you had a gentleman caller yesterday."

"A gentleman caller!" Jenny scoffed, abashed at the comprehension that Willy might have read her mind.

"A gentleman caller," Willy reiterated. "Tall, good-looking, and according to Steve, he had a strong handshake. So, what are we talking, Perrin? Is it true love? Wedding bells are gonna chime?"

"Oh, please," she groaned, feeling her cheeks flame with color for no good reason. "He was an old friend who happened to catch me on the Channel Five news and decided to look me up. What is with you guys, anyway? Haven't you got anything better to do than meddle in other people's lives?"

Willy gave her an innocent shrug. "Hey, you can't blame us. Steve thinks of you as the daughter he never had."

"He has a daughter."

"Yeah, but you're the one he *never* had. As for me..." Leaning across his desk, he presented her with a woebegone look. "You know I've had a crush on you since the first day we met."

"You've had a crush on everyone since the day you were born," Jenny pointed out with a laugh. "And the first day we met we practically came to blows over possession of the corner desk in the Framingham office.''

"That desk was *mine*."

"I claimed it first."

"You *stole* it." He joined her laughter for a moment, then grew sober. "Steve worries about more than your weight. He worries about how come you never go out with anyone. So do I."

"Cripes. What a pair of busybodies." She occupied herself with the container of milk, opening it and jamming a straw into the spout so she wouldn't have to look at Willy.

"To our knowledge you haven't dated anyone since Framingham. You were seeing that guy from your law school class for a while, and then it fizzled, and since then... nothing."

"How do you know I haven't been seeing anyone since then?" she challenged. The instant she spoke she realized her stupidity in prolonging the discussion, but it was too late to retract the words.

"You come to all the office parties alone."

"And you come to every office party with a different woman. You're the one we ought to be worried about, Willy."

"I mean, celibacy was considered fashionable in the mid-eighties, but—"

"Enough!" She held her hand up for emphasis. One thing she definitely did not wish to discuss with Willy Taggart was celibacy.

He stared at her for a moment and apparently decided he had needled her enough. "So, how's the trial going?"

"Fine." Her irritation gradually abated. She forgave him for prying; he meant no harm.

"Good jury?"

"I guess we'll know when they hand down their verdict."

Noting her lack of interest in his potato chips, he twirled the bag back to himself and helped himself to a handful, scattering crumbs across his auto-thefts dossier. "You've got yourself a hot one, Jen. Any media types in the audience?"

"Lots of folks taking notes. The *Globe*'ll probably cover it well, and you know the *Herald* drools like Pavlov's dogs whenever there's a rape story. That woman who does art for Channel Seven was in the front row, too."

"Oh, yeah?" Willy seemed impressed. "Anyone else of note keeping an eye on the proceedings?"

Yes, one person of very special note. But she wasn't going to mention Luke to Willy. She wasn't going to have him giving her a hard time—or giving her an unnaturally soft time, either. She wasn't going to provide him and Steve with something new to gossip about by telling them that her "gentleman caller" had been at the trial.

For heaven's sake, Luke was her friend. He was the only man she could imagine bringing with her to an office party, the only man she could imagine meeting after work, as she used to meet Mark Hawkins after work during her ill-fated attempt at a relationship when she'd first begun working at the district office in Framingham.

Luke was the only man she could imagine kissing her on the cheek and not sending her into paroxysms of despair.

What he sent her into was...uncertainty. Anxiety. A faint queasiness she wished was simply a reaction to the overstuffed, aromatic sandwich lying on her desk in front of her. The lunch Willy had so generously bought for her wasn't what was causing her stomach to knot up, though. It was a belated aftershock from Luke's kiss, accompanied by the keen, fearful understanding that if she did make room for him in her life, he might try to press beyond friendship, might try to kiss not her cheek but her lips. Might try to become her lover again.

He was someone she had once loved, after all, someone she had considered marrying. He was a man who had swept her up in the exhilarating vulnerability of romance, and already, without any apparent effort, he seemed to be eroding the defenses she had spent the last seven years constructing with the assistance of psychologists, aerobic training, meditation and judo.

What if he broke through? What if he dismantled her carefully wrought emotional armor?

She couldn't let that happen. If only she could wrest a guarantee from him that he would never seek anything more than friendship from her, if only she could trust him.

If only she could remember how to trust.

ALL HER MISGIVINGS notwithstanding, the first thing she did upon entering the courtroom the following morning was search the seats for Luke.

He wasn't there, and she tried to convince herself that it was just as well. She nodded to a couple of reporters she recognized, then moved forward to where her witnesses were seated: the campus security officer who had responded to the health center's call; Trisha Vincent's roommate, who had brought Trisha to the health center the night of the attack; and the rape-crisis counselor who had accompanied Trisha through her physical examination and the collection of forensic evidence. As Jenny greeted her witnesses, reviewed the morning's schedule and reassured Trisha's roommate, who was nervous about participating in a criminal trial, her eyes frequently darted around the room, looking for Luke.

She ought to be glad to know she wasn't the center of his extremely well-centered life. It was a sign of sanity on his part that he'd realized it would be more fun to spend his day baking in the sun at the beach rather than sitting in a windowless air-conditioned court chamber six stories above sea level. Maybe he'd decided to wile away the day ogling the beautiful bikini-clad women sharing the beach with him, sizing them up as potential conquests. Perhaps he understood that nothing sexual could ever exist between him and Jenny, or perhaps the notion of something sexual with her had never even entered his mind.

This was good. His absence was a good thing.

Stewart Shaw entered the room with his sulky young client in tow. Jenny exchanged a few words across the aisle with Stewart, then settled herself at the prosecution table. At exactly nine o'clock the judge took his seat and gaveled the court into session. Jenny's first witness of the day was sworn in, and after skimming her notes she rose to begin her examination. As she strode forward, she allowed herself one final survey of the half-filled courtroom and swore to herself that she was pleased not to see Luke.

An hour later, with Officer Seborg of campus security still on the stand, reviewing for the jury the contents of his written report on the incident, Jenny noticed the door at the rear of the courtroom inching open. She allowed herself the briefest glance toward the rear of the room, and her eyes met Luke's.

All her mental exhortations went forgotten as she experienced a rush of unadulterated joy.

Not wanting to break the rhythm of her examination, she hastily dropped her gaze to her copy of the report. "You say here the victim was very upset, Officer Seborg," she noted. "Can you be specific about what led you to that conclusion?"

The security officer embarked on a description of Trisha Vincent's tears, her shivering, her incoherence. Jenny nodded; she and Officer Seborg had reviewed his testimony several times before the trial, and she had already committed most of it to memory. Allowing her concentration to lapse momentarily, she thought of Luke taking his seat at the back of the room and shaped a small, private smile.

He wouldn't kiss her cheek today. She wouldn't let him. Nor would she let his arrival at the court divert her. He was just a summer citizen of the Commonwealth observing a public trial. He was just her friend.

She couldn't deny it. For better or worse, he was her friend. And for better or worse, knowing he was nearby elated her.

HE WATCHED, once again mesmerized by her confidence and skill. Unlike yesterday, today she knew he was present. She had looked straight at him when he'd stepped inside the courtroom, and the corners of her lips had twitched upward into an enchanting smile.

Admit it, he ordered himself as he absorbed her graceful posture, her poise, the precision of her speech enunciated in that seductive voice of hers. *Admit it, you're falling for her.*

The possibility should have troubled him. He should have been disturbed by the fact that, after a monogamous two-year involvement with another woman that had ended only a few months ago, he could scarcely recall the color of Linda's eyes or the quality of her voice, yet now, less than a week after he'd stumbled onto Jenny, every single detail of her seemed permanently emblazoned on his soul. He observed the way she cupped her left hand and tapped her right index finger on her palm; the way the overhead lights captured the fiery highlights of her hair; the way she lifted her chin whenever she spoke, as if she thought this would make her look bigger or more imposing. The way her straight skirt hinted at the feminine outlines of her hips and thighs, and the two-inch heels of her shoes emphasized the surprisingly athletic contours of her calves. The way a tiny dimple punctuated the left corner of her mouth.

If he was falling for her, though, he was doing so in a manner vastly different from the way he'd fallen for her seven years ago. Then he'd been a drowning man, and she had been a lifeboat and a compass. If she hadn't exactly rescued him, she'd given him what he'd needed to rescue himself.

Much as he wanted to reciprocate now, she didn't appear to be drowning. Far from it, she seemed safe. Too safe, maybe. She had washed up on a deserted island and constructed herself a shelter, cultivated a garden and woven clothes out of tree leaves and grass. She had everything she needed to survive.

But she seemed so lonely.

It had nothing to do with lust; Taylor had missed the target with that guess. What Luke felt for Jenny transcended physical desire—which wasn't to say he would object to having sex with her. Leaning toward the aisle, he glimpsed her legs again, the delicate arch of her insteps and her slender ankles. Angling his head, he took note of the fluid line of her throat, accented by her simple, effective gold earrings. The suit she had on downplayed her curves, but that didn't stop Luke from imagining them, imagining her in his bed, seven years more experienced.

Oh, yes, he was falling, all right. Lust and all.

Court adjourned at one o'clock, and Luke waited patiently as the spectators around him exited the room. Jenny acknowledged him with a quick smile, then conferred quietly with the defense attorney for a minute. Snapping shut her briefcase, she strode up the aisle to Luke. Her smile widened, creating a matching dimple at the right corner of her mouth. "You're turning into a courtroom junkie," she warned.

"Just this courtroom," he said. "Just this trial."

He discreetly took her elbow as they left the room. For some intuitive reason, he prepared himself for the likelihood that she would pull away. When she didn't, he relaxed and molded his hand gently around the bend of her arm.

"It's really an interesting case," he remarked, having no difficulty discussing something intellectual and legalistic while his fingers were sending signals through his body about the dainty dimensions of her arm. "I mean, the Vincent girl's best friend took the stand and testified that Vincent and Sullivan had been dating for six weeks."

"So?"

"So, six weeks is a long time. These kids are past puberty. Things happen."

He detected a stiffening in Jenny as she halted at the elevator door and pressed the button. "It doesn't matter how long they knew each other. He raped her. Most women are raped by someone they know."

She was tense, bristling. "I'm not criticizing the prosecution, Jenny," he said, hoping to mollify her. "I think you're doing a great job. All I'm saying is, it's going to be tough trying to persuade the jury that after six weeks of dating her exclusively, Sullivan couldn't be expected to make certain assumptions. I'm not saying he's right," Luke hastily added when Jenny gave him a lethal stare. "I'm just saying he made a fairly typical assumption."

"Of course," she snapped, pounding impatiently on the summoning button when the elevator didn't arrive at once. "He made an assumption that if she didn't go to bed with him willingly he was free to force her, under threat of bodily harm.'' The elevator door slid open at last, and she slid her arm from Luke's hand and stormed into the vacant car.

He followed her in and the door whisked shut. "Jenny, I'm not trying to excuse what he did," he persevered. She seemed unjustifiably touchy about what he considered a calm, philosophical debate. He wasn't sure why, but he felt compelled to resolve the issue before the elevator door slid open again. "All I'm saying is, it's a hard thing to prove."

"Yes," she muttered, glowering at the panel of buttons on the wall adjacent to the door. "Men always assume that if they know a woman for a while and treat her nicely, they're entitled to do whatever they want to her. It's in their nature. Spend enough time with a woman and you've earned the right to jump her bones."

"You know that's not what I think."

"If you didn't think it you wouldn't say it."

"I *didn't* say it."

"You said that's what Sullivan thought and that's what the jury thinks. Heaven only knows, maybe the only reason you kept asking me out that summer was that you figured it was only a matter of time before you'd earn the right—"

The door began to open at the second floor, and he slammed his fist against the button to close it again. Then he turned to her. He was shocked not only by what she'd said but by the fact that she'd referred so bluntly to their love affair.

Bluntly and falsely. If she didn't know why he had kept asking her out that summer, if she didn't know how deeply he had cared for her, then she was crazy.

Abruptly chastened, he let his rage at her fraudulent charge slip away. She *had* been crazy for a while. The horror she'd been through had affected her mind. He shouldn't be startled if her memory of their relationship had been warped along the way.

"Jenny," he said softly. "You know that's not the way it was."

She, too, seemed chastened. She lowered her gaze to her hands, convulsively gripping the handle of her briefcase, and let out a shaky breath. "I'm sorry," she managed. "I shouldn't have said that. I guess...it's just...this case..."

"Okay." He pressed the ground-floor button, and the elevator began to move again.

Jenny's head jerked up. "Where are we going?" she asked, her eyes wide with something akin to panic.

"Out."

"I can't go out. I've got too much work to do."

"You've got to eat lunch."

"I was planning to have something at my desk. Luke, I can't go." The elevator door opened and, once again taking her elbow, he propelled her through the throngs of people to the nearest exit. She didn't openly resist him, but the look she gave him was scathing. "Luke, I have a lot of work to do this afternoon."

"And you'll get it done," he assured her. "Fifteen minutes isn't going to make a difference."

"Fifteen minutes?"

They stepped outside into the hot afternoon sunlight. "Just a walk around the block."

She opened her mouth to object, then shut it. Pressing her lips together in a grim line, she hoisted her briefcase higher and started toward the corner at a brisk, businesslike pace.

He should have let her drop off her briefcase at her office. Chivalrously he lifted the heavy leather bag from her hand and carried it for her.

The street was alive with midday traffic—congested sidewalks and the drone of automobiles cruising by. He didn't mind. He had to get her alone for a few minutes to find out what the hell was going on in her head. Forget about reviving their affair—their friendship was at stake. Their history. Not only her memories but his.

"Does every trial get under your skin like this?" he asked in what he hoped was an unthreatening way.

Her eyes resolutely forward and her hands shoved into the pockets of her blazer, she held her silence for a minute. Then, "No. This is a special one."

"Why?"

"Because..." She took a long, calming breath and let it out slowly. They turned the corner and she slowed her pace enough to imply she was beginning to unwind. "Because men treat women badly in this society," she explained dispassionately. "I'm not talking about you in particular, Luke. But as a rule...men treat women badly."

That was it, then. Some man had broken her heart. The detachment, the withdrawal, the subtle defensiveness that had become a part of Jenny's personality were a result not of the violence she'd suffered at college but of something that had happened since then. A man had treated her badly. She'd been in love with someone else and he'd hurt her and she'd developed a hard, protective shell.

He endured a strange mixture of emotions: jealousy, indignation, a hunger for revenge against the louse who'd won her heart when it should have belonged to Luke, the louse who'd won her heart and damaged it so severely that Luke might never possess it.

Sorrow for Jenny's pain, and for his own.

"Who was he?" he asked, steeling himself for a conversation he knew was necessary, even though he would rather avoid it.

Jenny flinched. "Who was who?" she asked, so quietly he could scarcely hear her above the din of street noise.

"The guy who broke your heart."

She didn't answer right away. She continued walking, her face pale in the glaring sunlight, her eyes squinting slightly and her lips once again taut. "What makes you think someone broke my heart?"

"Because it seems to be broken," he replied, aware that that wasn't an especially illuminating answer but unable to come up with anything better.

Again she lapsed into silence for a while. "I'm not enjoying this," she finally said.

"Neither am I, but I'll be damned if we don't talk about it."

She stared across the street. She stared at the buildings lining the sidewalk, at a delivery truck rumbling past, at a trio of frizzy-haired teenage girls giggling and eating ice cream cones—everywhere but at Luke. Her eyes glistened, maybe from the sun's glare, maybe from sadness. "It used to be so easy to talk to you," she said wistfully.

"Why is it hard now?"

"Luke, I haven't seen you for seven years."

"From the minute we met it was easy for us to talk to each other," he reminded her. He sensed her discomfort, but he couldn't let up. "You commandeered me, the way I commandeered you just now, and marched me around a block and we talked."

"It was a prettier block," she reminisced, managing a crooked smile. "And by the time we'd walked completely around the block, you had thoroughly ticked me off. I don't recall how."

Luke did. He'd ticked her off by trying to get her into bed. Chalk one up to Jenny's negative view of men.

"I want us to be able to talk like that again," he said.

At last she lifted her eyes to his. They were still glistening, a shimmer of tears magnifying their multicolored beauty. "I'd like that, too."

He stopped and turned her to face him. "Then *talk* to me."

He had to give her credit. A tear skittered down her cheek, and another, but her gaze didn't waver. At long last she was ready to stop evading him. "I keep thinking . . ." She swallowed, then began again. "I keep thinking you want more from me than I can give you."

He knew a kiss-off when he heard one. But he couldn't give up, couldn't walk away from her. He just couldn't do it. If she was setting him up for a fall, as Taylor had warned, he had to proceed on the assumption that he'd land on his feet. "What can you give me?" he asked.

"My friendship."

"Your honesty?"

She sighed and he heard the tremor in her breath. "I can't give you my secrets," she said. "But I'll be as honest as I can."

Did he dare to push her? Should he test her promise? "Tell me honestly, did someone break your heart?"

She searched his face, her breath still shaky, her lower lip trapped in her teeth. An eternity passed, and she shook her head. "No, Luke. No one broke my heart."

She appeared fragile to him, courageous yet exquisitely breakable. He suddenly felt as if he were trying to catch a butterfly with a flamethrower. If she was telling the truth, if no one had broken her heart up to now, he didn't want to be the first to do it. One more question might just break her.

"I'll take your friendship," he said, arching his arm around her shoulders as they resumed their walk. Almost imperceptibly, she leaned back into his arm until her hair brushed against the bare skin.

Maybe he was being absurdly optimistic, but that alone was enough to make him think that someday—soon, he hoped—she would be able to give him more.

Chapter Ten

"Ms. Perrin? This is Evelyn Vincent. Trisha's mom."

"Yes, of course." Jenny stretched the telephone cord across the kitchen to turn off the heat under the vegetables she'd been stir-frying.

It was Sunday evening, the end of a restful weekend during which Jenny had gone to an aerobics class, taken a bike ride, read the Sunday *Globe* from beginning to end and reviewed her notes for the prosecution's final day of testimony. Whenever thoughts of Luke had intruded she'd managed them, just as her therapist had taught her to do: "It is normal for certain thoughts to cause you distress," Dr. Slater had explained. "The key to managing your distress is to manage your thoughts. Master them. Focus on that which gives you strength, and use your strength to conquer that which upsets you."

Jenny focused on Luke's companionship, on the fact that he could kiss her cheek or touch her arm without destroying her equilibrium. She focused on his claim that if all she could give him was her friendship, he would accept it. She discovered enough sources of strength in her thoughts about him that she could combat the troublesome undercurrent of his questions about the state of her heart and about the man who had decimated her world.

She'd managed. A weekend had passed without Luke, two long days during which he'd probably socialized, partied, done all the things he would never do with Jenny. From that thought, too, she took strength.

"Ms. Perrin, I hate to bother you at home..."

"No problem," Jenny assured her caller. If she hadn't wanted to be bothered she wouldn't have given her personal phone number to the Vincents.

"I didn't think this could wait. Trisha is home with us this weekend and...well, she doesn't want to testify tomorrow."

"Doesn't want to testify? Mrs. Vincent, her testimony is the most important part of our case. I've been building up to it all along. I've saved her for my final witness because she's the most powerful voice the prosecution has."

"I understand, Ms. Perrin. Oh, Lord, I understand." Evelyn Vincent sounded distraught. "I've tried talking to her. You know I want to see that creep locked up, what he did to my baby. I want to see him suffer the way she's suffered. That is a mother's prayer, Ms. Perrin. I pray every day for that boy to suffer." She sighed, and her voice was muted when she continued. "But I can't force Trisha. She's been through so much already. She says she can't bear the prospect of going through the whole thing on the stand in front of all those people. I can't force her. She's already been through too much."

Jenny's mind raced. Without Trisha's testimony, she might as well give up and ask that the charges against Matthew Sullivan be dismissed. There was no other way to win the case. She had to put Trisha on the stand. "Can I talk to Trisha?" she asked Evelyn.

"Right now?"

Jenny considered. "I don't know that this is something we can work out over the phone. Would you mind if I came to your house?"

"No, of course not. But please, Ms. Perrin, I don't want my daughter coerced. She's been hurt enough by all this."

"I understand. I'll be there in half an hour, and we'll see what we can work out."

The Vincents lived in a modest shingled house not far from historic downtown Concord. Jenny had been to their house a number of times; she'd done most of her questioning of Trisha there. Because Concord was only a half hour's drive from Tufts University, Trisha had been spending more time since the attack with her parents than at her campus dormitory.

Evelyn Vincent answered the door wearing an apologetic smile. Jenny recognized in the older woman the same anguish she had seen in her own mother's eyes when Jenny had been struggling to recover. Although Jenny wasn't a mother, she could easily believe that a mother suffered her child's hurts as acutely as the child herself.

"I'm so sorry about this," Evelyn said as she held open the screen door for Jenny. "I think Trisha is, too. But she's already been exploited by that boy once and—"

"Let me speak to her," Jenny said gently, patting Evelyn's arm. "I'm not going to exploit her or coerce her or anything like that, Mrs. Vincent. I just want to see if I can make testifying easier for her."

"Why don't you go out on the porch?" Evelyn suggested, escorting Jenny down a short hallway to an enclosed porch at the rear of the house. "You'll be cooler out there. I'll go tell Trisha you're here. Would you like some iced tea?"

"No, thanks." Jenny stepped out onto the porch, sat on one of the upholstered wrought iron chairs and smoothed

her cotton slacks over her knees. She had chosen her outfit—the cream-colored slacks and a kelly green camp shirt—
for their informality. She wanted to gain Trisha's confidence and put her mind at rest. If Trisha was frightened
about appearing in court, she might well be frightened about
facing an attorney, even if the attorney was on her side.

After a few minutes Trisha appeared. A few inches taller
than Jenny, she had brown hair and brown eyes, smooth,
slightly rounded cheeks and a small nose. All in all, she
looked quite ordinary—and she *was* quite ordinary, at least
when it came to cases like this. Stewart Shaw had claimed
that Matthew Sullivan could be anyone's brother or son.
Well, Trisha Vincent could be anyone's sister or daughter.

At the moment, her girlish cheeks bore the evidence of a
recent crying jag. Clutching a soggy tissue in one hand, she
collapsed onto the nearest chair, kicked off her rubber bath
sandals, balanced her feet on the edge of the seat cushion
and hugged her arms around her knees. The position made
her look even younger than her twenty years.

"I'm really sorry, Ms. Perrin," she mumbled hoarsely.

"That's okay," Jenny murmured sympathetically. "I
know that what I'm asking you to do is very hard."

"I just—" Trisha dabbed at her eyes with her tissue,
swallowed and began again. "I just don't think I can do it.
My mom keeps saying if I don't testify Matt'll go free,
but . . . but there's always a chance he'll go free even if I *do*
testify, so what's the point?"

"The point is, if you testify, you're contributing to
justice." Jenny sensed the protest rising to Trisha's lips and
continued before Trisha could interrupt. "I know you think
I'm exaggerating, but I've been involved in a lot of criminal proceedings. It's cathartic for a victim to testify. It's
cleansing. It's a chance to be heard. Otherwise you go

through life with this unresolved thing inside you. It will eat at you, Trisha."

"It's already eating at me," the girl moaned, swabbing at her face with the tissue again.

"I don't mean this facetiously, but if you're going to feel bad either way, why not at least go with the way that might bring a conviction?"

"Because you said—" Trisha's gaze moved around the cozy porch "—you said Matt's lawyer is going to ask me all kinds of questions about how I told Matt I loved him and everything, and like, how far I let him go with me on other dates and stuff, and...it's going to be so embarrassing, Ms. Perrin. Like, it's so personal, what he did to me and—I mean, how do you talk about something like that? It's, like, my body, and..." Her arms tightened around her shins and she rested her chin on her knees.

"You have nothing to hide," Jenny reminded her in a soft, heartfelt voice. "You have nothing to be ashamed of."

"But what he did to me—"

"If he attacked you with a gun, would you be ashamed to talk about it in court? If he attacked you with a knife? He assaulted you, Trisha. What he did to you had nothing to do with sex. It was an act of violence. Maybe it's embarrassing if you think about it as a sex act, but it *wasn't* a sex act. It was an act of violence, only he used his body instead of a gun or a knife. You're the victim of a violent crime. You're not to blame. You did nothing wrong. This boy did a vicious, hurtful thing to you, and he deserves to be punished, just as much as he would deserve to be punished if he beat you with his fists."

Trisha stared at her. A few tears trickled down her cheeks, but she didn't argue. "I guess..." she mumbled, swabbing her cheeks one last time. "I guess, when you think about it that way..."

"That's the only way to think about it."

"Okay," Trisha capitulated, her voice barely above a whisper. "I'll testify."

IF LUKE had been impressed by Jenny's performance in court on Thursday and Friday, he was spellbound on Monday. It was obvious that she was dealing with a dreadfully skittish witness in Trisha Vincent, yet Jenny's gentle, sympathetic questions elicited the most devastating testimony the prosecution had produced.

Over the weekend Luke had tried not to think about her. He'd been about as successful as he'd been trying not to think about her seven years ago, which was not very successful at all. At Taylor's request, he had taken Ellie, the vacationing financial whiz, out for pizza and miniature golf on Saturday night so Taylor could woo her cousin without interference. Suzanne had appeared at the breakfast table with Taylor Sunday morning, which implied that they'd had a more exciting night than Luke and Ellie had.

Not that they'd had a bad time. They'd gotten along well enough, and they'd both understood that they were doing a good deed for the lovebirds. But before tackling her second slice of pizza Ellie had asked Luke pointedly whether he was involved with someone else, and before he could stop himself he'd replied that he was.

Admittedly that involvement was an unfathomable thing. Jenny didn't love him. She wouldn't give him more than friendship. And she'd all but admitted she couldn't be totally honest with him.

He was challenged, puzzled, frustrated...and wildly, dangerously tempted.

So what if, in pursuing Jenny, his ego got knocked around a little? That would be preferable to spending the rest of his life in ignorance. It had taken him seven years to learn as much as he now knew about her. He was desperate to learn more.

At least that was what he'd thought about over the weekend. In court on Monday, what he thought about was her deft, sensitive handling of her witness, Trisha Vincent.

The girl was obviously tense, but Jenny's tone soothed her. She spoke quietly, addressing the witness personally, injecting just the right amount of compassion to console the girl without patronizing her. Jenny's demeanor awakened Luke's memory of the night, long ago, when she had approached a bum at Dupont Circle. She hadn't castigated the poor man or condescended to him. What she'd given him was her attention, her concern, her humanity.

"The thing is," the girl was saying, sitting tall in the witness box, looking directly at Jenny, at the jury, even at the accused, "it didn't matter whether he loved me or I loved him, because what he did was violent. He was angry and he did it to hurt me. He wrestled me onto the bed and he pinned me down and he said, 'I'm tired of you holding out on me,' and he told me to shut up, and he hit me in the mouth. He told me I had to do this because he had taken me out a lot of times and I owed it to him. He told me most girls put out on the first date and I must be sick not to want it, and then he did it. It had nothing to do with love."

"Did you say no when he asked you for sex?" Jenny asked.

"Yes."

"Did he hear you?"

"Yes."

"Did you scream?"

"Yes, until he hit me in the mouth."

"Did you fear for your life?"

"Yes."

Luke wished he could take back the fatuous comments he'd made last Friday, about how men made assumptions about the women they dated. No wonder Jenny had gotten so angry. What this girl had suffered had nothing to do with the behavior of frisky young men high on their own hormones.

Jenny questioned the girl a bit more, then thanked her and invited the defense attorney to cross-examine. As he'd been doing throughout the trial, Sullivan's attorney frequently raised his eyebrows skeptically and shot conspiratorial looks at the jury. "Did Mr. Sullivan force you to go to his room?" the attorney asked, and with marvelous aplomb the girl replied that going to a boy's room wasn't the same thing as agreeing to sex. Luke issued a silent cheer.

The defense attorney worked hard. He did whatever he could to cast aspersions on the girl's character. He mentioned a previous boyfriend of hers, and Jenny sprang to her feet with an objection. The defense attorney questioned the girl about the prevailing morality on campus, and she'd shot back that peer pressure was no reason to have sex against your will. The lawyer jabbed, but she refused to go down.

By one o'clock the cross-examination was done, and the judge excused the girl with the reminder that she might be called back as a defense witness. She nodded with great dignity and walked to the prosecution table to wait for adjournment. As soon as the judge banged his gavel and swept out of the courtroom, Trisha crumpled in her chair. Jenny wrapped her arms around the girl and hugged her.

The sight moved Luke. No matter how aloofly Jenny treated him, she still had an abundance of mercy to shower on those who needed it. Maybe her own experience as a crime victim enabled her to empathize with what Trisha Vincent had been through. But he'd be willing to wager that even if Jenny had never had a personal brush with violence she'd be just as sympathetic. She'd cared about street people without ever having lived on the streets, hadn't she? She'd cared about Luke without ever having felt neglected by her father.

No matter how much she'd changed, no matter how much she'd *tried* to change, her benevolence had remained intact.

With one arm still wrapped around Trisha's shoulders, Jenny walked the girl up the aisle to where an older woman sat. After thanking Jenny, the woman escorted Trisha out of the courtroom.

Jenny turned to Luke. She appeared both drained and exhilarated.

"You won," he said confidently. "That was incredible, Jenny. You won."

"I wish." She looked heavenward for a moment, then laughed. "Tomorrow Stewart Shaw is going to start the defense, and we may lose everything we gained today. But—" she cut him off before he could argue "—we gained a lot. She was great, wasn't she?"

"*You* were great."

She shook her head. "I wasn't the one on the stand, having the most intimate details of my life made public." Beckoning him to follow, she strode back to the prosecution table to pack up her papers. "I will admit to one major accomplishment. I managed to get her up there."

"Was there a chance she wouldn't testify?"

"Last night she was adamant about not taking the stand. I had to pay her a visit and change her mind." Jenny snapped shut her briefcase and chuckled. "After convincing her, maybe convincing the jury will be a piece of cake." Her chuckle dissolved into a satisfied smile as she gazed up at Luke. "I'm glad you were here to see it."

"So am I."

"You weren't here when the session started, and I thought, damn, he sat through all the boring stuff and he's going to miss my best witness."

"It's hard for me to get to Cambridge by nine," he explained, permitting himself a moment to savor the news that she'd been watching for him, marking his arrival and taking pleasure in it. "It's a long drive. But I made it, and it was worth it. You've already convinced the jury. You're home free, Jenny."

She laughed. "I ought to get you some pom-poms and a megaphone," she teased, preceding him up the aisle and out of the courtroom.

"I think you ought to celebrate," he remarked as they headed down the hall to the stairs. "Can we have lunch today?"

"Oh, Luke, you already know the answer. I've got too much work."

"Then let's celebrate with dinner tonight." He deliberately kept his tone light. He didn't want her to feel pressured.

She scrutinized him for a moment, weighing his invitation. "I'm really beat," she said. "This morning took a lot out of me. I was planning to head straight home after work. But . . . if you'd like, I'll make dinner for us."

"Are you sure you want to do that?" he asked. "I mean, make dinner. If you're tired we could eat takeout. I'm not fussy."

"All right. Takeout."

"You'll have to tell me where you live, and I can pick up some dinner for us on the way to your place."

"Do you know Route 9 in Framingham?" She drew him to the side of the hall out of the flow of pedestrian traffic, pulled out her legal pad and jotted down directions for him. "There," she said, handing the sheet of long yellow paper to him. "I should be home by six. And I'll pick up the takeout. I know the neighborhood restaurants. Six o'clock." She closed her briefcase, gave him a quick wave and vanished into the crowd surging toward the elevator.

He spent the day being a tourist in Boston, walking the Freedom Trail with all the enthusiasm of the social studies teacher he was. At five-thirty, after purchasing a bottle of Cabernet Sauvignon, he joined the hundreds of thousands of rush hour commuters jamming onto the Mass Pike, escaping to the suburbs for the night.

Her apartment complex was easy to find, although actually seeing it took him aback. It was exactly as she'd described it: a cluster of modern terraced apartments scaling a hill above Route 9 and overlooking a vast, picturesque reservoir. It seemed like the sort of complex in which a young, upwardly mobile lawyer would live—but Luke was still having difficulty acknowledging that Jenny was a young, upwardly mobile lawyer. She'd been such a free spirit when he'd known her in Washington, waltzing through the city with her hair tumbling down her back and her body swathed in airy earth mother dresses. If she hadn't switched tracks somewhere along the line, she would probably be living in a rickety but enchanting old Victorian house with plants on every windowsill and wind chimes clanging on the back porch.

The setting of her residence helped to remind him that he had not come to Jenny's home for romance. He had come to drink a toast to the grand conclusion to her prosecution and to learn more about her, to find out why a woman with a heart as big as Jenny's could be so afraid of opening it to love.

He parked his Hyundai in a space reserved for visitors, entered Jenny's building and rode the elevator up to her floor. She answered the door dressed in a summery slacks outfit of pastel green. Her face was devoid of makeup, her hair brushed casually back from her face, and her eyes seemed brighter than usual, complemented by the lime-sherbet color of her blouse. The Tory button earrings were gone; in their place were gold hoops. Her feet were bare.

"Come in," she invited him, leading him through the entry hall into the living room. "Did you have any trouble finding the place?"

"No," he said, taking in the room's austere decor—Danish modern couches and Parsons tables, a chilly abstract hung on the wall, not a single houseplant. He hastily glanced back at her bare feet. The sight of her cute pink toes reassured him, and he smiled and handed her the wine bottle.

"Thank you." She returned his smile, then squinted at the label. "Does it go with Mexican food? I picked up an assortment of dishes at El Torrito. I hope you like them."

He trailed her through a dining alcove into an efficient well-applianced kitchen. One pristine white counter was spread with foil-lined containers that emitted piquant aromas. "It smells great," he declared.

She crossed the room to a cabinet and pulled down two goblets, then produced a corkscrew from a drawer and handed it to Luke. "Why don't you do the honors while I pop these into the oven?" she suggested as she loosened the lids of the containers. "They could use some heating up." She organized the containers on a cookie sheet, slid it into the wall oven and adjusted the dials.

She seemed awfully chipper. Whatever her feelings for Luke, she was apparently happy to have him over for dinner. Away from the tensions of work and the pain underlying her cases, perhaps she was able to shed some of her protective shell. Maybe she would recognize that Luke had come here with no preconceptions, no driving needs or macho assumptions, no desire other than to deepen their friendship in whatever way he could.

Maybe, if she let down her guard enough, he might be able to find out where she was hurting, why she seemed lonely, how he could help.

The smile she sent him as she turned from the oven was so bright he was hard pressed to believe she was hurting anywhere at all. Her buoyant expression mesmerized him, warmed him, distracted him so much he fumbled with the corkscrew. "Ow!" he yelled as its sharp point punctured the tip of his index finger.

Clicking her tongue, Jenny glided to the sink. As soon as he was beside her, she positioned his hand under the spout, washed his finger and toweled it dry. "That corkscrew always jams," she said contritely, "and then it pops out and stabs you. I think you need a Band-Aid."

Wrapping the paper towel around his finger, she marched him out of the kitchen and down a short hall to the bathroom. Unlike the living room, the tiny bathroom was filled with warm touches. A wicker shelf above the toilet held a spray of dried flowers and an apothecary jar of bath salts; a plush white terry robe hung from a hook on the back of the door; the towels bore a vivid rainbow design, and a mirrored tray beside the sink held Jenny's toiletries. She opened the medicine cabinet above the sink and rummaged in it for antiseptic and bandages.

He scanned the shelves in front of him, aiding her search. His gaze snagged on a plastic disk containing a circular arrangement of pills. Birth control pills. The realization zapped through him like a jolt of electricity.

One part of him responded with excitement that she was sophisticated and prepared, that if by some quirk of fate things heated up between her and Luke tonight, she would be ready. Yet he felt a strange disappointment as well. He remembered the night they'd become lovers, when they'd exuberantly depleted her roommate's supply of condoms. There had been something innocent about Jenny then, something honest and unpremeditated and beautifully ingenuous. The circular container of pills in her medicine cabinet forced him once more to acknowledge how much time had gone by, how much Jenny had changed.

It was a ridiculous reaction, totally unjustifiable. But he couldn't help himself.

"There you go," she said, reminding him that while he'd been lost in thought she'd been taping his finger. "I'll send you the bill."

"Don't worry, I'm insured," he joked feebly.

They returned to the kitchen, where he concentrated on uncorking the wine bottle without further injury. By the time he'd filled the two goblets and handed one to Jenny, his mental turmoil had waned and his smile felt natural.

"Let's go out on the deck," she suggested, leaving the kitchen for the dining alcove, one wall of which contained glass sliders opening onto her terrace. "It'll be a few minutes before dinner's ready." She stepped into a pair of leather sandals by the door, slid it open and led Luke outside.

Her terrace overlooked the reservoir. The surface of the water was glass-smooth, reflecting the verdant woods surrounding it and the cloudless sky above it. "It's a beautiful view," he commented, moving past the deck furniture to the railing and leaning against it.

"The view is the nicest thing about this apartment," she said, and he had to agree. Joining him at the railing, she took a sip of her wine. "This is good."

Belatedly, he tapped his glass against hers. "Here's to your spectacular performance in court."

She gave a self-deprecating laugh. "We should be drinking to Trisha Vincent. She was the one doing all the hard work today."

Luke consumed some wine and studied the petite woman beside him. Her modesty didn't seem false, yet he saw no reason for it. "It amazes me," he remarked, "to think you almost didn't become a lawyer. You really are good at it."

She snorted.

"I wouldn't have been anywhere near as good."

"I bet you're a wonderful teacher."

He considered, then confirmed her guess with a nod. "As a matter of fact, I am."

"Tell me about it. Are you tough with the kids? Do they think you're cool? Do all the girls get crushes on you?"

He laughed. "If they do they don't mention it to me."

"Do you wear tweeds and make your students read the great books?"

"God, no. That would be boring." He ruminated for a moment. "I'm more of a gonzo-style teacher, I guess. Social studies can be dull if you don't juice it up."

"How do you juice it up?"

"Well...for example, in the class I teach on Third World studies, we play a game called 'Who Gets the Bomb?' Each of the kids is named the leader of a different Third World country, and each of them has access to a single nuclear warhead. They have to research their countries and decide who their worst enemy is—who gets the bomb."

"That's grotesque!" Jenny scolded, although she was laughing.

"They learn a lot, not only about their country's history and politics but also about the repercussions of their decision. Some of them actually decide to dismantle their bombs, once they've come to terms with the devastation they could cause. Last spring I had a real slick kid who decided to sell his bomb to one of the other kids for ten million dollars, which just about doubled his country's GNP.''

"It sounds like he's got a future in government."

"You'd better believe it. He wanted me to help him get a summer job on Capitol Hill, like the one I had in Senator Milford's office. He's too young; I couldn't do much for him. But he's going places, for better or worse.''

Jenny turned to face Luke. Her eyes were still bright, sparkling with intelligence and energy, and her hair was lustrous with coppery streaks in the fading sunlight. "I'm so glad you became a teacher, Luke," she said earnestly, all traces of amusement gone. "You seem content."

"It's all because of you," he said, adopting her tone. If she wanted to talk seriously, if she wanted to bump up against the past, that was fine with him. "I don't know if I've thanked you for everything you did for me back then—"

"I didn't give you much of a chance," she muttered, lowering her eyes.

"Then give me a chance now." He slid his thumb under her chin and tilted her head back so she had to meet his gaze. "Thank you. For everything."

"I didn't do much," she whispered.

"You just opened my eyes and put my head on straight and saved my life."

"And then vanished."

"Vanished," he agreed, startled by her unflinching honesty. "And then reappeared." Without shifting his eyes from hers, he placed his wine on the glass-topped table, then eased her goblet from her hand and set it down beside his. He slid one arm around her waist and lifted his other hand to twine his fingers through the glossy silk of her hair.

He hadn't come here for this, and if she made the merest show of resistance he would back off. He waited, giving her the opportunity to rebuff him.

Her eyes remained locked with his, glittering with emotions he couldn't interpret. Her body remained inches from his; her shoulders remained proudly square. The only sign of nervousness in her was her breath, which became short and shallow.

His respiration was uneven, too. His heart was pounding. Simply imagining what was about to happen put his nervous system on alert.

He leaned toward her. She didn't stop him.

Her lips were so soft, soft and velvety against his. Exercising restraint, he concentrated solely on them, brushing and stroking them with his mouth, not daring to venture further.

Her eyelids fluttered but stayed open, her eyes still fixed on his. She raised her hands to his sides and arched her fingers along his ribs. It would take little effort on her part to push him away.

She didn't.

He slid his arm more snugly around her, pulling her a fraction of an inch closer. He angled his head. Gently he nipped her lower lip.

She moaned and closed her eyes. Her fingertips dug into his sides.

Oh, God, he wanted her. He wanted her more than he'd ever wanted a woman before. More, even, than he'd wanted her seven years ago. He felt her self-protective layers melting like ice beneath the sun, liquefying and slipping away, bathing him with the promise of more.

His tongue danced across her lips, and with another helpless moan she opened her mouth. He stole inside, tasting, drinking her in, devouring her. His body grew taut and his arms drew her fully to himself, letting her know exactly what she was doing to him, exactly how much he desired her.

With a cry, she jerked her head away. The sudden motion caused him to release her, and she stumbled back from him. Her eyes blazed with panic and she pressed her knuckles to her mouth. Her breath came in labored gasps and her cheeks went from crimson to waxy white in the fraction of a second.

What? What went wrong?

"The dinner," she mumbled vaguely, darting toward the sliding glass door. "I'd better go check the dinner."

And once again, she vanished.

ALONE IN THE KITCHEN, she headed straight for the sink, turned on the cold water and doused her face. Her lungs hurt from the deep, ragged breaths she was taking, and her legs were rubbery. She felt sick and weak and despicable.

The amazing thing, she realized as the splashes of icy water shocked her brain back into a lucid state, was that she hadn't minded Luke's kiss at first. She had almost enjoyed it.

For the first time in seven years, she had actually enjoyed kissing a man.

She'd reveled in the subtle persuasion of his lips, their warmth, their life. She'd experienced pleasure as he'd raveled his fingers into her hair, as he'd closed his arms around her. Her body had been suffused with a strange glow, a sensation of tingling expectation that seemed to stir awake from some distant, long-suppressed region of her soul.

Then he'd shifted, pulling her closer and pressing into her. She'd felt the voracious hardness of him, demanding and unbearably male, and all that sweet, syrupy pleasure had shriveled up into a dry, withered knot of fear. She'd had to run. She couldn't deal with this.

Some things were simply beyond her ability to manage.

She heard the distant sound of the glass door sliding shut. Then Luke's voice from the kitchen doorway: "Are you all right?"

"I'm fine," she said, still hunched over the sink, hiding her face from him, feeling cowardly and queasy. "Dinner's ready." Mustering what little strength she had, she turned from the sink, carefully keeping her back to Luke, and walked to the oven to turn it off.

He didn't speak. His silence magnified every other sound in the room. She heard the dull pop of the wine bottle being reopened, the slosh of the glasses being refilled, the squeak of the oven door's hinge as she shoved it shut.

She wondered why he didn't just take off, get out of her life, find himself a normal woman.

He wanted to know. That was why he'd come here, why he kept coming, kept stalking her. They had once loved each other intensely and that love was gone. He wanted to know why. If only it didn't hurt so much to talk about it, if only she weren't so determined to let the past recede into shadow and put a good face on the present, if only she wasn't so damned afraid....

She had never testified. Now, seven years later, before a jury of one, perhaps it was time.

She put the steaming dinner entrées on a tray and brought them into the dining area, where she'd set the table for two. Luke followed her, carrying the wineglasses. They took their seats, facing each other across the table. He watched her, attentive, patient, wary.

You have nothing to hide. She was haunted by her own words, words spoken to give Trisha the strength to testify. *You have nothing to be ashamed of.*

"I was raped," she said.

Chapter Eleven

"I know."

Jenny gaped at him. "When did you figure it out?"

"Three minutes ago," he said. "When you broke from me and ran inside."

She dropped her gaze to the feast arrayed before her—enchiladas, tamales, quesadillas, rice and guacamole. She had no appetite. "I'm sorry," she mumbled.

"Sorry?"

"I should have told you before."

After a pause, he nodded. "It would have clarified a lot."

"Oh?"

"The way you've been handling your court case, for instance," he elaborated. "The way you get so riled up when you talk about it." He lifted his glass to his lips, swallowed some wine, and added, "The way you dropped out of my life."

"I had to, Luke, I—"

"I know. You broke down. I'm not criticizing you, Jenny, so stop apologizing." He tempered his blunt words by extending his hand across the table to hers, covering it, stroking his thumb against her wrist. "If you'd been mugged...I could believe you would suffer emotionally, but I don't think you would have cut me off like that. A rape, though . . . it's different."

"Yes." She concentrated on the soothing pattern his thumb was sketching on her skin. "I keep trying to convince myself that it's just like any other violent crime. Someone hurts you, and if you're lucky you recover and get on with your life. But it's not a crime like any other, Luke. It hurts you in places that never heal."

He squeezed her hand. "If you don't want to talk about it . . ."

"No, I do," she insisted. "I owe you—"

"You don't owe me anything."

"I do. I've lied to you, Luke." The words spilled out in a rush. She would never be able to discuss this with Luke again, so she had to say it all now, at once, before she lost her nerve. "I lied about the crime—"

"Not really."

"And I lied about your letters. I got all of them."

His thumb stilled. Even without looking at him she could feel his eyes on her, first quizzical, then wounded, crystallizing into coldness. She didn't have to see him to know how icy they'd become.

"I thought . . ." She sighed tremulously. "I thought I was doing you a favor by clearing out of your life. I wanted you to find a woman who was healthy and whole, who could love you in every way. I couldn't, not after . . ." She drifted off a minute, loathing the quiver in her voice but unable to stifle it. "I couldn't. I loved you enough to want something better for you."

"Oh, God." Though whispered, his words carried anguish and anger. "What made you think I wouldn't want you?"

"Think?" She let out a caustic chuckle. "One thing I wasn't doing much of was thinking."

"But afterward, I mean, after you got better."

"I'm still not better," she snapped. "I'll never be better, don't you see? Some things haven't healed."

He scrutinized her. She had neglected to turn on the light, and as the sun drifted westward it threw shadows over the table. She wondered whether the darkness in his face was a result of dusk or his own confusion. Both, probably.

She had to tell him. If she wanted catharsis, she had to testify. No more lies. The whole truth and nothing but. "I love you, Luke," she confessed, her voice low and rich with emotion. "I did then and I do now. I love you."

"Jenny—"

"But we can never have a relationship, not a complete one. I can't . . . I can't have sex anymore. I hate it. It hurts. I've tried, Luke, I've gone through therapy and I've dated a few men. I've tried. And it—" she closed her eyes, afraid of how he might react "—it disgusts me. I can't help it. It disgusts me."

His thumb came to life again, moving slowly, consolingly over the pulse point in her wrist. "You're on the pill," he observed.

She wasn't sure how he knew that, but she saw no need to deny it. "Yes. In case I get raped again." A bitter laugh escaped her. "Going through it was wretched enough, but then, afterward, I had to face the possibility of a pregnancy. I went crazy, Luke. I demanded an abortion. I demanded a hysterectomy. It turned out I wasn't pregnant, and I guess I should be grateful the doctors didn't listen to me. But the fear that I might have been... For a while I was on tranquilizers, and then I went on the pill. If it ever happens again I've protected myself. I've learned judo and I take my pill every day."

The shadows lengthened until they shrouded the entire dining area. Luke remained silent, stroking her wrist. Several minutes elapsed, and then he rose from his chair and eased her out of hers. He guided her into the living room, onto the couch. Sitting next to her, he arched his arm around her.

She tucked her legs beneath her and nestled against him, her body folded in on itself. His chest formed a solid cushion for her head, and his arm sheltered her. She wanted him to protect her. She wanted him to carry her back in time, to make all the pain go away.

She wanted the impossible.

"He was a classmate?"

She nodded.

"Smith is an all-women school."

"I was taking a class at UMass," she told him. "It was an advanced seminar in educational philosophy at the School of Ed. There's a five-college exchange program where Smith students can take courses at other colleges in the area, and I signed up for this course at UMass."

"And you were dating the guy?"

"Dating him? No. I was in love with you."

His fingers drew soothing circles against her upper arm. She snuggled closer to him. He wasn't making the pain go away, but somehow, when she curled up within the curve of his arm and absorbed his strength and stability, the pain seemed easier to bear.

"He wanted to date me, though," she continued, resting her head against the soft white cotton of his shirt. "He asked me out dozens of times. He wouldn't give up, even when I told him I was in love with someone else." She sighed. She knew she was inhaling Luke's bracing male scent, the spicy aromas of their uneaten dinner, the clean fragrance of her apartment, but her nostrils filled with the odors of pine needles and decomposing leaves, one smell tangy and one musty. A shiver ran down her spine.

Apparently Luke sensed her sudden discomfort. "If it hurts too much to talk about . . ."

"I want to talk about it," she insisted. "Unless you don't want to hear."

"I want to," he assured her, touching his lips to the soft red wisps of hair at the crown of her head. "Whatever you want to tell me, I want to know."

"His name was Adam Hastings. He was brilliant but very disorganized. He was clinically a manic-depressive—at least that's how his lawyer plea-bargained it."

"There was never a trial?"

"No. He had himself voluntarily committed to a psychiatric hospital and everyone told me I was fortunate not to have to go through the agony of a court trial."

"Is he still hospitalized?"

"I don't know. I don't want to know." She swallowed. "He never seemed particularly unbalanced to me. We were friends. He was awfully persistent about trying to get me to go out with him, but he was a good person—I thought. I was so stupid."

"No, Jenny." Luke grazed the crown of her head with his lips again. "You're not stupid."

"Not anymore. I was then. I trusted everyone. I thought that if you treated people with kindness they would be kind right back to you. I thought that no matter what they were like on the surface, everyone was blessed with inner goodness. It never occurred to me not to trust Adam. I didn't know how not to trust."

Luke sighed. His chest rose and fell against her cheek, and he pulled her closer to himself.

"It was a Wednesday in October," she continued determinedly. "The Wednesday before you were supposed to visit. I was at UMass for the seminar, and afterward Adam asked me for my help on a research assignment. I told him

I didn't think we were allowed to collaborate, and he begged me to help him anyway, and we argued long enough that I wound up missing the bus back to Smith. He offered to drive me back to campus. So I got into his car.'' She smothered a reflexive groan of self-loathing. Her parents, her doctors and her therapists had all labored tirelessly to convince her she'd done nothing wrong in accepting a ride from a classmate, and most of the time she believed them. But every now and then, when she thought about how different her life might have been if only she'd refused his offer and waited for the next bus...

"He drove right past the campus," she said, her voice cracking. Luke encouraged her with a hug. "He started hounding me about why I wouldn't go out with him, and why wouldn't I give him a chance, and he was so much better than whoever it was I was in love with. And—" she grimaced at her memory of how obtuse she'd been "—I *still* didn't think I was in any trouble. I just thought he was a bit overwrought. I told him I'd be happy to talk it through with him for the sake of our friendship, but I wished he'd take me back to Smith first. And he kept driving. He kept driving...."

Her voice drifted off. The smell was growing so intense she almost gagged. Pine needles and rotting leaves, autumn decay. Twigs and rocks. She couldn't go on.

She couldn't stop.

"He took me to a park. It was getting late, and no one was around. He made me get out of the car and go into the woods with him, and all the time he kept saying he was going to make me love him. And then—" She was silenced by another wave of nausea.

"You don't have to tell me," Luke murmured.

The deep, smooth texture of his voice lulled her. She closed her eyes and cuddled impossibly closer to him, so close she was practically sitting in his lap. She *did* have to tell him. If she didn't, if she stopped now, it would be another defeat. Adam Hastings would have triumphed again.

"He threw me on the ground and he raped me." She sounded unnaturally calm, even to herself, but that was the only way she could force out the words. "I screamed, but no one was there to hear me, and I tried to push him away but he was much bigger than me. He just shoved down my jeans and climbed onto me and raped me, and he kept saying this was going to make me fall in love with him. And when he was done I started crying, and he said that if I didn't love him it meant he must have done it wrong and he'd have to do it again. So he pulled the rest of my clothes off, and he tried to get me to make him hard again, and when I refused he hit me. And that seemed to excite him, so he kept on hitting me until he was aroused enough to rape me again."

"Jenny..."

She realized that Luke's arms had become as tense and rigid as steel, that his breath had grown harsh. Against her ear his heart drummed in a savage rage.

When he'd said she didn't have to tell him, maybe what he'd meant was that he didn't want to hear. He didn't want to hear about how chilly and damp the ground was, how the rocks and twigs dug into her flesh, transforming her skin into a map of bruises and cuts, and how she screamed until her throat was too raw to make any sound at all, and how the nightmare went on and on, again and again, time after torturous time until the sun set completely and the air became frigid. And how, hours later, Adam closed his pants and kicked her in the ribs for good measure and said, "Well, if you didn't like it there must be something wrong with you," and sauntered off, leaving her alone in the night, naked and battered, surrounded by towering pines.

Maybe Luke didn't want to hear. But she told him anyway. Just so he'd understand. Just so he'd know why she could never be his lover.

"I REALLY THINK this is what we're looking for," Taylor was saying as he refilled their mugs with coffee. Morning sunlight streamed into the kitchen, burning Luke's eyes. Even in a less glaring light, the documents Taylor had placed before him would have registered as a meaningless blur.

"The price is a little high, given the current market conditions," Taylor continued as he removed a quart of milk from the refrigerator and brought it to the table. He poured some into his mug, stirred it, and scanned the documents. "There's room to negotiate, though. And even at the asking price, I think it's feasible. The profits have been outstanding. We'd be buying a business with a great reputation and a loyal clientele. Their menu is limited, but I can work with the chef on that. He's had the training. He says he's willing to expand. The place has an ideal location, its off-season traffic isn't bad and I can pull off the financing." He sipped his coffee and eyed Luke inquisitively. "So? Say something."

"Why should I say something?" Luke asked. "I'm supposed to be the silent partner."

"You're planning to sink fifty grand into the deal. You're entitled to an opinion."

"My opinion," Luke said, shutting the folder of documents and sliding it across the table to Taylor, "is that in the four years since you bought the Haven you've doubled profits and gotten a two-star review from the *Globe*. I have faith in your judgment. If you say this place is a good investment, I'm not going to argue."

Taylor scrutinized his friend thoughtfully. "What's the matter? You look strung out."

"I'm not strung out," Luke said defensively. Hoping to forestall further questioning, he shielded himself with his mug and drank, even though the coffee scalded his tongue.

"Then what is it? You're going through withdrawal because you're missing a day of the trial?"

In truth, Luke had been very anxious to be in the courtroom today, not so much because it was the first day of defense testimony but because he didn't want Jenny to think she'd frightened him off by what she'd revealed. If she'd allowed him, he wouldn't have even left her apartment last night. He would have spent the entire night holding her, cradling her, whispering words of comfort even though he knew such words were empty and useless, even though he acknowledged that, as pained as he was by what she'd told him, he could scarcely begin to imagine the pain she herself had suffered.

He would have stayed all night but she wouldn't let him. She'd asked him to leave and he had, but only because he knew he'd see her again the next day, and the next, and the next. Now that she was back in his life, he had every intention of remaining firmly in hers.

When Taylor had accosted him early that morning before he'd left for Cambridge, and implored him to stay home so they could discuss the investment toward which Taylor was leaning, Luke had reluctantly caved in. He could give his best friend this one day. But he'd telephoned Jenny's office and left a message that he would definitely be there tomorrow.

He couldn't bear the possibility that she would misinterpret his absence. He couldn't bear to let her think he was deliberately keeping his distance. Last night she had cut her soul open and let its terrifying contents bleed onto him. As shaken as he was by what she'd said, her honesty had been the most profound expression of love.

All he wanted was to be with her. Courtrooms, trials, restaurants and investments were irrelevant. He wanted Jenny.

"Things were quiet at the Haven last night," Taylor noted, selecting a banana from the fruit bowl at the center of the table and methodically peeling it. "I thought you'd be showing up for dinner. We could have talked about all this—" he indicated the folder "—then."

"Yeah, well . . . I didn't make it."

"You had dinner in town?"

"I had dinner with Jenny," Luke confessed, staring into his coffee.

Taylor shook his head. "She's sucking you in, pal."

"Shut up."

"Hey, come on, this is Taylor you're talking to. I'm the guy who put out the fire the last time she burned you, remember?"

"She loves me," Luke said slowly, addressing his mug. "She loves me, and I love her."

"Great," Taylor muttered sarcastically. "You love each other. I'm moved to tears."

Luke exhaled. He couldn't tell Taylor the truth about Jenny. He had won her confidence last night. To tell Taylor any of it at all would betray her trust.

Trust. That was really what it was all about. Jenny loved him, but she was incapable of trust. She'd gone from someone who didn't know how not to trust, as she'd put it, to someone who couldn't trust anyone at all.

Worst of all, she'd lost the ability to trust herself.

She had taught him how to trust himself seven years ago, how to listen to his own heart. Now he had to do for her what she'd done for him, especially since the message her heart was sending her, the message she seemed unable to trust, was that she loved Luke.

"So, you both decided that you love each other," Taylor summarized a few minutes later, as he and Luke drove west into Yarmouth to have another look at the restaurant Taylor was thinking about purchasing. "Would you care to be specific about how this love expressed itself?"

"No."

Taylor shot him a sidelong glance, then turned his attention back to the traffic clogging Route 28. "Judging by your wildly euphoric mood, I suppose it's safe to assume you didn't get any last night."

"Zip it, Taylor."

"I'm just trying to get a handle on this thing. The last time you and she were in love with each other, you told me she was outstanding in bed."

"I was twenty-one years old, then," Luke muttered. "Twenty-one-year-olds talk too much."

"In other words, I'm being immature?"

"Precisely."

"I don't mean to pry," Taylor defended himself somberly. "I care about you, buddy. You and I go back a long way. If you really think you and Jenny have a shot this time, tell me what I can do to help."

Luke eyed his friend with a newfound gratitude. Maybe Taylor's behavior had bordered on crass, but he meant well. "You could stop asking so many questions."

Taylor nodded. "How about, I could also leave town for the weekend?"

"Leave town?"

"Suzanne invited me to spend the weekend in Boston with her."

"No kidding?"

"It's going to take some rearranging at the Haven, but I think Bev Cioffi can cover for me. As far as the house, it's all yours."

Luke's brain kicked into high gear. He could invite Jenny down to the Cape. They could loll on the beach, lounge on the deck, drive up to the National Seashore for a picnic or dine out in elegance. She could unwind and empty her mind of thoughts about the trial. She could relax. She could accustom herself to the fact that Luke was her friend.

And then, after dinner, after a moonlit stroll along the water's edge... maybe he would win her full trust. Maybe he would prove to her that what she'd suffered at the hands of a mentally deranged classmate had nothing at all to do with making love.

One evening seven years ago in Washington, Jenny had turned to Luke and declared, "Tonight you'll stay with me." Maybe, if the stars were with him, if he convinced her to trust him—and herself—she would turn to him and say, "Tonight I'll stay with you."

SHE HAD long ago perfected the art of maintaining an unruffled facade even when her thoughts were in upheaval, and she put that talent to use when Luke didn't show up at court on Tuesday. She carried off the cross-examination of Stewart Shaw's first three witnesses with deftness and accuracy. She performed calmly, flawlessly.

And all the while her soul twisted in anguish at the understanding that she had scared Luke away. The one man she'd dared to trust didn't want anything to do with her, now that he knew the truth. She'd scared him away.

The phone message waiting for her at her office quelled her anxiety somewhat: "Can't make it today. I'll be there tomorrow. Have lunch with me, PLEASE. Luke."

"He insisted that I capitalize 'please,'" the receptionist said contritely.

Having lunch with him would be out of the question, of course. Her mornings belonged to the Sullivan trial and her afternoons were devoted to a criminal harassment case in Waltham that was scheduled to go before a grand jury next week. She was willing to nibble on a sandwich at her desk to keep Steve and Willy off her back, but going out for lunch with Luke would consume more time than she had to spare.

Yet the next day, when she saw him in the courtroom at nine a.m.—which meant he must have left Cape Cod by seven—her resolve melted. By one o'clock she was exhausted from the intensive cross-examination of the parade of character witnesses Stewart Shaw had marched through court. She was hungry, she was frazzled and she was so relieved to see Luke that she couldn't imagine declining his offer of lunch.

"We can't linger over a fancy meal, though," she warned him. "I've got—"

"A ton of work," Luke recited with a grin. "So we'll eat fast." Taking her elbow, he ushered her down the hall to the elevator. "The defense really put on a show today. How many people are they planning to drag in to say what a swell guy Sullivan is?"

"Their witness list was ridiculous," Jenny muttered. "They listed twenty-five character witnesses—everyone from Sullivan's kindergarten teacher to his high school sweetheart. You'd think people were lined up outside the lawyer's office, begging for the privilege of telling the jury that Matthew Sullivan is an angel."

"Are they allowed to call up that many character witnesses?"

"I presented my objections," she told Luke as they left the elevator on the ground floor and made their way outside. "But the judge said that on a charge as serious as rape he's got to cut the defense some slack. I just hope they don't put the entire list on the stand."

"You handled today's witnesses wonderfully," Luke observed.

Jenny shot him a dubious look. What she'd done in court that morning was only her job. "Wonderful" seemed an overstatement. "You don't have to pump me up, Luke. I'm a good lawyer, but I'm not wonderful."

"Don't be modest," he countered, holding open the door of a neighborhood eatery and waving her inside. "If you weren't wonderful, this case would have been dismissed by now. It would have never gotten past a grand jury."

"How can you say that? The man committed a crime. He—"

"I know what he did, and I agree that it's a crime," said Luke. He fell silent as a hostess approached and led them to a table, but once they were alone he continued. "I'm the son of a lawyer, Jenny, and one thing I've learned is that not every case is black and white. It doesn't matter what happened. It doesn't matter that a real crime might have been committed. What matters is, how will it play in court? In anyone else's hands, Jenny, this case wouldn't have played well at all."

She wanted to refute him but she couldn't. When Steve had agreed to let her take the case he'd said much the same thing; and when, seven years ago, she'd asked the police whether it would be possible to bring charges against Adam Hastings, she had been told the same thing. Acquaintance rape was never a black-and-white situation.

"You think I'm going to lose, then," she concluded grimly.

"No. I think you're going to win. But it's not because your case is easily winnable, Jenny. You'll win because you're good." A waitress came to their table, and he ordered a beer for himself and a soft drink for Jenny. "So, when do you think the case will go to the jury?" he asked.

"Tomorrow, I hope. Maybe Friday. It depends on how long Shaw continues with the testimonials. He's still got to put Sullivan on the stand."

"But you'll be free for the weekend," he half asked.

"In terms of this case, yes. Once it goes to the jury, there's nothing more I can do. But I've got another case to prepare...."

"Come on, Jen. You deserve a day off."

"I deserve a year off," she said with a laugh. "However—"

"However, you'll settle for a day. Come to the Cape, Jenny. I'm staying right on the beach. We'll lie on the sand and stare at the clouds."

What a tantalizing thought. She couldn't remember the last time she'd spent an entire day doing nothing more significant than staring at the clouds. Even when she'd gone home to Illinois for Christmas she'd brought work with her.

The harassment case in Waltham needed a lot of work before it went to the grand jury. But still . . .

"I burn easily," she said.

He grinned. "So we'll douse ourselves in sunscreen and stare at the underside of a beach umbrella."

"I really shouldn't."

"You really have to."

Her litigation skills abandoned her. She could come up with no effective counterargument. She couldn't tear his allegations to shreds or undermine his certainty. The man was right. She really had to get away for a day.

"All right," she murmured. "We'll stare at the underside of an umbrella."

Chapter Twelve

She was dressed in white.

It wasn't the same outfit she'd worn in Washington; this one was a cool white below-the-knee skirt with a slouch-shouldered jacket to match; under the jacket she had on a tank top of a tangerine shade that went well with her hair. It was a crisp, summery ensemble, lacking the gauzy, lacy dreaminess of the clothing she'd worn the night Luke had fallen in love with her, and worn again the night they'd consummated their love.

But she looked just as beautiful now as she had then. Despite several generous applications of sunscreen and the protection of the striped beach umbrella Luke had found in Taylor's garage, Jenny had acquired a dusting of golden freckles across her nose, cheeks and forearms. The sun had ignited her hair, imbuing it with licks of flame that a late-afternoon shampoo before dinner had done nothing to extinguish. Her eyes were bright. Her face glowed.

Even if she left for home right now, Luke would consider this day a rousing success. They'd spent hours on the beach talking, dozing, sipping tall drinks and talking some more. Luke had described his students to her, discussed some of the new concepts he was planning to implement in the fall and filled her in on his phone conversation with his mother that morning: she had entered a bridge tournament at the club, his father had convinced a powerful trade association to let him represent their interests in Washington, and Elliott's daughter had recovered completely from the chicken pox. Jenny had told Luke about the first time she'd visited the Cape, to spend a September weekend with three of her law school classmates. It had rained nonstop the entire weekend, by the end of which the four of them were scarcely speaking to each other.

The only time Jenny had mentioned the Sullivan trial was early in the day when she'd informed Luke that the jury, which had received the case the previous morning, had not yet reached a verdict. "I don't know if that's a good sign or a bad sign," she'd admitted. "Frankly, I'd just as soon not think about it for a while."

"Then let's not think about it," Luke had readily agreed. As far as he was concerned, emotionally charged subjects were off-limits for the day. Trust was built on trivial matters as much as significant ones. After ten leisurely hours discussing little of importance in each other's company today, he believed they'd done a lot of building.

"I'm sorry your friend Taylor wasn't at his restaurant," she said, leaning out over the deck railing and letting the evening breeze toss her hair. "I would have liked to meet him."

"He would have liked to meet you, too," said Luke.

"Please tell him I think the Haven is wonderful."

"I will." He rested his forearms on the railing, welcoming the warm, salty wind against his face. His skin tingled from its exposure to the sun. The sky was a deep blue and the water lapped the sand in a soothing rhythm. "Would you like something to drink?" he asked her.

"No." Reluctantly she turned from the lovely vista beyond the deck. "I really should be heading for home."

The moment of truth had arrived. Luke reminded himself once more that, no matter what happened next, the day had been excellent. If she said no, if she couldn't bring herself to trust him fully, he would try not to be disappointed.

He snagged her hand with his to prevent her from backing away. "Stay," he said.

"It's getting late."

"I don't mean stay another hour. I mean *stay*."

She peered up at him thoughtfully. To his great relief, she made no move to escape. She met his imploring look with one of indecision and wariness. "I can't do that," she said, clearly aware of what he was getting at.

"Please." He didn't mean to beg, didn't mean to overwhelm her or pressure her but...damn. He wanted her. He'd been wanting her since the moment she'd arrived, dressed in her attractive white outfit and carrying a tote bag full of beach things. His longing had increased when she'd joined him on the deck a half hour later, clad in a form-fitting one-piece swimsuit. All through the day, as she'd lain beside him in the umbrella's shade, he had admired her slender legs and womanly curves. When she'd emerged from the water after an invigorating swim, her skin shimmering with water, her swimsuit clinging to her torso and her hair slicked back, he'd had to fight the impulse to grab her and kiss her.

"Luke. Don't do this," she mumbled, averting her gaze even though her hand remained in his. "I can't—"

"You can," he insisted with quiet force. "*We* can."

"No. I can't." Her voice broke, and she ducked her head and blinked away a tear. "This is why I avoided you for so long, Luke—I was afraid you'd want more than I can give you, and—"

"I know you're afraid." Gently, slowly, he drew her to himself. "I love you, Jenny. I won't hurt you." He closed his arms around her trembling shoulders and kissed the top of her head. "The only thing I'm afraid of is losing you again."

"If we do this, you will," she warned, her words muffled as she buried her face against his chest. "It won't work. I can't do it. If I try, I'll fail and it'll be a disaster, and I'll hate you for it."

"It won't be a disaster," Luke assured her, praying that he was right, praying that their love was strong enough to overcome even this. Praying that, just as Jenny had worked a miracle for him seven years ago, he could work a miracle for her now. "Trust me, Jenny," he whispered. "Please trust me."

Leaning back, she stared up at him. Her eyes held an accusation. "You planned this, didn't you? You had the house to yourself for the weekend, and you planned to have me spend the night."

"Yes." He couldn't lie, not when winning her trust meant so much.

She continued to stare at him, less reproachful than reflective. "You understand what this means. You're ready to risk our friendship. Because it's going to be ruined if you do this. It's going to be destroyed."

"It's a risk I'm willing to take," he swore, silencing his own private doubts. He was no Romeo, no acrobat. He had no secret talents or surefire moves when it came to sex. All he had was his love for Jenny. God only knew if that would be enough.

She gave him a final assessment, then sighed and slid out of his arms. "All right," she yielded. "Let's go and get it over with."

Not a good attitude. He felt countless misgivings nattering inside his skull. Willfully he fended them off. He couldn't afford to fail. Too much was at stake.

He ushered Jenny into the house and upstairs to the guest bedroom that had been his home for the past month. The drapes were open to let in the moonlight; an ocean breeze wafted through the broad screened windows. Jenny surveyed her surroundings, taking note of the neat piles of textbooks and magazines, the small stack of unanswered mail on the dresser, the bathrobe draped over a hook on the closet door. She drifted to the window and stared out, her arms crossed tightly over her chest and each of her hands gripping the opposite shoulder.

He came up behind her, bowed and kissed her fingertips. He heard her sharp intake of breath and tried not to be discouraged by her nervousness. He kissed her hand again, then lifted it from her shoulder and rotated her until she was facing him. "Relax," he whispered as he slid her jacket down her arms.

"That's easy for you to say," she joked lamely. Her eyes were glassy with tears.

He arranged the jacket over the back of a chair, then nibbled a path across her shoulder, grazing over the narrow strap of her shirt until he reached her throat. She stood rigidly before him, her arms at her sides and her eyes wide open.

The last time he'd kissed her she had been aroused—at first, before she'd freaked out and run away. Clinging to that memory, he skimmed the warm hollow of her neck with his lips, working his way upward to her chin, to her lips. He cupped her cheeks and tilted her head. "Kiss me," he urged her, touching his mouth to hers again and again. "You kiss me."

Tentatively she moved her lips against his. He positioned himself so his body wouldn't accidentally brush against hers. He couldn't rush her. He had to let her take charge, direct each step, comprehend that she was in command.

She covered his lips briefly with hers, then pulled back and sighed. "That's nice," he murmured, his words filling her mouth. He angled his head and slid his tongue over her lower lip. She sighed again, a tremulous whisper.

"Let's lie down," he suggested, sliding his arm around her shoulders and leading her across the room.

She sat on the edge of the bed, removed her sandals and eyed him uncertainly. She looked so small all of a sudden, so vulnerable, a slight, fragile figure perched precariously on the edge of the double-width mattress. "Luke," she said, her voice trapped in her throat. "I'm really scared."

Oh, God, so am I, he almost blurted out. "Don't be," he said aloud. "I love you." He sat beside her, combed his hand through her hair and pulled her mouth to his. His kiss this time was less polite, less restrained. He let his tongue slide along the seal of her lips until she relented and allowed him entry. At the moment their tongues met he groaned.

So did she.

His fear vanished. He captured her hand and drew it to his face, inviting her to stroke his smoothly shaved cheek, his jaw, his hair, his neck. At some point her hand began to move on its own, tracing the broad ridge of his shoulders and then roaming forward to his chest. He tore open the buttons of his shirt and pulled back the fabric. Timidly she slipped her hand inside.

The sensation of her fingers on his warm, sun-bronzed skin sent a dazzling charge through his nervous system. The muscles beneath her questing hand tensed with excitement. She ventured further under his shirt, running her fingernails experimentally across his ribs and down to the flat surface of his abdomen. Bumping against the waistband of his slacks, she flinched and broke the kiss. "I'm sorry, I—"

"Oh, Jenny, Jenny..." His voice emerged hoarse and uneven. "Touch me anywhere you want. It feels so good." To emphasize the point, he tugged his shirt completely off and tossed it to the floor.

Her eyes grew round, reflecting a combination of wonder and apprehension. After a brief hesitation she let him guide her hand back to his chest. She watched herself stroke him, watched her hand as it roamed across the smooth expanse of skin, bashfully skirting his nipple en route to his shoulder. He watched, too. He'd never realized how erotic it could be to watch a woman's hand moving on his body.

"I should stop this," she muttered, even as her hand continued its meandering journey about his torso.

"Why?"

She let her hand fall to her lap. "If I get you too—too aroused, you might—" Unable to complete the thought, she closed her eyes.

"Lose control?" he finished for her.

She gave a tiny, anguished nod.

"Trust me," he whispered, bringing both of her hands to his lips and kissing each palm. Then, carefully, he gripped the edge of her shirt and lifted it over her head. He felt nearly palpable waves of tension emanating from her; she stiffened perceptibly when he unclasped her brassiere and dispensed with it. Her eyes glinted with sheer panic. "Trust me," he repeated, his voice a soothing purr as he explored the soft, creamy skin of her naked shoulders, lingered for a moment on her delicate collarbone, then drifted down to caress her breast.

As his hand curved around her sensitive flesh he felt her shiver, felt her fight against her own reaction—and lose. Her nipple budded, her breath grew short, and suddenly, without premeditation, he found himself drawing her down onto the bed, lying beside her, pressing his mouth to the sleek underside of her jaw and feeling her throat vibrate against his lips as she moaned.

She arched her back, pressing into his hand. Her hips twisted, and she dug her fingers into Luke's back, clinging to him as his mouth blazed a path to her breast. He sucked gently until she moaned again, and then harder, feeling her writhe, feeling her defenses dissolve, feeling her awaken to her capacity for pleasure. "Luke," she gasped. "Luke..."

He raised his head. "Do you want me to stop?"

"No." It was a capitulation, a celebration. A confession of her own sexual rebirth.

He rose and kissed her lips, then sat up and reached for the button of her skirt. Thinking better of it, he instead directed his attention to what remained of his own clothing. During her assault, she'd been naked while her attacker had remained dressed. Luke didn't want that to happen now. He didn't want anything to resemble that terrifying incident.

As soon as he was fully undressed he glanced at her. She stared at the straining fullness of his erection, her expression inscrutable.

He took her hand once more and curled it around his hard flesh. "It's okay," he whispered. "I love you, Jenny." As soon as he released her hand she pulled back from him.

She needed time. No matter how imperatively he wanted her, he mustn't rush her.

Still unable to read her expression, he took a deep breath and unfastened her skirt. She lifted her eyes to his face, as if she couldn't bear to watch him undressing her. He slid the skirt off, and then her panties.

She was so beautiful, so very beautiful. He skimmed his hand down her body, pausing at her breasts, at her midriff, at her belly, at the sharp point of her hipbone. Her breath emerged in short, frantic gasps; her eyes never left his.

He moved his hand lower, prepared for her to halt him. She didn't.

She felt moist, slippery, melting with readiness. A hot spasm of desire whipped through him, stringing every sinew in his body taut. He slid his finger deeper and she cried out, not in protest but in rapture. "Now," she breathed, clutching at his shoulders and urging him onto her. "Now."

It was too soon. He wanted to be sure, wanted her so primed there was no chance of her not being satisfied. He wanted her on top, so she could be in control.

Yet she *was* in control. If she wanted him now, he would obey. If she wanted him on top he would oblige. If he wanted her to trust him, he had to trust her.

He braced himself above her and she grabbed his hips, pulling him down. He tried to hold back but she was so soft, so buttery, and her embrace was so demanding. He yielded to her wishes and his own aching need.

The instant he penetrated her he experienced a clash of emotions, pleasure warring with fear. She was much tighter than he'd expected. "Jenny," he murmured, lifting his head to view her.

She stared back at him, her eyes dry and her mouth pinched with fear. He bent to kiss her and she turned away.

"Jenny."

"It's okay," she whispered, clenching her hands against his hips, refusing to let him withdraw.

"You're so tense..."

"No. It's okay. I'm okay."

He didn't want her to be okay. He wanted her to feel what he was feeling, the fierce splendor of it, the seething, pulsing magnificence of it. He wanted her on fire. He wanted her to climax around him the way she had seven years ago, the way she had when there was nothing between them but love.

The understanding that it wasn't going to happen sliced through him like a shaft of ice. He felt himself going slack.

She shifted her hips, reviving him. When she turned her face back to him he detected acceptance in her eyes. "It's all right," she whispered, sliding one hand up his spine to the nape of his neck. "I love you, Luke. It's all right."

Her distant look implied that she had given up on the possibility of attaining fulfillment. "I want you with me," he implored, touching his lips to hers. Her hips rose to his, again and again, and he couldn't resist the sensual rhythm of her movements.

"I'm here."

"Not the way I want you to be."

"I'm here," she repeated, then turned her face from his once more and pulled his head down to her shoulder. He attempted to wedge his hand between them, to stimulate her with his fingers, but she pushed his arm away. Anxiety twined with desire inside him, each feeding the other until his soul begged for deliverance. His release came in a final, shuddering surge, leaving in its wake an overwhelming feeling of dismay.

"Jenny?"

He propped himself up and she let her arms fall from him. As soon as he was off her she rolled away, drawing her knees to her chest and presenting him with her back. She said nothing.

He touched her shoulder. "Jenny?"

She was weeping. Silent sobs racked her body, and she shrugged off his hand and twisted into an even more self-protective posture, shutting him out.

They'd been denied their miracle.

SHE DESPISED HERSELF for behaving this way. Luke had done nothing wrong. As a matter of fact, he'd done everything as right as possible. Even now he was still doing things right: gliding his hands up and down her back in a tender massage, kneading her shoulders, murmuring quiet, placating words more important for their tranquilizing sound than their literal meaning.

But she couldn't stop crying. She'd come so close with him, she'd been so aroused, so receptive. She'd never felt more sure of herself than she'd felt tonight with Luke.

It didn't matter, though. As close as she'd been, she had ultimately failed.

She'd realized the truth the instant he'd thrust inside her. Was this supposed to feel good? Had she once upon a time derived enjoyment from this invasive, aggressive act? How? What had she done then that she could no longer do now? What had she thought? Why didn't it feel good anymore, not even with Luke?

At least she didn't hate him. He'd done his best, and it was a sign of how much she cared for him that she hadn't felt sick during the act. He had been sensitive to her, patient, compassionate. Once she'd realized it wasn't going to work for her, she'd done whatever she could to make it work for him.

She had obviously failed as miserably at satisfying him as she had at achieving her own satisfaction. What a mistake this had been. What a pathetic, wretched folly.

"We'll try again," he was whispering, and she groaned in anguish. "Jenny, we got this far. I'm sure that if we keep trying—"

"I don't want to keep trying," she lashed out, sniffling away her tears as her despair gave way to bitterness. "I want it to happen automatically, the way it did the last time we made love. We didn't have to try then. It just happened."

"That was then, Jenny. I'm sure it will be better next time. I'll go slower."

"No, it's not your fault. You were wonderful. It was me. I warned you, I can't do this."

"Did it hurt?"

"No."

He inched his fingertips along the delicate bones of her spine, rubbing out the tension. "Was it awful from beginning to end?"

She sighed. "No."

"Then we'll try again, after we've both rested a little."

"No."

He pressed gently on her shoulder, and she let him ease her onto her back so he could view her face. He brushed her hair back from her tearstained cheeks. "I'm not giving up on you, Jenny. For God's sake, don't give up on yourself."

"You arrived on the scene kind of late," she argued, wishing he weren't so damned considerate. "I didn't just give up on myself. I've been living this life for seven years, Luke."

He offered a lopsided smile. "So maybe I arrived late. But I finally made it on the scene, and all in all I'd say we've made a promising start." He continued to stroke her hair back from her face, tucking it behind her ears and letting his fingers drift sensuously over her skin. "As far as I can tell, this scene involves two adults who've loved each other for a long time. Call me crazy, but I think we can work it out."

"You're crazy," she obliged. To her amazement, she felt herself smile. "Oh, Luke..." Fresh tears stung her eyes, and she closed them. "Failing at sex is bad enough. But failing with you is infinitely worse. I don't think I can bear to try again."

"We didn't fail," he assured her. "That's the thing of it, Jenny. We went a fair distance. Next time we'll get farther. We didn't fail tonight. We've only just started."

She didn't agree. She didn't want to test the limits of her endurance by making a second attempt. If they were smart—and they both were—they'd quit while they were ahead.

"I think I ought to go home," she said.

"No." He bowed and kissed her forehead. "Sleep with me."

"Forget it," she snapped, her tone laced with suspicion.

"Jenny, I'm asking you to *sleep* with me. That's a part of love, too. Sleeping together, and dreaming together, and holding each other. I want to spend the night next to you in bed."

Dubious, she searched his face for a clue as to his intentions. What if he initiated another humiliating foray into the world of inadequate sex? He'd already made an ominous remark about "next time." What if "next time" happened within the next hour?

If she felt the least bit coerced by him, that would be the end of it. She'd scream, she'd hit him, she'd fight back with everything she had. Years of self-defense lessons had to be good for something.

Lord help her, what was she thinking? That Luke was going to rape her?

Yet how could she trust him? He was a man.

A man who loved her.

A low sob choked her throat as she confronted her deepest fear—not that she would never enjoy making love again, but she would never be able to trust a man again. She wanted to trust Luke. She wanted it more than anything in the world.

"I'll stay," she whispered, then turned abruptly away so he wouldn't see her tears. "I'll stay."

THE DREAM CREPT up on her subtly, unexpectedly. In it she was floating on an undulating cushion of warmth. Every fiber in her body was relaxed, lethargic. Her respiration was slow and deep, each breath filling her with an inexplicable serenity.

Someone was with her in the dream, but she wasn't afraid. He was a man, a friend, the source of the warmth. She had no idea how she knew this, but she knew.

Lips on her breast, languorously sucking. It seemed so real, in the way dreams sometimes seemed more real than reality itself. The lips moved from one breast to the other, kissing, licking, bathing her in shimmering pleasure.

If she woke up the feeling would stop. Keeping her eyes shut, she nestled her head deeper into the pillow and sighed.

He was moving down her body. Luke. In her dream she saw him, his large, virile physique, his honey-brown skin and honey-sweet eyes. If she was awake she'd be alarmed, but she wasn't awake, and she wasn't afraid.

He kissed the surface of her belly, then continued down.

The warmth began to condense, to contract into a tight, localized knot of heat. She felt hands on her thighs, caressing them, spreading them. His mouth touched her and she jerked awake as the knot grew precipitously hotter and tighter. She felt Luke's hair against her thighs, his hands cupping her hips, his tongue stroking her.

A strangled moan escaped her. The sensations he elicited were excruciating, painful and blissful all at once. She couldn't breathe. She couldn't move. Every bit of energy concentrated itself deep inside her, in a place over which she had no power.

She fought for control, but Luke refused to cede it. A wave of dread swept through her and then evanesced.

She couldn't control this, so she stopped trying. She put her faith in Luke. She trusted him. She trusted him and let go.

Her body shook with convulsions, profound, cataclysmic, ravishing pulses of ecstasy. She was floating again, held aloft on the healing current of her own liberation. Laughing and crying, she groped for Luke and urged him up onto her. With a powerful surge he fused himself to her, and her body erupted in more convulsions, mind-boggling, heart-stopping, soul-shattering spasms as he moved within her. She felt him stiffen, heard him groan, absorbed the tremors of his body cresting inside her.

With a weary sigh, he sank into her arms. She clung to him, savoring his weight, the dampness of his skin, the uneven rasp of his breath against her cheek. After a minute she heard the low, throaty rumble of his laughter. Leaning back, she twisted to view his face—and saw that his eyes, like hers, were filled with tears.

Chapter Thirteen

"And he said, 'This wine tastes awful!' So I tasted the wine, and it was magnificent. We're talking about a '74 Bordeaux. You could take a sip of this stuff and die happy. And he's spluttering and wincing and making a big to-do until his wife finally smacked his arm to shut him up. Then she looked at me and said, '*I'll* take the wine. Just bring him a Pepsi.'"

Taylor laughed politely. So did the real estate broker at the far end of the conference room, where she was refilling the coffee mugs. Luke was too distracted to smile.

This was supposed to be a preliminary get-together between Taylor and the owner of the restaurant in Yarmouth, a chance for them to feel each other out. The business looked good enough on paper, but Taylor was too shrewd to go forward with a purchase without ascertaining that all the numbers were true.

Luke admired Taylor's thoroughness. Indeed, he had complete confidence in Taylor's ability to assess the restaurant's value. So what the hell was he doing at this meeting?

He was here not only because Taylor had asked him to come but because Jenny had asked him not to come to Cambridge. "You'll be bored silly," she insisted. "There's nothing to do but stand around biting your nails when the jury is out. I plan to spend the morning preparing my evidence for a grand jury hearing on Wednesday. I'd love to see you for dinner if you'd like to come up in the evening, Luke, but really, it's deadly hanging out at the courthouse waiting for a verdict.''

He believed her. Yet he couldn't imagine that hanging out at the courthouse would be any more deadly than listening to a superannuated restaurateur reciting limp tales about all the phony wine connoisseurs he'd encountered in the course of his career. Luke had been sitting with Taylor and the old coot in the realtor's conference room for over an hour. He was restless.

"Is there a telephone I could use?" he asked the broker as she returned to the table with the refilled mugs.

"Right this way." She led him out of the conference room and pointed him toward an empty office across the hall. "Press nine to get an outside line."

"Thanks." He stepped into the office, shut the door and smiled the smile of a newly released prisoner. When he spotted the telephone console on the desk, his smile expanded.

Two minutes of Jenny's time, that was all he'd ask of her. Just a brief bit of contact to keep him going until he met her for dinner. Just a chance to assure her that the love they'd found together over the weekend was real, that no matter what had happened in the past or would happen in the future, his feelings weren't going to change.

If Saturday night had been intense, Sunday had been no less so. He'd awakened in the early hours, aglow with the joy of having Jenny next to him. The moonlight spilling in through the window glazed her face in silver, imparting an exquisite delicacy to her features. Seven years after he'd lost her he had found her again. She was here, she was his, and for the first time since those tumultuous weeks in Washington so many years ago, he felt as if his life was complete.

For the first time since then, he believed in miracles.

She stirred beside him, issued a sleepy groan and opened her eyes. As soon as they came into focus on Luke, she returned his smile.

"Did I wake you?" he whispered apologetically.

"No." She edged closer to him, letting her head come to rest on his shoulder.

Her hair felt silky against his skin. He kissed her temple. "Let's make love," he said.

"No." At his surprised look, she explained, "I don't want to press my luck."

"Jenny, what happened before wasn't luck. It wasn't a fluke. It's going to happen again and again."

"You're pretty sure of yourself, aren't you?" she teased, although he detected a strong hint of insecurity in her tone.

"I'm sure of you, too." He ran his hand down her side, following the narrow frame of her rib cage, the steep slope of her waist, the feminine rise of her hip. Then he slid his hand back up, detouring around her arm to fondle her breast. He stroked it seductively, taking pleasure in the instantaneous hardening of her nipple, in the involuntary movement of her hips.

She moaned softly. "Luke, don't."

He immediately pulled his hand away. He was more perplexed than disappointed. She had enjoyed his caress, responded to it. Why did she want him to stop?

"This is all so—so strange," she answered without prompting. "I'm not used to it."

"Neither am I. But I like it."

She smiled and shifted even closer. "So do I," she murmured, brushing her lips against his neck. "Just hold me, Luke."

He held her. He wove his legs through hers and wrapped his arm snugly around her narrow waist.

"I'm still scared," she confessed.

"About making love with me?"

She shook her head. "I'm scared because I have to—to relearn myself all over again. I don't know if this makes any sense, Luke, but—it's as if I have to rethink everything and figure out who I am all over again. It's like..." She fell silent, evidently searching for a way to clarify her thoughts. "When I was a little girl, my grandmother was almost completely deaf. After about eight years this new surgical procedure was developed, and she had it performed on her, and suddenly she could hear again. It was a big adjustment for her."

"It was an adjustment she must have been thrilled to make."

"She was," Jenny told him. "So am I. But it's scary. I've spent so long getting used to not feeling certain things. Now I have to get used to feeling them again. The ground keeps shifting under my feet. I'm afraid the next shift might knock me over."

"There doesn't have to be another shift, if you're happy with the way things are now."

"My happiness can't prevent earthquakes," Jenny argued. "I can only control so much of my life. If it all starts shifting again—"

"I'll be there to catch you."

She sighed. "I have to be strong on my own, Luke. I have to know I can be safe even if you aren't with me."

"I'll always be with you."

She chuckled at his stubbornness. Her breath tickled his chest. "Be real, Luke. I still have to go out into the world every day. It's a dangerous place. There are too many..." Again she drifted off.

"Men?" Luke guessed with a self-deprecating grin.

"You said it."

"So you'll go back to your office and keep prosecuting the bad ones. And each time you nail a creep the world will be a little bit safer."

"You make it sound simple."

He heard his own words mocking him. Hadn't he complained, seven years ago, that things were never as simple as Jenny claimed they were?

If things hadn't been simple then, it had been because he'd refused to view them simply. Some things *were* simple, though. Seven years ago he'd learned the simple truth about himself: He couldn't earn his father's love by being obeisant, and he couldn't find true happiness unless he listened to his heart. And today, he understood some simple truths about Jenny. Making love could satisfy her, and she needed him as much as he needed her.

None of which altered another simple truth: No matter how many violent men ended up behind bars, a few would always manage to escape the law. "Okay. It's not simple," he conceded. "But you'll do everything in your power to bring the bad guys to justice. It's your job. It's what you've chosen to do, and you do it wonderfully. And I'll do my job and try to set all the potential creeps straight before they leave school. Weren't you the one who made that idealistic speech about molding children's minds?"

"I don't think I'll ever be idealistic again," she said sadly.

"That's all right. I'll be the resident optimist. You can be the cynic. We'll cancel each other out."

"A match made in heaven," she declared with a laugh.

A match made in heaven. Even though he knew she'd been joking, he'd liked the sound of that on Sunday. He liked it just as much today.

He strode across the office to the desk, lifted the phone, pressed nine and then the digits of Jenny's office number.

The receptionist answered, and Luke identified himself. "May I speak to Jennifer Perrin, please?"

"I'm sorry, she's in a meeting now. Can I take a message?"

His shoulders slumped. He'd gotten out of his meeting; why couldn't she get out of hers? Didn't she know how much he wanted to hear her voice?

He chuckled at his own impatience. He'd existed for seven years without her in his life. Surely he could wait a few minutes to talk to her. "When will she be done with her meeting?

"Who knows? I guess when the press is done questioning her."

"The press?" His pulse accelerated slightly. The only reason he could imagine her facing the press right now was if—"Did the jury reach a verdict in the Sullivan case?"

"Ten minutes ago," the receptionist informed him.

"And? What was it?"

The receptionist hesitated for a moment, then said, "They voted for acquittal."

He cursed. It was bad enough that Sullivan would walk—certainly people guilty of worse crimes had gone unpunished. But *this* trial, Jenny's trial... He couldn't bear to think what losing might do to her. She had scars that even Luke couldn't eradicate. She'd told him point-blank that she was still afraid, that she would never feel totally safe. Especially not with men like Matthew Sullivan at large, men who were nice-looking and well educated, men who looked and acted and were viewed by society as totally normal.

He never seemed particularly unbalanced to me, she had said, describing another Matthew Sullivan, one with a different name, living at a different time and a different place but suffering from the same brutal, evil psyche. *We were friends.*

Over the past weekend Luke had labored with all his might to teach Jenny how to trust. After a verdict like this, how could she ever trust anyone? How could she trust Luke? He was the epitome of mental balance, and he was her friend.

"Is she all right?" he asked the receptionist.

"I beg your pardon?"

It dawned on him that by implying that Jenny might be unhinged by the verdict he was jeopardizing her position in the D.A.'s office. "Is Jenny disappointed?" he amended.

Again the receptionist paused before answering. "Verdicts are a matter of public record, Mr. Benning. The personal reactions of our attorneys aren't."

If the receptionist couldn't tell him, it must be bad. Maybe Jenny had broken down in court. Maybe she was right this minute ranting and raving before the press corps.

"I'm sorry to take up your time," he said quickly. "Please tell Jenny I called." Then he slammed down the phone and headed back to the conference room to say goodbye to Taylor and the others.

He completed the trip to Cambridge in under an hour and a half, but never had a drive seemed so long to him. In his haste, he almost forgot to lock his car after parking it, and he ran to the courthouse building with the speed of an Olympic sprinter. Too anxious to wait for the elevator, he dashed up the stairs to the second floor. Emerging from the stairwell, he tore down the hall to the D.A.'s office and burst through the door. "Where is she?" he demanded of the receptionist.

She peered up at him suspiciously. "Where is who?"

"Jenny Perrin. I'm Luke Benning."

"You telephoned earlier, didn't you?" the young woman said, her eyes narrowing on him. "I gave her your message."

If Jenny had tried to call him back she wouldn't have been able to reach him. If she *hadn't* tried... He didn't even want to consider what that might imply.

"Where is she?"

"She's in a meeting."

"Still?" An hour and a half fencing with reporters? Or had she told the receptionist to lie to Luke so she could hide from him? "When I telephoned, she was in a meeting," he said, bearing down on the woman behind the desk, hoping to intimidate her into revealing Jenny's whereabouts.

"That was a different meeting," she said placidly. "Right now she's with District Attorney Blair."

"Fine." Not bothering to request permission, he barged down the corridor of partitions, searching for Blair's office, ignoring the receptionist's shout of protest. Through an open door he heard voices, and he peeked into the doorway to see Jenny's genial, bald-pated boss standing in front of his desk, two other men in business attire facing him, and in the center of this trio of towering men, a petite red-haired woman in a chic gray suit and spectator pumps.

Seeing how tiny she looked amid the men wrenched Luke's heart. Not caring about the consequences, he stepped brashly into the office and called her name.

They all turned to stare at him. And then Jenny's lips curved in an enchanting smile of surprise. "Luke! What are you doing here?"

Her smile was the most reassuring sight in the universe. It banished his anxiety, slowed his pulse, neutralized the overabundance of adrenaline pumping through his body. She was okay. She had survived. She was stronger and tougher than even he had given her credit for being.

"Hello," he mumbled, abruptly embarrassed by his rude invasion of this professional confab. "I'm sorry to interrupt—"

"No, that's all right," Jenny said. "We're basically done here. You remember Steve Blair, don't you?" She gestured toward the district attorney, who nodded at Luke in recognition and extended his hand. After they'd shaken hands Luke was introduced to Jenny's fellow assistant D.A., Willy Taggart, and the third man, a police lieutenant from Somerville. More handshakes, and then Jenny excused herself and led Luke out of the room.

"What are you doing here?" she asked again as they walked down the corridor to her own cramped office.

"I heard about the verdict."

"Really? How? The local newscasts won't be on for hours."

"I called to talk to you, and the receptionist told me."

Jenny nodded and crossed to her desk, which was uncharacteristically messy, scattered with papers and folders. She eyed the disorder, then turned her back on it and faced Luke. For the first time since he'd found her, she didn't look happy. "So. You know."

"You seem to be taking it well," he observed, although his voice rose in a question.

She took a deep breath and let it out. Then she shook her head. "It stinks," she said tersely.

"You did the best you could."

"I don't know." She shrugged. "That's what Steve and Mike were saying in Steve's office. Willy was just there to offer moral support." She sighed again. "We have no grounds for appeal. It was a fair trial. There's nothing more I can do."

He scrutinized her. "How's the girl?" he asked. "The victim—is she all right?"

"I talked to her on the phone as soon as the verdict came down." Jenny's voice faltered slightly, and she lowered her eyes. "Needless to say, she's devastated. I promised I'd drop by her house this evening and talk to her. I know you and I are supposed to have dinner, but . . ."

"This is more important," he said. "We'll eat later, or— whatever. You'll go and see her right after work."

She sent him a look of gratitude. "I was hoping you'd understand."

Something in her expression—the defiant tilt of her chin, the metallic glint in her multicolored eyes—puzzled him. Her words implied that, although justifiably disappointed, she had come to terms with her loss. Yet he sensed a strain of resistance in her, something below the surface, contradicting her superficially calm acceptance of the courtroom defeat. "What are you thinking?" he asked.

She met his steady gaze and one corner of her mouth lifted in a wry half smile. "Do you know why I lost the case? I'll tell you. Because *these things happen*. The same reason I was raped. *These things happen.* It's not my fault, Luke. It wasn't my fault seven years ago, and it's not my fault now. It's this society we're living in. The jurors were candid about it. They thought Sullivan was a jerk and a louse and a rat, but hey, that's men for you. Two of the jurors came over to me after court adjourned and spelled it out. They said, 'What he did was wrong, but that's what men do. That's how they operate. They've been that way since the beginning of time. You can't criminalize the male instinct. *These things happen.*'"

Luke absorbed her words. He couldn't refute the truth in them, even though he wanted to. "These things *shouldn't* happen," he muttered.

"But they do. And there isn't a hell of a lot I can do about it, except keep on fighting."

Keep on fighting. His soul filled with a profound exhilaration at her quiet pledge. It really was simple after all. What a person could do was keep on fighting.

One loss couldn't destroy Jenny, not anymore. She was already gearing up for the next battle. She was no longer willing to run away. She was too angry, too spirited, too principled to give up.

This was the Jenny Luke had fallen in love with so long ago—strong, self-righteous, noble and fearless. She was back, in full flower.

"Do you know how much I love you?" he murmured, crossing the room and gathering her into his arms.

"It better be a lot," she said as she nestled her face against his shoulder. "You got me through this, Luke. You got me through the verdict, through the press conference, through the whole thing. I ducked into the bathroom for a minute because I thought I might want to cry, but I didn't. The urge vanished. I just thought about you, and I felt better."

As thrilled as he was by her words, he didn't see what he could have done to help her through her frustration and sorrow. "How did I help?"

"You didn't give up on me. You kept on fighting." She leaned back and looked squarely at him. "When we believe in something, that's what we have to do. I used to know that, and then I forgot. And you taught me all over again. You're a very good teacher." She rose on tiptoe and kissed him. "I've always believed in you, Luke, but you taught me to believe in myself. It was something I needed to learn."

They kissed again, a deeper, fuller kiss. If Willy hadn't entered the cubicle and cleared his throat loudly, they might have continued kissing forever. When Jenny broke from Luke, he felt mildly chagrined, but she didn't look the least bit abashed. "Knock next time," she reproached her colleague.

He gave Luke a thorough inspection. "This is your gentleman caller, I take it."

"This," Jenny declared, sliding her arm around Luke and holding him tight, "is my gentle man."

My gentle man. Luke decided that sounded right, not just the "gentle man" part but the possessive pronoun. Especially that.

Epilogue

His mother stood amid the confusion of the kitchen, sipping Evian from a highball glass. "Help me out, Luke," she said, brushing a wisp of ash-blond hair back from her brow and gazing around her. "I know Aida put the cranberry sauce somewhere, but I can't seem to find it."

Aida was Luke's parents' housekeeper. She had been given the day off for Thanksgiving, but she'd spent the past several days helping to prepare the feast Luke's mother was about to serve. Aida had cleaned and dressed the turkey, boiled and mashed the turnips, prepared the sweet-potato casserole, chilled the wines, cut the greens for a salad and baked the bread. Luke's mother had managed to assemble most of the meal, which had all been cooked according to Aida's instructions and was now spread out on the kitchen's various counters, awaiting removal to the dining room.

Luke opened the refrigerator and located a cut-crystal bowl brimming with homemade cranberry sauce at the back of one of the shelves. "Here you go," he said, presenting it to his mother with a theatrical flourish.

From the dining room came the shrill sound of Elliott's daughter explaining the seating arrangement to her oblivious younger brother. From somewhere near the foot of the stairs, Elliott was hollering to his wife to bring him the diaper bag.

Luke's mother took another swig of mineral water and laughed. "Every year it's a zoo," she muttered. "I suppose I should be grateful you all still want to come."

"You know we wouldn't go anywhere else."

"Not even to Jenny's parents?" she asked, giving Luke a canny look. "I'll bet they're a lot easier to take than we are."

"We'll visit her folks for Christmas," Luke said. "They understood that we couldn't manage such a long trip twice in two months. It's hard enough on us that we're shuttling back and forth between Long Island and Boston every weekend."

"Speaking of which, how's the job search coming?" his mother asked as she untied the apron she'd been wearing over her silk hostess pajamas.

"I've already gotten an offer from the Billerica school district," Luke told her. "I'm still waiting to hear from Newton and Belmont. One way or another, Jenny and I are going to have the same address next year."

"And then you can start making babies," his mother advised.

He knew she was teasing, and he gave her the appropriate response—a groan and a grimace.

His mother scanned the kitchen one last time. "I'll start bringing this stuff to the table. You go lure the lion from his lair."

With another groan, Luke departed from the kitchen to fetch his father from the study where he holed himself up every Thanksgiving, avoiding all contact with his family.

James Benning hadn't even acknowledged Luke and Jenny's arrival at the house an hour ago. In fact, Luke hadn't seen his father in months. The old man had refused to attend the wedding—a small civil ceremony performed by one of Jenny's friends on the Massachusetts bench—and he'd made no bones about his displeasure that Luke had gone and married that gullible, mouthy little snip of a girl from Washington, D.C. "That was just a mindless infatuation," his father had snorted when Luke had informed him, over the phone, that he and Jenny were going to get married. "I know she went to a good college, but—what's her background? What on earth can she bring to a marriage?"

Everything, Luke had nearly answered. *Joy and purpose, faith and trust.* "I'm not marrying her for her dowry," he'd muttered. "And I'm sure as hell not marrying her to earn a pat on the back from you."

"Well, you sure as hell won't get one," his father had snapped back before passing the phone to his wife.

That conversation three months ago was the last time Luke had spoken to his father. They'd been estranged for so long, James Benning's reaction to the marriage didn't faze Luke. At least his mother had come to witness the wedding, along with Elliott and his family, Jenny's parents, Taylor and Suzanne and a few of Jenny's friends from the D.A.'s office.

Given his father's cold reaction, Luke would not have been surprised if Jenny refused to go to the Benning home for Thanksgiving. But when he'd mentioned his mother's invitation, she had urged him to accept. "Sooner or later your father and I are going to have to confront each other," she'd said.

Now the time of confrontation was upon them. Jenny and James were going to have to sit at the dinner table together. Even if James tried to ignore her, she would never ignore him.

Sighing, resigning himself to the inevitable unpleasantness of their meeting, Luke headed down the hall to his father's retreat at the rear of the house. To his astonishment, he noticed that the door to the study had been left ajar. Several feet from the doorway, he heard Jenny's distinctive voice floating out of the room.

It wasn't proper to spy on one's own wife, but Luke couldn't resist. He hovered in the hallway, eavesdropping.

"You're wrong, Mr. Benning," she declared.

"I've lived a lot longer than you, child," his father argued. "And I've learned a lot about the way things are done in this world. People use the law to get what they want. Period."

"Maybe the real issue is that different people want different things. Some people may want money and power, and they use the law to get it. But some of us use the law to illuminate society and bring about justice."

"Still the idealist, aren't you?" James retorted. "When are you going to grow up, young lady?"

"If growing up means becoming a cynic..." Luke heard the unexpected sound of Jenny's laughter. "I'll tell you, Mr. Benning, I've been there and it wasn't so hot."

"I'll grant you this, Jenny," James muttered. "You do have what it takes to be a good lawyer—a quick wit and a sharp tongue, and a lot of nerve."

"It doesn't take so much nerve to have a friendly debate with your father-in-law," Jenny claimed, still chuckling.

"Friendly?" his father countered, and then started to laugh, too. "If this is your idea of friendly, your grip on reality is even weaker than I thought."

"Actually, I'm so hungry I'm beginning to lose consciousness. I wish they'd call us for dinner already."

"You could use some fattening up," James noted. "Are you and Luke planning to have children?"

Jenny dissolved in fresh laughter.

While she was clearly quite capable of defending her professional views to Luke's father, Luke didn't think she should have to put up with grandparent-style meddling from the old man. Hurrying to the door, he tapped on it and edged it wider. "Hello, Dad," he said, hoping his face didn't betray his shock at seeing his father and Jenny seated side by side on the puckered leather sofa, convulsed in mirth.

James glanced up and reflexively scowled. "Your wife is giving me a hard time."

"You're giving her a hard time, too."

"I'm trying, but she isn't letting me," his father complained. "A few minutes alone with her and I'm almost looking forward to discussing laundry detergents with Elliott. I hope you came to tell us dinner's ready, because if it isn't I'm going to the club."

"It's ready," Luke announced, moving to the sofa and offering Jenny his hand. "And the club is closed on Thanksgiving."

"Don't remind me," James harrumphed. He heaved himself to his feet and stalked out of the room.

Luke helped Jenny up and kissed her cheek. "You didn't have to socialize with him."

"I chose to," she said. "See how fearless I'm becoming?"

"Well, here I am to rescue you," Luke said gallantly. "Not that you needed any rescuing."

"He's not so bad," she remarked.

Luke tucked her hand into the crook of his elbow. "He's awful," he argued with a grin.

She disputed him with a shake of her head. "Not only is he not so bad, but I think he actually likes me."

Luke gazed down at her. She looked vibrant, blooming with health and intelligence. Her eyes sparkled, her lips curved in a generous smile and her cheeks were marginally rounder than they used to be, thanks to her concerted effort to gain weight. But the source of her beauty wasn't her glowing complexion, her striking coloring or her alluring figure. Jenny's was a beauty born of confidence and optimism.

"Of course he likes you," Luke agreed, speaking for himself as much as his father. "He can't help himself." Abruptly he pulled her to a halt and touched his lips to hers.

She wrapped her arms around him and deepened the kiss, sharing with him the inner beauty of her soul, the deep, quiet, infinitely loving beauty of a woman who had conquered fear.

"Let's go give thanks," she whispered once the kiss ended.

Smiling, he slid his arm around her shoulders and walked with her into the dining room.

Silhouette Sensation

COMING NEXT MONTH

STARTING OVER
Kathy Clark

Rusty Russell never stayed in one place for long, but Kate Cramer was hoping he'd settle down. Her husband's helicopter crash had left her vulnerable and desperate. She was expecting her first baby, her business was on the brink of bankruptcy and she needed Rusty — not only as a pilot.

Rusty found his priorities changing as he put Kate's business back on its feet and helped her bring tiny Shanna into the world. But would Kate want him to stay *if* his suspicions were true?

SOMETHING OF HEAVEN
Marilyn Pappano

Remember Gabriel Rodriguez, the charming but ruthless cop from *Guilt by Association*? He wanted someone found. He wanted the answers to some twelve-year-old questions. So he hired Rachel Martinez, a former cop and a former love, to get the job done.

Rachel wanted nothing to do with Gabriel; she still remembered the cruel words that had driven her away. But, when the only man she'd ever loved asked her to discover if he was a father, she couldn't turn him away. He promised it would be strictly business…

Silhouette Sensation

COMING NEXT MONTH

FIRES OF SUMMER
Catherine Spencer

Susannah Boyd thought a small rural town would be a good place to bring up her young son Ben. Several years ago, her infant son had been kidnapped and her husband killed so, naturally, she didn't like taking risks.

Travis O'Connor was a pilot with a rather peripatetic lifestyle but once he'd seen Susannah he knew his wandering days were over. Could he convince Susannah he was a safe gamble?

THE ECHO OF THUNDER
Linda Turner

Alex Trent was an honest but tough lawyer, which was why his bank robber client told Alex where the evidence that cleared him of murder was hidden — along with the proceeds of the robbery!

Jessica Rawlins had been raised in the mountains where the money was hidden and she blamed the mountains for her husband's death. She didn't want to guide Alex, who'd provoked her right from their first meeting, but he made her an offer she just couldn't refuse...

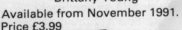